Credits:

Edited by Mollie Traver and Linda Ingmanson

Cover Design by Deranged Doctor Design

ALEX LIDELL

GREAT FALLS PROTECTOR

POWER OF FIVE BOOK 7

THE CADET OF TILDOR

SIGN UP FOR NEW RELEASE NOTIFICATIONS at https://links.
alexlidell.com/News

CONTENTS

PART I: ENEMY TYES

PROLOGUE

Owalin

Stepping out of the Gloom into what Owalin liked to call his war room, the male stretched his spine and inhaled the hot, slightly moist air. As well as the war room had been decorated, with its thick carpets and gilded porcelain jugs of the best wines, it was still a cave inside a mountain. Instead of windows and towering views, there were earwigs and smoky torchlight. And that had gotten old years ago.

It would change soon, though. To be precise, in nine days. Taking a seat at the head of the polished table, Owalin regarded his gathered lieutenants, forcing himself to nod courteously even to the dimwitted human lord at the table's end.

"Status?" Owalin asked.

"The Prowess Trials begin in six days," Han said, walking over to where the Academy map was pinned to a wall for the room to see. The shifter was still in his animal form, his blunt human features irritating Owalin irrationally. "Most of the activity will take place in the newly constructed arena, which is conveniently open to aerial entry and should pose little problem in securing. However, the nature of an ongoing event means knowing which monarchs will be viewing the competition when is unpredictable. Fortunately, the Trials will culminate in a victory ceremony, when all the royals will all be present in the arena to present the medals. "

Owalin nodded. It was almost too convenient for Han's personal whims that the best time for the assault was to come *after* his pets' game, but there was little reason to fight on this point. Han never made it a secret that racing his pets was important to him, and Owalin didn't believe in taking away privileges when nothing warranting discipline had occurred.

"Master Zake." Owalin turned to the grizzled lord at the end of the table stuffing his face full of Owalin's finest provisions. "Have you people in place to secure positions amidst the staff?"

"The servers' guild that's been contracted to assist knows where to place its loyalties," Zake said, wrinkling his nose as if answering questions was beneath him.

"You will personally supervise them, of course?" Owalin didn't need to add that this would mean playing the role of servant himself.

Zake's muddy eyes flashed, the beginnings of a sharp protest crossing his pockmarked features, but one look at the hard faces around the table had him bowing his head. "Of course. Though I don't understand why we are going through the trouble. Just walk your army out of the dark like you did yourself not minutes ago."

Owalin took a breath, mastering his voice before speaking. "Access to the *Gloom*, Lord Zake, is blocked in the mortal world. The small rip in the protective fabric that allows me to cross the threshold extends not far beyond these caves." *Which, you dimwit, is the whole reason we've taken up residence here for decades.*

"The moon's position during Ostera gave us greater reach for a short period, but even that was limited to sections of the forest." Krum, Owalin's chief wardsmith and the oldest of the Night Guard, said in a slow, measured voice. The silver-haired male sat twisting a pair of stone spheres around each other in the palm of his hand, appearing for all the world to be absorbed in his game. "We will only use the Gloom passage to release the caged sclices to entertain the squatters outside the Academy walls. When it's time."

Krum's hypnotic voice tickled the air in the room, making even Owalin's skin crawl. "Fortunately, unlike the infinitesimal tear in the fabric separating the Light and Gloom from the mortal world, the wards shackling our magic are an entirely different beast. One that can be trapped and bled."

"Will you be ready to bring the wards down on my command?" Owalin asked Krum.

The corner of Krum's thin mouth rose, his attention still on his spheres. "Would you like a short test?"

"By all means."

Krum's smile widened, then froze. "Were you ever able to locate those wild fae, Han?" he asked. "The ones who ran amok of our patrol on the night of Ostera?"

Han's jaw tightened. "No."

"Hmm." Krum shrugged. "Well, I do hope they are not doing anything stupid just now. Brace yourselves." With that, the balls in Krum's hand stopped dead.

1

Lera

"Coal!" I grip the male's elbow, shamelessly steadying myself against him as a sudden wave of energy rushes through my core. The mortal shackles binding my magic violently spring open, the cords of power escaping with such force that it's all I can do not to ignite the forest around us in raging wildfire.

The starlit sky seems to spin above me, the rich scents of fern and pine and sticky sap exploding inside my mouth. Strength vibrates in my muscles, surges of life pulsing through me with every heartbeat. My fingers still digging into Coal's rock-hard forearm, I draw in a breath brimming with life—

And all but choke on the next as the phantom shackles choke my magic once more. Bile rises up my throat, everything inside me clawing at the restraint no matter what my better sense tells me. I don't care what's right and wrong just now. I care about nothing but the part of me I just glimpsed and lost all over again. Reaching down into the coil of magic inside me, I throw my will blindly against the shackles. Again. And again. And again.

"Easy, mortal." A strong arm hooks around my back, and Coal brings me in front of him, his beautifully carved features only inches from mine, his metallic scent drowning out the rustling night. Taking my face between his callused hands, the warrior tips back my head, studying me intensely with piercing blue eyes. "I felt it too, the sudden release of magic. But not anymore. Everything is back to normal now."

Normal. I force air into my tight lungs, the safety of Coal's grip on my face returning me to my senses. That shouldn't have happened. As good as the magic feels, it has no place in the human world. *Stars,* we came here to prevent this very disaster.

"Does this mean we failed?" I whisper. "Are the wards completely down?"

"Not yet." Coal runs his hands down my arms, then puts his palm into the small of my back and turns us on the path back to the Academy. "Though I imagine it's safe to say that we aren't the only ones in the mortal world who want to fiddle with the bloody things."

Looking down from the ridge where Coal and I ventured to survey the small army of campgrounds growing on what were recently sheep fields, I shake my head at the neat rows of tents. Torches and lanterns flicker in every direction, distant shouts and bursts of laughter echoing up the valley. By now, less than a week out from the Prowess Trials, the whole place has transformed from an isolated sleepy town to the makeshift capital of a new world, the Academy's flag atop the keep tower flapping like a beating heart.

All are in high spirits, impatient for the coming games—and completely unaware of the potential danger lying in wait.

"You know"—I pull aside a prickly branch before it whacks me in the face—"with not so much as a loose sclice in the Great Falls woods for nearly two months now, I actually thought things might be shifting in our favor."

"I didn't."

"Yes, but you just like killing things."

Coal gives me a menacing look and quickens his pace so I nearly have to jog just to keep up with him. His tall, sculpted body cuts so easily through the night, it's as if the air moves aside for him, every muscle in his powerful thighs and backside outlined under his tight black pants. If he's going to make me run back, at least I can enjoy the view.

Deprived of killing sclices and other nastiness, the male has been channeling his pent-up frustration into correcting what he declared a deficiency in my training. "Now that I remember what you are, there is no reason to coddle you in the ring," he'd informed me two months ago before launching into a new morning torment routine that has the other cadets keeping their distance from me, lest some of Coal's inventiveness splashes their way. "Plus, the more time you spend in Shade's company, the better. So, I'm doing us all a favor."

Even these nightly patrols—with little else to occupy us—have become training opportunities, Coal stopping us in random moonlit clearings for near-silent sparring sessions. They usually start with me being pinned to the ground with no warning, furiously trying to free myself—and sometimes end with my back on the ground or against a tree, racing just as breathlessly to wrap my legs around Coal's naked waist and fit him inside me.

The bond's magic may be muted here in the mortal world, but the mating instinct feels just as strong—sometimes overwhelming now that Coal has his memories back. Tree bark or desk lamp or bedframe be damned.

By the time Coal and I return to the library, Arisha and Gavriel have the place littered with books, maps, and notes. So far, we have all the hundreds of temporary staff camps marked on a chart, along with schedules of soon-to-arrive royals. The pot of red ink we've prepared to mark places of recent blight activity stands untouched, and it has for months.

"Tell me you two killed something today," Arisha says, her back to the door as she juggles a journal in one hand and Minion—the two-pound kitten she found last week in the newly built arena's scaffolding—in the other.

I shake my head. "No."

Sticking his furry little orange head over Arisha's shoulder, Minion hisses at Coal and me, showing a tiny mouth full of needle-sharp teeth.

"The night is young," Coal tells the cat darkly.

Arisha turns, cuddling the vicious little feline as she glares at Coal, her wire-rimmed glasses askance over her narrowed blue eyes. Her freckles stand out more starkly now on her pale face after too many hours spent inside, deep in research—morning training being the one exception. Arisha may have expected Coal, upon learning the truth, to look the other way whenever she decided physical training wasn't the best use of her time—but he disabused her of that notion with one raised brow and a great deal of running.

The warrior crosses his large arms over his chest, the sheer power exuding from him filling the room. Even with my amulet dulling my senses, his metallic musk makes my skin prickle, my body longing for the feel of his—as it seems to do approximately every few hours.

"I liked him better when he didn't know he was a bloody legendary fae warrior," Arisha tells me. "And that amount wasn't much to begin with."

"Good. There is little to like." Grabbing one of her braids, Coal moves her out of his way as he takes a chair across from Gavriel. "When wards erode naturally, does it look like a steady decline or flashes of on-and-off activity?"

Gavriel takes off his glasses, cleaning them against the lapel of his robe. "Steady. Wards turning on and off is purposeful activity." Despite an utter lack of progress in finding a way to mend the shattering wards, the man still knows more about how they function than any of the rest of us. "Might I hope you are asking out of academic curiosity?"

"That one has as much academic curiosity as I have coordination," Arisha mutters.

"There was a moment today when we had full access to our magic," I say, joining the others at the table as I recount the event, the Guild members' faces getting progressively darker with each word. "Could it have been a glitch or something like the opposite of Ostera?"

Dislodging Minion, Arisha walks to the celestial reference text, her mouth moving through complex calculations before she shakes her head. "No. And even if there was a lunar influence, it would be nothing this stark."

"So someone—let's presume it was the Night Guard—pried the wards open on purpose?" I say. "But why now, and why only for a moment?"

"It stinks of a bloody mouse trap," says Coal. "The Prowess Trials at the Academy to gather the royals, a sudden lack of Mors rodents to keep the prey from spooking, and now the magic jaws poised to snap shut." The male growls his frustration, slamming his hand down on a side table.

Minion, crouching low on Arisha's shoulder, hisses.

"The royals will be sitting ducks, and the bloody reality is that no matter what we do, we can't keep an eye on all of them at once," says Coal. "It will be a bloody massacre before we even get to the scene of battle."

I rub my eyes with the heels of my hands. Coal is right. Without knowing how and when the attack will come, we can't position ourselves to stop it—and telling this to Sage is more likely to get us thrown out of the Academy as anything else, where our ability to do something will drop to a heroic zero. The headmaster's precious Prowess team and their parents are going nowhere.

I freeze.

Precious Prowess team. The eye of this whole blasted storm.

The fragments of an idea start forming in my mind. "Maybe Coal and I are only two people," I say slowly, the fragments knitting tighter together, sending dread spiraling into my gut. "But I think I know how to get us into a better defensive position."

2

Lera

"MEAWRRR!" With a battle cry that far exceeds his tiny body, Minion leaps off the arena scaffolding, bounces off Coal, and lands in Arisha's arms.

Coal and I step away in unison, into the shadow of the towering bleachers.

In the brightly shining sun that makes my underclothes stick to my skin, the new arena looms over the Academy's vast central courtyard, an oval monstrosity of soaring wooden struts, canvas-walled changing rooms for each team's athletes, and a tall white-tented platform on one side where Sage and his most honored guests will watch the ceremonies. And, in just a few days' time, the students' final exams.

Where before the massive structure only annoyed me, now it makes my breath come short. The plan I hatched last night feels like an absurd dream this afternoon, presided over by this abomination of wood, canvas, and steel.

The grandiose stadium is just one of many changes to sweep over Great Falls, transforming the Academy grounds from a somber, orderly fortress to…whatever this is. The smells of sawdust and ovens working overtime permeate everything now, drowning out summer grass and nodding flowers. And as if the construction sounds and constant buzz of voices weren't disrupting enough, we have to build in extra time to get from the dining hall back to the library, where we're headed now for a postlunch Guild meeting, as we can't simply cut across the grass anymore.

No corner of the Academy has been left untouched. Every spare room of the keep is being set up into suites for the soon-to-come royals, and most of the east practice rings have been disassembled to create a separate riding arena for the equine events. Their brightly painted jumping fences are already in place. Colorful flags representing every kingdom, the Prowess Trials, and the Academy itself hang from seemingly every surface and tree limb, the ribbons catching on branches as often as fluttering in the wind. The *snap snap snap* of standards is so voluminous to my immortal hearing that it feels like an invasion of tiny drummers has settled into every nook and cranny.

The Prowess Trials, I've learned, divide into three disciplines: control, combat, and constitution. Control, by far the premier tier of the competition, has athletes of Tye's caliber navigating their bodies through spectacular, and seemingly incompatible-with-life, feats. Far below that, combat includes the swordsmanship, horseback riding, and archery competitions, while constitution includes the more basic running, jumping, and lifting events.

"There you are, Minion." Arisha nuzzles the orange-striped kitten, who rubs his ears against her with pious love. "I was so worried."

Coal rubs the three long bloody lines on the back of his hand. " I thought Sh...*Ruffle* was taking care of...that," he mutters to me with a glower, as if I have anything whatsoever to do with the fur ball. "What kind of self-respecting wolf is unable to get rid of a two-pound threat?"

Cuddled in Arisha's arms, Minion turns his head and yawns at Coal, leisurely extending the razor-sharp claws of his front paws.

"It's not Ruffle's fau..." My words trail off at the sight of a lithe red-haired male exiting the keep. My whole body tightens painfully, as it always does now when I see Tye. With his fast healing and faster talking, my reporting him to Shade led only to a ten-day rest from his training regimen. Not long enough to get him pulled from the team, but plenty long enough to have him—and all the Prowess athletes— declare me their arch nemesis. "He is never going to forgive me, is he?"

"I wouldn't," says Coal.

Tye is his quint mate just as much as I am—which doesn't stop me from wanting to punch Coal's perfect mouth for siding with the bastard.

My hands tighten around the strap of my book satchel to avoid the temptation.

The helplessness thunders through me. We were never supposed to be in the Trials. If Tye had stepped aside, it would have defused the whole disaster. Bought us time to try to stop the Mors threat before more human lives are lost. Not only that… When I spoke to him in the bathhouse two months ago—the last time I truly saw him up close—Tye looked like a victim of torture, not training. Yet it is me, not Han, who he believes is out to ruin his life.

"The reason he feels so hurt is because you matter to him," Arisha says softly, the empathy in her voice shifting to a warning that I'm tired of hearing. "Which, by the way, isn't going to make this harebrained plan of yours any easier."

Before I can answer, Minion hisses at someone behind me. Escaping Arisha's hold, the kitten bounces off Coal's shoulder and scampers away.

Coal curses, tiny spots of blood seeping down his arm from under his sleeveless black shirt. "Is it in my power to give a passing grade to any cadet who brings me that demon's hide?"

"As of this morning, it is." River's deep voice twists all three of us around. My eyes widen at a bloody gash running along his strong jaw. "That thing is responsible for three of the maids leaving service." His gray eyes shift to me, a tingling sensation running across my skin and prickling my sex as the humor in his gaze turns to an inscrutable intensity.

Over the past two months, in spite of my best efforts, River's reined himself back to bloody professionalism, which he seems determined to hang fast to even as it kills us both. The occasional slips, like the time two weeks ago when the male brushed a stray lock of hair behind my ear without thinking, his fingers trailing down my jaw before he caught himself, have ended with blazing red cheeks and a sudden need to end the tutoring session midword, while my breath still came in short spurts.

The whole complicated compote makes me almost fear the next time our skin comes into contact, accidentally or otherwise. And long for it so fiercely, I'm worried I'll go insane.

A direction I'm heading in presently, despite my best efforts. Stars take me, but with River's commanding presence suddenly beside me, his impossibly tall, muscled body dominating the courtyard, even the grand arena feels small. My thighs moisten with the memory of what exactly hides under all that tailored silk—starting with a ridged abdomen and rock-hard pectorals, a taut V of muscle leading down to a—

"Good morning, ladies." River's polite greeting makes me jump, the hot brush of his eyes against mine leaving little doubt that my thoughts weren't as private as I hoped. River clears his throat. "Coal. Might I have a minute of your time?"

Coal wordlessly falls in step with the commander. As the two walk away, their heads bent close in discussion, I watch their broad backs, wondering suddenly what River's veil-clouded mind made of last night's sudden burst of magic. Maybe there's a way of asking about it in our next study session without sounding daft—well, any dafter than I already sound trying to explain the intricacies of Ckridel trade policy or how to measure the sides of a triangle.

Arisha's soft murmur of confusion pulls my attention. Taking a folded piece of paper out of her pocket, she frowns. "High strike right. Pivot step left. Low parry. It goes on for a while like this." She blinks up at me, her glasses making her look like a frizzled owl. "I just found this in my pocket. Isn't this Coal's writing?"

I peer at the neatly written list. Yes, the list is most certainly Coal's. More to the point, it lists a sequence he and I have warmed up with regularly, especially in the early days of my training.

"Is this—" Arisha starts.

"A sequence that you are to memorize in case you find yourself needing to perform before an audience." A small chuckle escapes me, and Arisha's frown deepens. Fortunately for my friend, no exams are held for physical training, but with such an influx of visitors, there is no telling who might be watching what. For all his bickering with Arisha, Coal is quietly attempting to preserve her dignity. "I know the other side of this dance. So if we were partnered up…"

Arisha swallows, her cheeks pinking as she quickly puts the note away and starts walking once more toward the library. "Your males are a lot more complicated than they seem, aren't they?"

"If—" Someone shoves me hard from the back, and I stumble forward, managing to keep from falling on my face only by virtue of stomping into the puddle before me, the mud splattering all over my blue satin gown. Twisting around to see who hit me, I see Tye and Katita walking away toward the entrance of the arena, Tye's laugh piercing the air between us.

My stomach twists. Grabbing a clump of mud, I launch it will all my strength, the gray-brown patty hitting the back of Tye's head with a satisfying thump.

Tye stops. Turns. Looks down at me from his great height.

In the bright sun, the male is devastatingly beautiful, with his broad chest and sweat-matted red hair framing a square jaw. Each movement of his body sings with controlled power, the corded muscles shaping his red-and-gold exercise tunic. Beads of sweat along his temples reflect the sunlight, making his skin shimmer. Large, callused hands that I've felt along my body so many times before now open and close against his sides.

A smile that doesn't touch Tye's cold emerald eyes curves along his face, somehow making it even more breathtaking. And cruel. The glinting silver earring only adds to his aura of danger—only now, that danger is directed toward me. *So this is what it feels like.* "Lady Leralynn. Did I inadvertently disturb you? Inexcusable. Shall I help you to the infirmary to see if any injury might have befallen you?"

"We might need to evacuate Lera to safety," Katita adds sweetly.

Swallowing, I conjure a smile as genuine as Tye's own, even as my heart squeezes. "On the contrary, it is I who should be thanking you. I only put this dress on to appease Arisha, and you've finally given me a reason to change before dinner. Excuse me." I start walking away, only to stop two steps later, my racing blood taking over better reason. For better or worse, I suddenly want Tye to know the plan I concocted last night over the protests of the rest of the Protector's Guild. I like it no better than they do, but it is the only way of having one of us at the very center of the highest-value targets at all times, ready to respond if —when—the Night Guard strikes. "I almost forgot—I expect to be your teammate soon, Tye. Welcome news, I'm sure."

"You?" Katita throws her head back with a laugh, her curtain of blonde hair gleaming in the sunlight. "On our team. I cannot imagine I heard that right."

My gaze shifts to the princess, my heart thudding in my chest. "No, you didn't, Your Highness. I don't intend to be on *your* team at all."

"There is only one team. I knew your math was bad, but surely you can count to one if you use your fingers," the princess says haughtily, though her turquoise eyes now flicker with unease.

I smile at her. "Yes. But I'll be competing for your swordsmanship spot on it at tomorrow's practice. Excuse me."

3

Tye

"She can't just join the Prowess team less than a week ahead of the Trials." Katita's indignant voice whittled away at the thickness of Tye's thoughts. They were near the cadet dorms already, though he didn't remember walking here, his mind still riveted to Lera's taunt.

Her on the Prowess team. Those lush curves he'd claimed and bottomless eyes he'd stared into, now just cruel reminders of her betrayal. In his face, each and every damn day.

"Right?" Katita repeated, putting emphasis into the word as she reached for Tye's elbow. Ever since Lera had sabotaged Tye by reporting him to Shade, Katita had used it as an unveiled opportunity to get closer to him. Sidling up to him at mealtimes, partnering with him in class with a silky hand on his arm. Tye let the princess play at flirting for the simple reason that Katita's father was the king of Ckridel and held all the strings to Tye's future—not to mention that it made Lera furious—but he had to admit that the attention was starting to chafe.

Tye pulled back from the princess's reach. "Of course she can," he said over his shoulder, only barely able to hide his irritation. "She is good with a bloody blade, and it wouldn't take long to learn a few extra rules."

"Surely Master Han would not allow such a thing."

"Han cares about winning, Kat. Do me a favor, and win the damn challenge round, because having to share the arena with a backstabbing vixen is more than I can handle just now." Without waiting for Katita's reply, Tye slid into the dormitory and out the first window he found. After climbing swiftly to the roof, he settled onto the sun-warmed stone that had become his choice of refuge in past months.

With his back against one of the two chimney columns, he braced his elbows atop his bent knees and tried to focus on the colorful flapping standards that had transformed Great Falls Academy into a stage. *His* stage. The culmination of everything he'd worked his entire life for, reaching its final zenith. A parapet from which the woman he had stupidly fallen in love with had tried to shove him off.

Stars, Lera's betrayal still hurt. And it was Tye's own fault. He knew that Prowess training and women don't mix—knew it better than anyone. And yet, despite his better sense, despite the too-vivid memory of what his last attempt at combining the two had led to, Tye had let his guard down again.

Granted, Lera offered an overwhelming temptation. Despite their short acquaintance, her musical laugh and bravery and what Tye had thought was a deeply kind heart had started to fill the void Tiga's death left inside his soul. Leralynn's intoxicating lilac scent brightened the world's colors and sounds, whispering promises of great adventures—of *life*—just beyond sight. Yes, it was all so very tempting that Tye had lapped it up like a dimwitted pig, not realizing the extra scraps only ensured a faster butchering.

And as it turned out, Leralynn of Osprey butchered with the best of them.

Tye's fingers curled into a trembling fist, the morning of her betrayal unfurling bitterly in his memory. It had been well before dawn, and Tye had just slipped into the bath. Since starting to train with Han, he'd made a habit of bathing in private—his body was edging the limit of its endurance, and he knew better than to trust outsiders to understand that it had to be so, that the costs his training exacted had to be paid.

When he heard the bathhouse door whisper open, the lass's lilac scent drifting in on warm moist air, Tye knew at once that he should leave. But he didn't. Of all people, he was blindly certain that he could trust Lera—with his secrets, his dreams, his pain. With everything. So he'd let her see him, revealed the costs of his chiseled muscles and gravity-defying flips, of what it took to claw his way out of the nothing that he was born into.

He'd expected Lera's understanding. Had secretly hoped that there might be a person—just one person—whom he might rest his forehead against for a few moments of reprieve. Instead, Lera turned his secret into a weapon to be used against him.

That very day, she reported Tye to the healers—not even from some misplaced concern over his well-being, but because it was a means to an end. She'd gotten it into her head that the Prowess Trials were a frivolous game and needed to end.

It was only with Han and Sage's interference that Shade agreed to return Tye to training after ten days instead of three weeks, but even that time off had hurt Tye's chances. No, not chances—*chance*. Tye had only one shot. Without this victory, he'd return to poverty by summer's end, with nothing but the memory of Tiga's death and his failure to keep him company.

All because he had trusted Lera. No more. There was only one reason Lera would want to get onto the Prowess team, and that was to destroy it. So Tye needed to destroy her first.

4

Lera

I return to my room to find Coal sulking against a wall and Shade's wolf sprawled on my bed with his belly and four giant paws up in the air.

"If this is a send-off gathering for my Prowess tryouts tomorrow, I hope one of you brought cake." I toss my books onto my bed, making Shade sneeze with indignation, and conjure a relaxed posture for my males' benefit. In truth, my stomach has been tight ever since I announced my intention to Katita and Tye. The ire in the male's emerald eyes still sends shivers through me.

Shade whines, sensing the tension in the room, but stops abruptly at a look from me.

Coal remains silent.

"It is our one chance to have someone on the inside with the royals. Keep an eye on the high-value targets," I say to my tight dress stays, making a poor attempt at undoing them elegantly. The dress slumps to the ground at my feet in a sad blue heap. "It's our best positioning option, and it would be folly not to take it." I finally turn to Coal, his blue eyes hooded in a fair imitation of a rain cloud. "You think I can't hold up through a week of Han's training?"

Coal's gaze skitters to Shade, who—damn him—slinks out through the open door instead of staying to defend me. Before I can say anything, the warrior snags me around the waist, pins my back to the wall, and looms over me, one bare, corded arm braced on either side of my face. The heat of his body simmers the air between us, his masculine scent filling the space. "You know exactly what I'm worried about, mortal." His voice is low. Dangerous. "And it isn't Han's training. Shall I demonstrate the problem?"

My heart stutters, and I lift my gaze to find my footing outside Coal's intense scrutiny. Over the past two months, the male has insisted on replaying the scene from Zake's stable, as if determination could make my body unfreeze on command. Returning my attention to his face, I trace its hard angles, lined with a worry that he tries to cover with authority. I square my shoulders the best I can with my heart now racing. "You have nightmares too, Coal. And I've not seen you sit out a battle from fear that something may trigger you."

His eyes spark, and he leans closer. "I've lived with my demons for several hundred years, Leralynn. Let's not confuse the issue. More importantly, my flashbacks spur me to fight for my life. Yours leave you paralyzed like a rabbit for slaughter. That's the difference. Until you have it under control—"

I put my hand on Coal's chest, feeling his heart pound beneath the hard muscle. "If I wait until everything is perfect, there may not be a mortal world to save." I slide both hands down his abdomen, watching his pupils dilate as I hook his shirt hem and slide my hands right back up. Muscle by perfect muscle, his stomach reveals itself, then his chest, his nipples hardening in the cool air. He pulls off his shirt automatically, before he even has a chance to realize he's being distracted. "As to my demons," I continue in a low voice, "I think it's safe to predict that when the Night Guard attacks, they'll be trying to kill me, not whip me. So if you'd like to actually be helpful tonight—"

Coal growls softly and spins me around, pushing me back onto the bed hard enough that it rattles against the wall. The bastard has caught on.

He prowls over me, sniffing my neck like an animal scenting his mate. "This isn't over," he says into my ear.

"Whatever you say, *Lieutenant*," I say impishly, pulling my slip up to my waist. I won this round, and he knows it. He's already too far gone to turn back now.

He bares his teeth and grinds his hips into mine so hard, I can't help but moan—then he disappears.

I look up with a furious protest on my lips only to find him standing in the middle of the room, unbuttoning his fly so carefully, I want to howl in frustration. He looks up, a wicked gleam in his eyes. "You're not the only one with methods of persuasion, mortal."

"I'm going to kill you," I say breathlessly.

"You can try," he says.

Then he's back on top of me, thrusting so deep and true that I have to bite his shoulder to keep from screaming.

THE DOZEN CADETS on Han's Prowess team are running up and down the gleaming arena steps when I stride onto the sands, my palms slightly sweaty against my thighs.

Inside, it's even hotter than I imagined—and even more intimidating. The high sun reflects blindingly off the long oval of sand and metal competition equipment, the bleachers reaching dizzyingly high into the air. I see a tall horizontal bar somewhat like the one Tye used to practice on in Lunos, and my heart squeezes painfully. It smells like dried sweat in here, with a coppery undertone of blood that makes my stomach turn.

I was obviously insane to think this was a good idea.

And I also see no other option.

Unlike the Prowess cadets, who now exclusively wear Academy colors even for physical training, my training grays are drab against the flapping flags and bright paint of the arena.

Han's darkly handsome face is unreadable as he marks me, crooking a finger to order me closer. His hair and brows shine like onyx under the oppressive sun, making his blue-gray eyes even more striking.

As I come up, swallowing hard against the stench of wrongness that leaches from the male like a body odor, he points to a spot in the sand, then turns his back to me to watch his athletes. They're fast and leanly muscled, hardened after weeks of training. Still no match for fae—but possibly the closest humans can get. "Puckler, you are running stairs, not crawling them. Start over. Tyelor, another stone."

Following Han's gaze, I see Tye with a pack of stone weights strapped to his back. At Han's order, the male trots to a pile of additional pieces, adding a mix of stones and sand to his pack. The male's red hair is soaked with sweat, dark splotches saturating his uniform shirt. His face is hard, eyes eerily emotionless. It hits me all over again how strange it is to see Tye as a stranger, behind such a high wall that I can barely see my friend, let alone my playful, passionate mate. Even worse, my body *does* recognize him, yearning toward his like a dog toward a treat, betraying me every time I lay eyes on his messy red hair and feline movements.

"Tyelor will need to put in extra effort to make up for the time your idiocy cost him," Han says quietly, almost casually, still watching his charges. "Is there a reason you are violating my sands this morning?"

I clear my throat. Han knows why I'm here. Everyone does. The very air in the arena is humming in protest at my appearance. Putting my hands behind my back, I give the male a partial bow. "I would like to try out for the swordsmanship slot, sir."

Han makes a noncommittal sound in the back of his throat, then walks a circle around me as if examining a filly for purchase. "I was under the distinct impression that you were not a supporter of our team or sport," he says, coming to rest before me again. "Your attempt to get my top athlete banned from the competition was rather clear evidence of your intentions."

"I made a mistake despite good intentions," I tell Han, though the words are meant for Tye. "I hadn't fully considered the likely consequences of my actions, and I apologize for the inconvenience."

Still adding weight to his running sack, Tye gives no evidence of having heard me.

"Is there a reason I should care about what you *meant* over what you *did?*"

Without waiting for a reply, Han walks away from me, yelling at three cadets about their running form before ordering the whole lot into push-up position in punishment for someone's slow time. The attention he gives the students grudgingly reminds me of Coal, though the similarities between the two end there. All of Coal's training is anchored in survival; Han's draws inspiration from victory—not the athlete's triumph, since it seems the cadets working in the ring are as expendable to him as racing dogs—but his own.

Which, at the moment, works in my favor.

After a few long seconds, I give up on the game and stride up to

Han's side. "You want me on the team because I'm better than Katita," I say, making no attempt to keep my voice quiet or respectful. "And you want to win. It's as simple as that."

Han turns his head, an amused gleam sparking in his eyes. "There is that," he agrees, then raises his voice. "Circle up."

The sweaty bodies forming a circle around Han and me vibrate with menace, each face telling me exactly how they feel about my presence. I wonder whether they are surprised by the challenge or have been waiting for this moment for a long time. Eyes shoot to Katita, who is taking her time drinking from a water bucket before striding forward as if she owns the sands. Not bothering to stop at the outer circle with the others, the princess goes right to Han. "Is it time to take out the rubbish, sir?"

Han lifts a brow. "That depends whether you can do it."

Katita's eyes flash to me. "With pleasure."

"What if we don't want her on the team, sir?" Tye's clear voice rings out over the sands. "I, for one, little care what she can do with a blade. The damage she can do with her mouth is enough."

The murmurs of agreement skittering around the circle don't hurt nearly as much as the venom in Tye's voice. My jaw tightens, my chin raised in high defiance as I try to pretend that none of it matters.

Han's mouth twists into an unpleasant smile. "Tyelor. Yes, you'd know the damage she can do with her mouth firsthand, wouldn't you?" His nostrils flare, and he tilts his head, his smile growing. Almost as if he's scented the males on me—which is impossible. "Fortunately, if you keep your cock in your pants, that can be minimized."

Tye's face reddens, the hate-filled glance he shoots at me so painful, I have to dig my fingers into my palms to keep my face straight. My lips want to tremble, my eyes to fill, but either would end my time here in a split second.

The smile fades from Han's lips. "If anyone else here is under the impression that their opinion matters, they can join Tyelor in an extra ten-mile run this evening." The noise stops, the only sounds suddenly the heavy breaths of the waiting cadets. Han snaps his fingers at Rik, ordering him to bring a pair of practice blades while he addresses Katita and me. "The round will be three minutes. Standard Prowess rules: No contact with the head allowed; points will be awarded only for blows that connect with enough force to have caused significant damage were the blades sharp or else slices across vital areas." Han draws a line over my pulse on both sides of my neck. his fingers cold. "Start back to back. Any questions?"

The last is directed at me as Katita plainly knows the Prowess rules forward and back. I do as well, Coal having cursed the damned things for a good half hour before coming to terms with them. *"Why in stars' name would you train yourself to avoid head strikes?"* I can still hear him growling with indignation as he threw the rules into the flames. *"Are we training for the common case of a headless opponent?"*

"No, sir," I tell Han, reaching for the practice blade Rik extends toward me. The boy pulls back at the last moment and throws the sword at my feet, wiping his hand on his pants when I reach down to pick it up.

"Positions," Han orders.

Despite knowing this part was coming, turning my back to Katita is the last thing I want to do. Forcing my limbs to move, I twist in the center of the sand and feel the princess's warm back press against mine a moment later. Her delicate rose perfume would cover up the sharp scents of sweat and adrenaline for anyone else, but not for me. The girl is nervous. When I look up, I find Tye's beautifully sharp face two paces away, his emerald eyes ice.

"I wouldn't accidentally get too close to the circle. Just a bit of friendly advice," he says. The cadets on either side of him chuckle, then stop so suddenly that I'm certain Han gave a sign I can't see.

A heartbeat later, the instructor's voice rings out again. "Start."

5

Lera

launch into an over-the-shoulder forward roll the moment Han's order singes the air, getting distance from Katita before I'm even on my feet. The princess, who spun around instead, blinks once to orient herself to my presence. Finding me two paces away, she bares her teeth and rushes forward, her fury-filled volley forcing me into an unexpected defense.

Whatever Han has been doing with her over the past months is showing, the princess's already crisp strikes now filled with a savage power. From the hard glint in her blue eyes, the harsh set to her pretty pink lips, I'm certain Katita would have no qualms about killing me outright—practice or not.

Taking a deep breath, I ground myself in the now of the match, letting the rest of the world fall away. The harsh sun beating down on my shoulders, the circling hawk patrolling the sky, the shifting sands beneath my feet. None of it matters. Not even the wave of menace coming from Tye. Or so I tell myself. This match isn't about Katita or Tye or the trials. It is about keeping the mortal world safe.

Wap. Wap. Wap. The rhythm of our wooden practice blades fills the air with a familiar sound as I let Katita's strikes continue to come at me, though now it's by my choice. Studying the new power and speed of the princess's blows, exploring the small changes of style. Building a plan before making my move. And then I do.

Breath steady, I track the opening along the left flank that the princess leaves whenever she parries too quickly, and swallow a smile. My muscles coil inside me, my eyes locking on Katita's shoulders without ever looking at my true target. The blade in my hand snaps in a deadly feint, my blade swinging right toward Katita's temple before—

The girl's boot strikes my chest so hard that my breath catches, the watching cadets cheering with a cutting malice as I stumble back like a drunken sailor, little bothering to hide my confusion. I could have split Katita's skull—any self-preserving being would have tried to block the attack or step from it or… *Stars, I'm an idiot.* Regaining my footing and my wits at the same time, I curse myself again. Katita never even entertained the idea that my attack could be real because Prowess rules forbid contact with the head.

No wonder Coal was furious with the notion. A few months of drilling that nonsense into one's head, and grave things could come in battle.

"Love the new instincts," I murmur to Katita. The princess's heaving breaths fill the air between us, strands of fine blonde hair now plastered to her cheeks and forehead. "Ignore heavy things trying to bash your skull in."

"What are you doing here?" Her nostrils flare, her heart beating so quickly that I see it vibrate in her neck. She wants—needs—to win this round with the desperation of a stallion trampling his way to a mare in heat. Fevered and blind. "No one on this team can stand the sight of you."

I believe her. And little care. Unfortunately for Katita, I'm not looking to champion the Prowess Trials. I'm looking to champion the whole mortal world. There is no option to lose.

Hooking my foot behind her ankle, I drop the girl backward. Her eyes widen in indignation as she lands hard on the sand.

"Didn't anyone tell the dimwit that only strikes with a *blade* score points?" Puckler calls.

Ignoring the royal, I follow Katita to the ground, jamming my knee into a spot just beneath her rib cage so hard that she can't draw air. Grabbing the top of her tunic with one hand and the material beside her thigh with the other, I pull up on both pieces of clothing, bending the girl's body like a bow around my knee.

Calls of indignation race through the watching cadets, but I little care. I can see the losing struggle in Katita's face already. One heartbeat passes, her face turning dark. Two, and her eyes flash from fury to panic to pain. Three. The sword falls from her hand, her whole being now focused on nothing but dislodging my weight. On drawing breath. A bug trying to escape the burning sun.

Grabbing Katita's fallen sword, I slide the length of the blade against her neck, killing her over and over. "Did anyone tell you that dead by any rules is still dead?" I say. "Yield."

"No."

With a shrug, I put my blade right across her windpipe and press, the wood threatening the tender cartilage of her throat. The girl's eyes bulge, her hands gripping the sand, as her legs kick out uselessly.

"I can do this much longer than you'd enjoy, Your Highness," I tell her coolly.

"Go. To. H—"

"Forfeit." Han's voice rings out across the sand a moment before his hand closes on the nape of my neck, throwing me off Katita and face-first into the ground.

Spitting sand from my mouth, I rise in time to see Han drag Katita up by the front of her shirt, the girl's eyes glazed with unshed tears. "I didn't yield, sir." Her voice sounds small. Desperate. "We weren't standing, so Lera's strikes won't count for points. Please. My father is coming and—"

"And I'm not going to embarrass the Academy by letting him see the rubbish you just called a fight," Han finishes for her. His voice is ice, but he looks polished, calm—no sweat on his forehead, not a single black hair out of place. "If you can't tell death when it's pressing down on your throat, you're too dim-witted for the slot. Ten laps around the Academy, and when you crawl back, I'll let you stay on as an alternate." Throwing Katita onto the sand like he did with me, Han meets my eyes. Their cold blue-gray depths send an eerie shiver through me, and I have to fight not to look away.

"Let me be clear, Osprey—you've won Katita's slot by virtue of your mutual stupidity. One cadet was too idiotic to remember the rules and the other too dim to take reality into account."

I stand, dusting myself off, and, after a moment of considering, decide to keep my mouth shut.

Han snorts. "You have what you wanted. Whether you keep it—or survive it—is entirely up to you."

THREE HOURS LATER, I discover Han wasn't kidding about my survival being in question. While the rest of the team rotates through stations varying between general fitness and event-specific techniques, I spend the time in nonstop sparring sessions with whoever is an odd man out. The setup, which seems comfortingly familiar at the onset, becomes something else entirely when Han instructs the cadets to provoke me into breaking the rules and then punishes me each time I do.

A method—like everything else he does—designed to win athletics events and lose battles.

At the end of the training, Han tells everyone to get cleaned up and change into clean uniforms for the midday meal—which I realize I will now be eating with this group of vipers instead of Arisha. Despite that being the plan all along, I can't help feeling the uncomfortable twist in my stomach at the notion of sitting with a group that wants nothing more than to see me fall flat on my face.

Having busied myself retying my perfectly intact shoelaces to buy myself some breathing space, I'm the last to leave the sand, the keep tower's bell just beginning to strike the hour.

Or so I thought. Tye steps out of the shadow of the low side exit as I approach, one muscled arm blocking the door, his pine-and-citrus scent coated with bitter anger. For a moment, the sheer proximity of the male, his bare chest glistening with sweat as it shifts with deep breaths, tricks my mind into hope. Then my gaze lifts to Tye's ice-green eyes, and all that hope shrivels like a sun-dried grape. Taking a step back, I cross my arms over my chest and wait for him to say whatever it is he plans on tossing my way.

I'm too tired to fight. I just hope I'm too tired to feel too.

Tye advances on me with the menace of a prowling tiger, his powerful limbs picking their way across the sand. "What game are you playing at, Osprey?" His lilting accent has deepened, his shoulders spread, taking space and air as he looms over me. "First, you try to have me kicked off the team, and now, failing that, you go after Katita. What's your angle?"

Protecting the mortal world while you are busy twirling around a bar.

"Well?" Tye presses closer now with a threatening jostle, so close I can see every freckle on his sharply carved face, the small scar on his lip that I've kissed too many times to count. The flecks of silver in his eyes that dazzle when he's using his magic.

The leash I hadn't realized I had on my anger slips with a resounding pop. My teeth grind together so hard, they screech, my heart pounding against my ribs as all the heat in my body fills my face. I hated hurting Tye. I truly did. But even knowing his barbed comments are born of perceived betrayal and pain, I've had enough.

"What answer can I possibly give that you'd find satisfactory?" I demand, refusing to take a step away as I know the male is attempting to make me do. Though I initially considered telling him the truth— that I'm here to be able to respond should the Night Guard strike—I no longer trust Tye not to use my own words against me. Not to pass them on to Han. A groan rises through my chest, my nostrils flaring with hot breath. "I'm here because I want to compete."

"Since when do you care about the Prowess Trials?"

I look up at the sun to gauge the time. "Since about three—no, three and a half—hours ago. Now get out of my way."

Tye shoves me, the unexpected malice in it sending me backward to fall ungracefully onto the sand. I gasp, the small puffs of sand rising about me now sticking to my sweat-drenched uniform. "You are not welcome here, Osprey." He glares down at me, shaking his head. Then his voice lowers. "Either get yourself gone, or it will be done for you in a way I promise you will little like."

Without waiting for a response, he turns his back to me and walks out of the arena, his heels kicking up grains of sand. Catching sight of Katita waiting for him in the entrance and their exchanged nods, I know the warning was as much from her as from Tye.

Despite the shield of anger encasing my heart, my throat closes. No amount of Coal's harsh hand knocking me on my backside compares to being discarded by someone who still holds a piece of my soul.

6

Lera

By the time I collect a fresh uniform from my room and drag myself to the baths before midday meal, everyone seems to have heard about the new change in the Prowess roster—and not a single soul seems happy about it.

"She rigged it, you know." The girl's words, mixing with the steamy air, seem to press on me from all directions. "Katita was out of sorts last night, so of course, Osprey pounced on it."

"Why did Han even entertain that bit of rubbish after the lies she spread about Tyelor?" another girl answers.

"Maybe she offered him something. Down below." The first girl's voice drops. "I wager she is only on the team long enough for a certain cock to deflate."

Hating my immortal ears, I rebraid my annoyingly thick hair as quickly as possible, finish buttoning my tunic, and slip quickly from the bathhouse into the muggy outside air for the too short walk to the dining hall—where I can look forward to the company of my new teammates surrounding me once more. Less than half a day on the Prowess team and I'm already homesick for Arisha's company and Coal's morning brutality.

The tall stone buildings on every side of the courtyard seem to press in tighter now, invisible eyes peering out of every window, waiting for me to fail.

"Lady Lera of Osprey." Rik's low, self-satisfied voice catches me in the back, making me flinch. When he and Puckler catch up to me in the shadow of the arena's towering wall, our identical uniforms turn my stomach. "You will, of course, do us the honor of allowing us to escort you to the dining hall?"

Given that my last meaningful interaction with Katita's royal cousins involved a brawl in the stable where one of them tried to stick a horse bit into my mouth, I don't even bother feigning friendliness and quicken my pace. I might have to share a table with the bastards, but I don't have to breathe the same air as them a moment longer than that. "Difficult as the feat may appear, I can manage to find the mess hall on my own. So be good little lapdogs, and run along to Katita."

"Is that any way to talk to your new teammates, for however short a time?" On my right, Puckler moves so close that his arm presses into mine while his twin mirrors the motion on the other side. Their heavy bodies, rather than leaning down through training, have only gained more mass—they'll be the Prowess team's best weapons in the wrestling and strength categories. Puckler's voice drops. "We are under orders from Han to make sure you're seen appearing at the dining hall in team company. Personally, I'd rather be wiping my boots with your blood, but I'm not about to cross Han for the pleasure. At least not until we have your arse flying so far through the air from Prowess, you'll need a map just to find the ground again."

My jaw tightens. As much as I want to tell the pair off again, keeping close to the royals was the whole point of joining the team, so I can hardly complain about Han doing half my work for me. Forcing a smile—which I hope will irritate the hell out of the cousins—I offer the pair a mocking bow. "Then I will savor the honor of your company for as long as I'm worthy."

The brothers exchange too-knowing glances. "Fortunately for everyone, I'd not worry about having to savor the honor for too long, Lady Lera."

I stop, forcing the pair to stop with me, and twist to grab the front of Puckler's tunic. "What exactly are you talking about?"

Puckler pulls his lapel free of my grip, dusting off the invisible dirt I supposedly left behind. He quirks one dark brow, the curved scar at its corner seeming to smile with the movement. "I know better than to use the privilege of my position and run my mouth with the Academy's official news before it's been announced. You'll be told soon enough."

My stomach clenches, and I turn back to the cobblestone path quickly, hoping the pair might not notice the renewed tension gripping my neck. The last time Sage had official news, it was to bring the Prowess Trials down atop our heads. A small voice in the back of my head tries to tell me that the pair are full of horseshit, as they always are, but the sight of Sage—who tends to take meals in the privacy of his own suite—seated comfortably in the dining hall makes that thought disappear.

Of course, the only empty chair at the team's table is next to Tye, who pushes it away from him with his foot just as I approach. His fresh pine-and-citrus scent washes over me, bringing stinging dread now instead of pleasure. My body still recognizes its mate in that scent, still wants to react with every nerve firing, but I have to start protecting myself.

On the other side of the table, Katita smiles at me like a cat with a bowl of cream. At least she and Tye are not sitting together. Even with this cavernous distance between Tye and me, the hard wall in his eyes, I can't shake the dull pain that washes over me whenever I see them together—which seems to be all the time these days.

Ignoring the princess, I move my chair back into place and frown at the food, which is already on the table. Unlike the rest of the cadets, who choose meats and breads and cheeses from the offerings along the dining room wall, the Prowess table's fine red tablecloth is covered with unappetizing slabs of bland chicken and bowls of steamed, saltless peas. Reaching for the metal pitcher to pour myself a drink, I find water in place of the freshly squeezed juices I know the others are sipping now.

Feeling Tye's malice-laced amusement, I serve myself from the platters. If he can eat this, so can I. I certainly ate worse during my servitude to Zake, even if my new immortal senses remind me just how much the food resembles performance feed assembled for prized show animals. I'm about to consume my first forkful of near-mashed peas when Headmaster Sage taps a fork against his glass for attention. His bald head shines under the chandeliers, his hooked nose casting a deep shadow over his face.

"My lords and ladies, good day," he says in his usual nasally voice. "With our esteemed royal guests and athletes arriving within days to watch the Academy's first hosted Prowess event, I remind you that this is our greatest chance to show all the continent our athletic abilities, but also our academic prowess. In deference to these unusual circumstances, I will allow any student who feels too nervous to attempt the final exams before such an audience to self-select themselves out of the Academy now and re-enroll to repeat this year in the fall. Any student who attempts the final oral exams and fails, however, will be expelled immediately and without recourse. Please consider which course of action is right for you as you finish the meal."

As Sage sits, a sharp murmur of conversation rises around the dining hall at once—though none from those at my table, who don't seem surprised. I stare at the contents of my fork, which still hovers awkwardly in the air. So this is what Katita was so self-satisfied about. Whether I fail the exams or self-select myself out, the effect will be the same by the start of the Prowess Trials—I will no longer be on the Academy's team.

As brilliant as Katita's plan is, it is not her I'm worried about. It's River. He watches me at the Prowess table with such a lack of emotion in his gray eyes that whatever appetite I managed to summon fails at once.

Watching him walk stiffly out of the dining hall's side door, I swallow my food as quickly and silently as basic decorum permits, and, with a murmur about needing to get a book, excuse myself into the keep's long stone corridor. Afternoon light slants in through high slit windows, a stern reminder of the Academy's former life as a military fortress. Instead of turning toward the library at the far end of the walkway, I turn toward the large male making a study of one of the paintings hanging on the wall. His dark brown hair, usually so neat, is mussed on one side, evidence of stressed fingers combing through it. His body is straight and regal, but exhaustion rides in the shadows under his eyes—and something more, something so rare in that perfect face that it makes my insides cramp. Fear.

Coming up beside the deputy headmaster, I place my hands behind my back and hope that the words that have eluded me since Sage's announcement will miraculously spark to mind now. They don't.

Which means I don't know how to explain to River why I'm seemingly throwing out the months of time and effort he's invested in me. And not just that—months of *himself*. I know he's shared pieces of himself with me in that study that he never has with anyone else, save his imaginary wife.

I wasn't thinking about River when I made this decision, and there's no way to pretend I was.

"When were you going to tell me about the Trials?" River's rich voice brushes against my skin, the careful tightness in it making the hurt obvious. At least to me. This close to his broad back, his heat and intoxicating scent wash over me, and it's all I can do not to close the distance.

I swallow. "Sometime after I knew that I had made the team."

"I see." He rocks back on his heels, his gaze still on the portrait of Ckridel's King Zenith. As if he needs to find a place to look that isn't me. "And what do you intend to do now, in light of the headmaster's new rules?"

"The same as I was going to do before—take the exams and pass."

"So you are rejecting Sage's offer to repeat the year." It isn't a question. River runs a hand through his hair, making it stand up even more. "Why? It is an option better than either of us could have hoped for. No exams. A guaranteed return to the Academy. You've made great strides, but the extra time to work with the material will only help."

"And you want me to spend the summer away from the Academy."

River finally swivels to me with thunder in his eyes, his chiseled jaw as hard and stubborn as the rest of his rock-hard body. His face seems to sing with command, from his high cheekbones to the shadowed planes of his cheeks, and I'm reminded for the thousandth time how foolish it is to cross this immortal king. "You can bloody bet on it. There is danger here no matter what I do, and I'm not going to pretend to sound apologetic about ensuring your safety."

For a moment, I can't speak, his power seeming to fill the corridor, the Academy, the world, taking all the air with it. My hope diminishes with each breath—hope that maybe telling River the truth of why I need to stay might actually sway him. The last thing the male wants to hear is that I'm inserting myself into the greatest fire I can find—and I've too many other wars to deal with to fight River on this too. My chin rises. "I'm not running away—from the Academy, from exams, from whatever will or will not happen here. That much is in my power to decide, and I have."

River says nothing, turning back to the painting as if that might keep the hurt in his eyes from showing. It doesn't. His stiff back rises above me once more, a wall of intricate muscle outlined under his white silk shirt. I long to put a hand there, to run my finger down his spine as I might have done in the old days—when I was allowed to. "I was under the impression what you and I did for the past months was important," he says finally.

"It was important. It *is* important." My heart aches, my mind finally seeing what I must do. A way to keep my decision from appearing like a betrayal of all our time together. Glancing around the empty corridor, I dare to touch the male's hard forearm, the muscles beneath the silk so coiled that I feel his tension seep through the connection. "What you've done for me in the past months, the lessons and the patience and the learning—it's meant the world. You are the first who's ever cared enough, who I could trust to protect my dignity as well as my mind. I'm grateful. Eternally. I need you to know that." My grip on his arm tightens. "There is less than a week left until exams, and we've always assumed I would be taking them. I trust what we've been doing together, River. You should too."

The silence settling at the heels of my words is deafening. One heartbeat passes. Two. Then River pulls his forearm from my grip.

"Indeed, Lady Leralynn." With a formal bow, the deputy headmaster walks away, his footsteps echoing down the long stone corridor.

7

Lera

To my surprise, a full third of Great Falls' cadets take Sage's offer to repeat the year over, nearly all of them belonging to the smaller noble families who little worry that the withdrawal will reflect poorly on their kingdom. All the royal-blooded cadets stay, some more nervous than others. By the time I walk into Master Briar mathematics classroom the following afternoon, the Academy already feels pruned.

For a moment, I'm jealous of all those students headed home to their cozy castles in their fine horse-drawn carriages. With only three days until the start of the Prowess Trials—and oral exams—the tension within these walls has never been higher.

"Find your seats quickly, please," Briar calls from the front of what was a musty classroom until someone's inspiration exploded over it last night. The neat rows of writing desks are gone, replaced with wooden benches placed in a semicircle around a raised dais, a large slate propped on top of it like a crown jewel. The room's heavy drapes are pulled back strategically to ensure that the afternoon light falls on the center of the space while keeping the bench area in shadow. As with the rest of the Academy, flags representing all of the ten kingdoms stand along the back wall, adding splotches of mismatched color to an otherwise heavy wood-paneled room. A mini arena without the sand and athletics equipment.

Without the usual writing desk to hide behind, I make a bid for the last row of benches and sit behind the widest back I can find—which just so happens to be Tye's. Putting my books on the bench next to me to save a spot for Arisha, I take a deep breath, preparing myself for an hour of my hardest subject. But instead of slowing, my heart stops altogether. The low hum of conversation and perfume-saturated air nearly makes me miss a familiar woodsy scent.

River.

Nodding in answer to Briar's bow, the male puts his arms behind his back and stands off to the side as unobtrusively as a warrior of his size can manage. Despite surely having felt my gaze on him, the male gives no sign of having seen me in the crowd. *Fine.*

Arisha slides somewhat breathlessly into the seat I saved, and for the first time ever, I take in her drab gray uniform with envy. Anything would be better than this stiff costume. "Shouldn't you be sitting up front with…them?" she whispers, looking meaningfully at my Prowess uniform.

I curse, realizing both my mistake and the empty seat left for me right in the center of the Prowess team bench. Around us, several other people have plainly come to the same conclusion and now watch me with a mixture of interest and amusement. I bite my lip. Move or stay? Move or stay? Seeing more and more eyes glance my way, I carefully rise from my seat—to suddenly find myself the only one standing besides Master Briar and River himself.

I sit down quickly. Brilliant.

"If you are done with selecting seats, Lady Leralynn, might I start class?" Briar asks, adding to the heat already flooding my cheeks. When his gaze finally releases me, I slump in relief—which quickly fades with his next words. "Today, we will hold mock examinations to familiarize everyone with this year's…modified exam procedures. On exam day, you will enter the arena, whose setup this room now mirrors. When your name is called, you will approach the instructor at the side table, choose one of the facedown tickets, and hand it to him. The question on the ticket, which may be from any subject of study, is the one you will be answering for the exam."

"One question. One answer. No makeups." River's voice carries easily as he walks forward, drawing utter silence like a cloak behind him. In his fine wool jacket and fitted pants tucked into polished black boots, he looks every inch a commander. His eyes pass over me flatly as if I'm just another student—and maybe after yesterday, I am. By the time he stops beside Briar, the only remaining sounds are the benches' occasional protesting creaks.

Briar, who blanched as much as the rest of us at River's approach, clears his throat. "Fortunately for today, I have it on good authority that all the questions concern mathematics." Some of the students titter nervously, but my throat is too dry to acknowledge his poor attempt at humor. These ridiculous exams are nothing more than an exhibition for the sake of a powerful audience—designed for maximum drama and minimum boredom.

Taking out a stack of tickets, the professor lays them out on a small side table beside him. "All right, then. A volunteer, please."

Beside me, Arisha sits taller—looking a bit like Shade's wolf spotting steak left too close to a table's edge.

Briar smiles at her. "Lady—"

"Lady Leralynn," River says, interrupting Briar midsentence, eyes as implacable as brushed steel. "You appear to have been planning on changing seats when I came in. You may as well come all the way up here."

No. No No NO.

For a second, I'm certain that I've imagined River's words, that he would not purposely do this to me. But then the reality of the silence and watching eyes seeps through, my limbs lead-heavy as I get to my feet. *Bastard.* My heart, which had stopped beating for a moment, now leaps into a gallop. River is a bloody bastard.

Walking onto the dais as if ascending the executioner's block, I reach for one of the identical slips of parchment lying facedown on a small table. Heart stuttering, I pull out the one farthest from me and feel what little air is left in my chest leave it altogether as I hand it to Briar to read aloud.

Provided the measurements below, calculate the farthest acceptable point to place a catapult outside the castle wall to ensure the load clears it.

I can barely hear the master over my pounding heart, forgetting the numbers the moment he reads them. When Briar hands me the slip of paper, I stare at it with gut-sinking dread, willing for the words to rearrange themselves into something different. They don't. Nor does the formula that I know exists condescend to make an appearance in my mind. River and I have worked out problems similar to this in the past, but stars take me if I remember where to even start.

Benches creak as the cadets shift in their seats, the air in the room turning from heavy with tension to full of confusion and curiosity. Apparently, I'm supposed to be doing something now. Writing. Calculating.

"If I were in that castle, I'd be feeling pretty safe just now," Tye murmurs to Katita, his voice loud enough to ensure that I hear it.

Heat fills my cheeks, spreading through me as the rest of the class chuckles along with Tye's words, and River lets it happen.

"Lady Leralynn?" Briar prompts. "There is a small slate and chalk you may use for preliminary calculations, if you wish."

I pull down on my tunic, gathering whatever dignity I have left into my voice. "That won't be necessary, sir, as I don't know the answer. I will, however, be sure to study harder over the coming days."

8

River

Having ordered Leralynn to wait for him in his study, River knew the rest of the mock exam would be difficult to stand through. But the breath-stealing tightness in his chest still caught him off guard. He wanted—*needed*—to go after her. To explain that he wasn't being a bastard just for the enjoyment of it, but to make her understand the danger of the fire she toyed with.

His nails dug into his skin where he held his own wrist behind his back, his shoulders so stiff that they were starting to ache. The mock exams were still running, and it was taking every ounce of his willpower to appear to listen to the other students when, in truth, their words buzzed together in his mind. *Stars,* if one of them danced a jig in the middle of his answer, River probably wouldn't even mark it just now—though, fortunately, his reputation was enough to keep the cadets in line.

At least the cadets who were not Lera.

When the class ended, three more cadets having decided to repeat the year rather than risk expulsion, River gave Briar an ominously ambivalent bow and excused himself to his study. He'd given away nothing about whether he was pleased with the class's performance, for the simple fact that he couldn't very well have an opinion after having paid zero attention.

Outside the windows that River passed with every twist of the circular stairs, the Academy was unrecognizable. In addition to the monstrous arena keeping dominion over the courtyard and flags of every color strung up posts and trees and rigged ropes, the grounds seethed with the unfamiliar faces of staff hired to support both the competition and the soon-to-arrive royals. Maids and scullery boys, guards and cooks, carpenters and seamstresses—it was an invasion. One that made the Academy a target for whatever darkness was at work in Great Falls. And one that River wanted Leralynn to have no part of.

The girl was so much like Diana that it dried his mouth. Not just the large chocolate eyes that saw everything, the hips made to fit his body, the luscious heavy breasts that peaked impertinently at a slight chill—but the fierce passion and bravery and the silk thread of concealed vulnerability that roused his every protective instinct. Their study sessions had slowly turned into a gauntlet for him, an hour each day that toed a knife's edge between pleasure and pain—and left River aching all over for hours afterward. He'd controlled his body around her for two months now. Just barely. But his soul wasn't nearly as cooperative, and the imminent danger of the Trials was only making it worse.

River's heart stuttered, the irrational sensation of history repeating itself washing through him.

The morning Diana took the fall that ended her life, he had marked her horse's unusual friskiness and known that Diana's passion for riding was exceeding her skill. But he'd not stopped his wife from getting into that saddle. She'd have hated him for it. But she would still have been alive.

River would not allow himself to be the same coward when it came to Leralynn.

Taking the final flight of stairs, he found the girl sitting on the bench outside his office as wayward pupils were instructed to do. A bad sign that she hadn't simply let herself in like she usually did. The sunlight flowing through the window caught on her auburn hair, making it sparkle with the same brazen life that radiated from her creamy skin. Blood rushed to River's cock, spurring thoughts that very much did not belong in the upcoming conversation.

"Leralynn."

"Sir." Rising, Lera put her hands behind her back, her voice carrying nothing but cool stinging distance.

All right. They could play it any way she wished so long as she was packing her bags at the end.

Opening the door to his study, River stood aside to let Lera through, the girl taking all of five steps before stopping. Awaiting instructions. No emotion. No contact. Nothing. At least she wasn't afraid that he'd beat her, River thought. They'd come far enough that she trusted him not to.

But then he looked into her eyes and realized it wasn't trust he was seeing but a wall. A cold brutal wall. And no matter how much he wanted to protect her, he didn't think he could stand this.

"Leralynn." Coming to stand before her, River reached to brush his thumb along her cheek before his better instincts could stop him. It was smooth as silk, sending a frisson of heat up his arm. He longed to reestablish a connection, to chip away at the wall of hurt so they could speak.

"Don't touch me."

The words hit River in the chest, and he dropped his hand at once, though it made his throat tighten. Putting his hands behind his back to avoid further temptation, he gave Lera a small nod of acknowledgment.

"Yes, I set you up," he said, his voice steady as he gripped her eyes. "But it was the only way of getting the message to register, Lera. This time, you walked off the testing stage draped only in humiliation. Had these exams been real, you would see the end of the Academy. No recourse. Nothing. Not even I could bring you back."

No response. Just a silent chocolate stare.

"Do you understand me?" River demanded.

"Perfectly." Lera raised a brow. "May I go?"

After striding to his desk, River pulled out the withdrawal agreement and ink and laid them out for Lera.

"I am not withdrawing."

"You will return in the fall." He reached for the pen.

"I said no. I am not withdrawing. *Sir*."

River stared at the pen in his hand, trying and failing to make sense of Lera's words. When the pen snapped beneath the pressure he didn't know he was exerting, he felt something inside himself give way too.

"What exactly do you expect to happen at the exams?" he demanded, his voice rising in spite of himself. He longed to take Lera into his arms and shake reason into the girl. He couldn't do this again, watch a coming disaster and do nothing to stop it. Couldn't lose Leralynn without a fight. "That was a real exam question, Lera. And you failed. What the bloody hell do you imagine will change in the coming days?"

A muscle tightened in Lera's jaw, and for a moment, something other than cold iron flashed in that beautiful gaze. Regret. Hurt. Longing tempered with determination.

Crouching down, she picked up the broken halves of the pen and laid them on River's desk. "I imagine that days from now, I will take the exam and fail, after which time, I will be expelled from the Academy forever," she said with an evenness that sent a shiver down River's spine. Lera wasn't lying. She was…she was up to something.

Something that River had missed completely. His eyes narrowed. He was barking up the wrong tree altogether, wasn't he? His heart quickened, his mind racing to discard the reality he'd imagined in favor of the one in Lera's too-brave mind. And it scared the stars out of him.

"Is there anything else you need from me just now, sir?" Lera asked, pausing for a heartbeat that wasn't long enough for River to find his words. When she started walking to the open door, however, River beat her to it, shamelessly using his longer stride and reach to shut the wooden panel before the girl walked out of his life forever.

"An explanation," he said quietly. Not a demand, not this time. A request. "Please."

A muscle ticked along Lera's jaw, the hurt and anger she'd kept leashed flashing over her face. "If you'd bothered listening to anything I've told you since I arrived here, you wouldn't be asking that." She shook her head, her breath quickening. "You humiliated me today, River. I trusted you, and you twisted my trust into a bloody lash. So I'm done. We'll play by your rules. For another three days or so, at least."

River kept his hand on the door, his heart pounding against his chest.

"So if you've no reason to hold me here, *sir*, let me go."

The cadet was right. He had no reason to hold her. Not as the Academy's deputy headmaster. Not as anything. Except, somehow, these particulars had stopped mattering. Deep in his heart, an aching, raging fear that had started to roar minutes earlier was now slipping into his blood. If Lera crossed that threshold now, she wouldn't be coming back. And a primal, untamed part of River wouldn't let that happen, not without one hell of a war.

"No." The rush of blood was deafening in his ears. "You are going to give me a chance to fix this."

Lera yanked the door handle, the heavy wooden panel staying shut beneath River's weight.

"Let me go." Twisting around, she shoved his chest, her small palm thudding against him with a futility that would be humorous any other time. "I want—"

A growl that had nothing human in it rumbled from River's lungs. Grabbing Lera's wrists in the middle of her next swing, he twisted her around and pulled her back against his chest, her trapped arms now crossed over her chest. "I don't care what you want. What you are going to do is talk. However long it takes to get there."

9

Lera

*B*astard. Bastard. *Bastard.*

I yank against River's unyielding hold, his warm, rock-hard body pressing into my back. His chest heaves, his breath fast and hot against my hair, his bounding pulse hammering through my skin. Raw and unrestrained and so unlike the controlled River I know that my own primal senses spiral from my grasp.

I was going to walk out. And now I can hardly move, my muscles coil with tension and pain and a sudden flush of arousal that I hate as much as I hate the male himself right now. I want to run. To hit River with all my might. I want to bed him. Kill him.

"You set me up as a laughingstock." I twist my hand, trying futilely to claw the skin on his wrist.

"I needed you to understand." The escaped anger in his voice clips the words.

"That I'm an ungrateful charity case who doesn't know a good thing when it smacks her in the nose?"

"That I'm not letting you walk out of my life without a bloody fight!" As suddenly as River grabbed me, he pushes me away to brace his trembling hands on his thighs. His nostrils flare, the quick gasps of air so unlike him that I stumble.

Not walk out of the Academy. Out of his *life*.

My eyes widen. River's raw glare confirms what I heard. His face has gone pale, lips tight. He said more than he meant to, and he knows he can't take it back.

I shake myself, my mind screaming at me not to believe a word. He's an immortal king and I'm a peasant. A stray who wandered into the palace. Without the bond's magic, River can't want me—can't feel anything but a mix of pity and indulgence. Strip our souls to the truth, and I'm not meant to be River's mate—I'm his project.

My eyes sting.

With a soft grunt, River snaps from his crouch, centuries of training giving his great body a predator's honed power. Before I can move, he grips my hips with hard hands, lifting me clear off the ground. My legs dangle above the floor for one confused heartbeat before he sits me on the edge of his tall desk. Staking out a place so close to me that my thighs open to accommodate his body, the male brazenly puts his palms on either side of my face, locking our eyes in a vise-hard grip.

"You aren't a charity case." He spits the words, which seem to steam in the tension-filled air. Outside the window, a cloud shifts, a new tiny ray of sunlight now reflecting off the male's storm-gray irises. A muscle twitches in his square jaw, every line of his hauntingly beautiful face filled with feral intensity. "You never were. Ever."

"Then why—"

"Because I've fallen in love with you, damn it." River swallows, his gaze rushing to the ceiling as he breathes deeply. Desperately. "No matter how much I've tried not to. And now I can't bloody undo it. Can't let you walk out that door and never come back."

My mind stills.

"Leralynn?" River swallows again, the sound loud in the silent room. Leaning his head down, he lets his mouth hover inches away from mine, his woodsy scent filling me. Sharp and dangerous, like a cliff's edge. "Say something," he whispers.

My mouth is dry, the blood racing so quickly through my veins that the world dims at the edges. And yet, despite all the warning of my screaming mind, my body is drawn toward him. A mouse walking willingly toward a yawning trap that might still snap shut.

River closes his mouth over mine with a groan. After all these weeks without his skin on mine, the heat is intoxicating, the pressure of his velvet lips so perfect, I can't help but respond with a hunger of my own. His tongue sweeps across my bottom lip before slipping inside with immortal confidence.

A cascade of heat and power slides from my mouth to my bunching nipples and open thighs. My senses revel in River's leisurely exploration, his tongue sweeping slowly through my mouth once, twice, before the sensual kiss morphs into something different. Wrapping his hand in my hair, he plunges himself deeper into me, the assault primal and possessive and unyielding enough to lay his soul bare.

My breath hitches, my hands digging into River's shoulders, then sliding down over his bulging chest. I want more than a kiss. *Need* more than a kiss.

River's muscles flutter and coil beneath my touch, his chest and abdomen tightening more and more as I wrap my fingers around the hard bulge pulsating beneath his tight britches.

Gasping for breath, he pulls his mouth away from mine, his large pupils fevered with pulsating need. "We... I can't." His voice is breathless, as if he's calling from the midst of battle. We're crossing a line that, in River's veiled world, we've never before touched—the last line in the sand that the deputy headmaster inside River knows is there. "You are a student."

"I'm Leralynn." A pressure I didn't realize was building inside my chest strains and breaks apart, spilling into my simmering blood. The lies and half-truths and pretenses and assumptions. Emotions wash over me in an unforgiving wave, pounding against my heart until it all forms into a single clear thought. "I'm Leralynn," I say again, my voice filling with a power that's of my soul, not of magic. "I'm not a student. I'm not a lady. I'm not anyone you think me to be or want me to be. I'm not anyone but *me*. Know that as you make your move, River, and own it. Because I am."

River's jaw tightens once.

And then he rips open my uniform jacket so hard that the buttons ping as they bounce off the stone walls.

1 0

River

The *ping ping ping* of Lera's buttons against the stone walls of his office sent little shocks all the way to River's cock. *Good stars,* he wanted her, his heart pounding from the toxic mix of desire and bewilderment—it was a *cadet* writhing with expectation beneath his hands. And yet, Leralynn was so much more than that.

Her destroyed jacket fell to the floor with a satisfying plop, the wide cloth belt dropping next, then shirt and chest wrap. With their bindings gone, the girl's gorgeous breasts fell loose at once, the bunching pink nipples begging to be touched. Breath in his throat, River traced his thumb once around each tantalizing bud in wonder, savoring the feel of the delicate skin perking beneath his touch. He'd dreamt of this moment countless times, mentally traced these curves that he knew were not his to touch, but the dream paled in comparison to reality. Now that he was here, he knew no ready-dealt plan could do Leralynn justice.

Lera inhaled lightly, her pleasure at his touch making his cock throb so hard that his vision darkened for a moment. He drew a slow breath to calm himself, but the scent of lilac and arousal that filled his lungs had quite the opposite effect.

Hooking her legs around his hips, Leralynn pulled him in closer, gazing at the pulsating crotch of his britches with the same rapt attention he'd just paid her breasts. When her face rose, the sight of her full, slightly parted lips and penetrating chocolate eyes tightened River's heart into a fist.

Diana. This was Diana and yet not.

The girl's hands were on his shoulders now, yanking his jacket down his arms and tearing at his shirt with about as much respect as he'd shown hers. When his chest was finally bare, she spread her palms against it possessively, then slid them down his stomach to his belt with what he could have sworn was a purr, her eyes hot enough to melt steel.

River's heart stopped.

Sweeping his arm roughly over the top of his desk, he threw the documents and pens and everything that had seemed important just this morning right to the floor. To irrelevance. Grasping Lera around her waist, he flipped her belly down on the wooden surface, her legs dangling over the edge even before the last of the rolling ink bottles stopped clattering against each other. One hand beneath her hips, River pulled open her fly with a single tug, feeling his pulse echo off his cock as he slid her pants and undershorts off her round bottom all the way to her knees.

Beads of moisture already hung like ornaments on Lera's wiry auburn curls, more glistening arousal slathering the insides of her thighs. River rubbed over the wetness greedily, inhaling her need as it melded with his own. Her small mews of desire almost made him climax on the spot. *Stars,* the girl smelled *right.* Fresh and perky and a perfect fit for a jagged void inside his soul. A missing piece.

Deep inside River, something strange rumbled to life. His senses woke to every sound and sight, down to the slight crackle of Lera's coarse curls rubbing against each other as she clenched her backside in instinctual protection. The wet sounds of her pulsing sex practically moaned for touch.

Yet River wanted so much more than just to be inside Leralynn. He wanted to conquer her. To enter her so fully and intimately, to bring her to such heights of overwhelming pleasure that neither of them would ever forget this moment. He wanted to make her scream with ecstasy, until she knew—not just in her mind but in her soul—the answer to the challenge she'd put before him.

Heart and breath racing, he swirled his fingers through her slick folds without warning, making the girl moan loudly—thank the stars for thick stone walls—then plunged a finger so deep inside her, he thought she would retreat from the pressure. But she only pressed harder against him. A new trickle of arousal dripped onto his desk beneath her. Yes, Lera was more than ready for him—which was convenient, because he needed to be inside her now.

"I'm going to take you, Leralynn." River's words came low and raw. "I'm going to take you as you are. And show you who I am too."

Lera's backside undulated beneath his hand in response, her hitching breath frantic with need.

Yanking open his fly, River positioned the dripping head of his cock at Lera's entrance. He'd intended to go slow, to push inside with a gentle pressure to let the girl adjust, but Lera's frustrated growl put an end to that plan.

Gripping her hips, he sheathed himself inside Lera's channel in a single stroke.

11

Lera

 y back arches as River's impossibly large cock thrusts deep and hard inside me. I grasp desperately for the edge of the desk to brace myself. His sheer size momentarily overwhelms me, focusing my whole being on the hard, hot, slick cock that throbs powerfully inside my tight channel.

And then he starts pumping.

In and out, in and out, the head of River's cock slides through me, melting my bones to a pliable blazing metal. My sex clamps around his throbbing intrusion, my channel first trying to restrain the great force inside me, then to urge it on instead. Heat pools in my sex and simmers my blood, my need rising. Rising.

River's desk creaks under his powerful thrusts. Through the open window, the clamor of students calling to each other in the courtyard and the harsh sounds of construction are a distant reminder of where we are. Of who River is when he's not in this room with me.

This only sends a new spike of need through me, and I buck, urging River to go faster. Harder.

Instead of yielding to my demand, the male inhales sharply and grips my hips in an unyielding hold that sends a message of its own. He will take me for who I am—and give me who he is as well. A

59

commander. A warrior. An immortal king he does not remember he is, though his body does.

A whimper escapes my lips, turning to a desperate moan. Everywhere River's cock touches turns more sensitive, more hungry. Even with his hands on me, my backside pushes up to meet his powerful hips as they slam into me, the *slap slap slap* of his heavy sac coming a fraction of a heartbeat later. Again. Again.

Cock still moving inside me, River bends his body over mine. His hard chest presses into my back, his hands sliding along my outstretched arms as his woodsy scent caresses my nose. Pressed between the heaviness of River's hot body and the cool, unyielding wood of his desk, I feel the strange combination of being trapped and safe, captured and savored.

Then River's canines scrape along my neck, and my thoughts stop.

"I love you, Leralynn," he whispers into my ear. "You. As you are."

Before I can answer, he pulls us back just enough to slide his hand beneath my hips, his fingers tracing the hood around my swelling apex. Explosions of sensation race through my core, tormenting my thighs and toes and spine until I'm gasping for breath.

The combination of River's cock and teeth and fingers is like a set of blazing shackles that I can neither escape nor stand a heartbeat longer. The approaching edge of pleasure looms before me, as inviting as it is frightening for its cosmic drop. For the fact that under River's skillful command, I've no control of what's to come.

"River." His name is breathless on my lips, and I don't know if I'm begging him for reprieve or acceleration. My muscles clench, my channel tightening around his shaft as the building sensation courses higher and higher and—

The male sinks his teeth into my neck just as his thumb brushes over my exposed bud.

Every muscle in my body tightens down on my throbbing sex in an explosion of blazing pleasure. I scream, River's other hand clamping down on my mouth before the sound can travel too far. The restraint, his warm callused fingers that smell of my own arousal, only heighten the waves of spasms shaking my body. I gasp, shuddering beneath River's heavy body, as each nerve inside me fires, the world splintering around me. Around River's thickness. Again and again, until my legs weaken.

I return to my senses slowly, aware first of the smooth writing desk beneath my cheek, then the firm pressure of River's fingers massaging my lower back, then the final hazy realization that the male's large cock is still hard and throbbing inside me. Which means… Which means River is just getting started, while I'm a gasping puddle of drained muscle and sensitive sex.

Blinking myself further into reality, I realize that River has pushed my thighs wider apart, the cheeks of my bottom splitting open with a wet sound.

I try to close my legs on instinct and get nothing but a quickening pulse.

"You wanted me to take all of you, Leralynn." River's low voice and harsh, unsteady breaths play over my back, making my blood tingle with excitement. "And I will. I will take you completely."

Before I can reply—not that my sluggish mind could conjure anything that my traitorously dripping thighs wouldn't name a lie— River swirls a finger in my moisture and presses it with steady pressure past my backside's sensitive rim. The finger slides in easily and—even as I squirm against the intimacy of the intrusion—zings of maddening need shoot from the engorged nerves right to my apex.

Intimate. Yes. The taking is humiliatingly intimate, and yet River's presence fills a void deeper than my pulsing sex. The male behind me isn't toying with me, isn't just playing at bedding, but giving me the whole truth of his desires. Not because some magic compels him to, but because he wants to. Chooses to. Chooses *me*.

He may be a different man in his mind, but his needs and pleasures are the same as *my* River's. If I close my eyes, I can almost pretend we're back in Lunos, River bending me over his huge oak desk and taking exactly what he wants—showing me new heights of pleasure in the process. I trust that male with every inch of my body.

Beneath me, River's blunt fingertip suddenly traces all around my hood, the swollen bud inside it waking with magnificent shock. My toes curl inside my boots, and, as I draw a sharp breath against the blooming sensation, River's second finger enters my backside, stretching me stealthily.

The urgency growing around my bud has my thighs squeezing against River's unyielding knees, my thoughts focusing ruthlessly on the tiny spot that controls my body like a fishhook. The knowledge of how open I am to River, how fully beneath his command, somehow magnifies each sensation, my body rousing more and more without regard for common sense.

River traces my hood again, flicking just a hair too lightly over my apex. As I arch my hips into him with demand, his cock and finger withdraw from me altogether, the sudden emptiness devastating.

I whimper.

And then I feel the large head of River's cock pressed against my back hole.

On the heels of emptiness, the slow entry is excruciatingly filling. Holding my bucking hips steady, River's strong thumbs dig into the fleshy mounds of my bottom and rub in tiny firm circles. The deep, deep pressure rides the edge of pain, which morphs into molten pleasure as it releases muscles I didn't even know were tight.

My body welcomes him, though the fullness inside me is enough to make the world flicker.

Moving his hands, Rivers finds the sides of my apex again, playing my body's sensations like a musical instrument. When the fingers of his free hand slide into my slippery channel, offsetting the cock filling my backside, a renewed wave of heat ripples through me, making me moan into the desk.

My sex pulses hungrily, blindly. The slow *thrust thrust thrust* of River's cock seems to touch every nerve in my body at once. My fingers claw the table, my helpless legs buckling beneath his assault.

River pounds into me now, each thud of his hips and fingers striking right into the center of my engorged bud. The abused nerves of my channel and backside howl with sensation so overwhelming, I don't know how much more of it I can endure. Our breath is harsh against the stone walls, our bodies meeting in a driving, jerking rhythm, mindlessly seeking release.

A primal keen escapes my lips before I can stop it, my body spasming around River's fingers, colliding with the echoing ripples from his throbbing cock.

His thrusts quick. Harden. More and more until my sex is convulsing around him and his own breaths come in desperate grunts. His unyielding control sends tremor after tremor through me until—

"Now, Leralynn," the male commands, and the two of us topple off the cliff together.

1 2

Lera

I shiver on River's lap, my body curled against his damp chest, my heavy head resting in the perfect, muscled groove of his shoulder. Not that I could stand just now even if I wanted to. My mouth is dry, my skin beaded with sweat, my insides a pool of satisfied exhaustion. With the potent aftermath of the coupling seeping through me, I'm more relaxed than I remember being since stepping foot in Great Falls. As if River's firm command of my body filled a missing puzzle piece, the scattered pieces of my soul now clicking into place.

His large, callused palm strokes my hair and back, the rhythm echoing the *plop plop plop* of raindrops pelting the window.

"When did it start raining?" I mumble.

River chuckles. "Sometime between your first and second release."

Despite my having just done the deed, my cheeks heat, and I bury my face deeper in River's shoulder, his skin warm velvet against mine.

"You are beautiful when you climax, Leralynn," he says into my hair, his soothing hand still stroking my skin. "I could listen to that sound all day."

I could too. Unfortunately, we don't have that long. Somewhere in this room are the remains of my clothing and my problems—both of which need to be found sooner than later. Gathering my wits, I start to pull myself back from puddle to living being.

River squeezes my backside roughly. "Stay put before you trip over your own feet," he orders, taking charge in a way that makes me want to punch him almost as much as it makes me want to mount him and start all over again.

With a chaste kiss on the top of my head, River rises with me in his arms and sets me back down into his chair. The leather is cool against my naked skin, the soft cushion hugging my curled form. Striding around the room, Rover collects my clothes, his muscles shifting beautifully beneath his bare skin. I can't help but watch him, his dark hair mussed adorably, gray eyes hooded with delicious satiation I'd never seen in the Great Falls' deputy headmaster. How the male still has energy to bustle around when I can barely lift my head is a mystery of its own.

River stops to pour a cup of water from a chilled pitcher before returning to crouch beside me. "Drink."

The cold liquid is so stark against my blazing body that my eyes pop open like a child's toy.

A corner of River's mouth twitches. "I think I've worked it out, by the way."

"Something in particular, or the world in general? Because I'm not sure I can recall much about the world in general just now."

"I know why you joined the Prowess team." River's smile fades. "Why you won't take the offer to leave the Academy for the summer."

My hands close around the water cup, the chill suddenly desperately necessary to focus my heavy mind. Not fair of River to bring it up now, but I can't make him unsay the words. Can't undo the reality pressing in on me on all sides either. Shimmying to sit upright, I meet his penetrating gray eyes and wait for him to continue as the pattering of the rain against the glass intensifies.

"You've inserted yourself into the middle of any and all danger to befall this Academy ever since you set foot here, Leralynn. A habit that I've tried to talk, work, and punish out of you with no success to date. In that light, imagining that you've suddenly reformed and decided to leave the worrying of the Prowess Trials to me was utter folly all along." River swallows, his dear face so tight, I wish I could smooth it with my fingers.

"River—"

He shakes his head. "I promised to accept you as you are, Lera. And for that, it seems I must acknowledge what you are."

My chest tightens. "What am I?"

"A protector." River draws a deep breath, his glistening chest and shoulders expanding with it. "You won't stand aside and let other people defend the Academy because, deep down, you can't. It goes against your nature. You aren't inserting yourself into the middle of the Prowess competition because you've developed a sudden interest in showmanship, and you aren't refusing to repeat the year because you worry about the consequences of the delay. No. Everything you do, it's designed to get you to the hottest center of whatever inferno you believe most likely to happen."

My breath catches, each of River's words striking its target. *Protector.* The irony of the word choice isn't lost on me, but neither is River's own nature.

Now that the male understands what I'm doing, what will he do about it?

My fingers tighten around the water glass, which I drain quickly, my mind racing for footing. I'm swallowing the last mouthful, still settling on a response, when I hear nimble footsteps climbing the stairway outside River's study.

My eyes widen. River's do too.

Scrambling into the shirt that River hastily hands me, I discard the now-buttonless coat and wage war on my chest wrap while River kicks the writing supplies he swept onto the floor into the space behind his desk. Inks that survived the previous fall now open in protest at the new insult, spreading in dark puddles across the floor.

On the heels of River's too-keen words, the sight of him cursing as he simultaneously tries to lace his fly closed and dance away from the spreading ink puddles is almost enough to make me dissolve into giggles.

"Leralynn," River hisses my name in quiet warning.

I blink at him. Mark his fierce gray gaze. And double over in spasming deranged laughter that refuses to get itself under control no matter how hard I clap my hands over my mouth.

13

Lera

"Tyelor." River's control of his voice is a skill to envy. "What can I do for you?"

"Master Han sent me to track down Leralynn, sir." Tye slides his hands into his pockets, carefully avoiding my gaze. "Shall I tell him that Lera is unavailable?"

My mind sobers to the twin blows of Han's name and Tye's cool gaze, harsh reminders of the world beyond this office—beyond River. Despite our hasty cleanup efforts, the smell of our coupling hangs too thick for a fae to miss—especially Tye. I weigh the merits of saying something about it outright, but end up just straightening my tunic instead. Giving River the formal bow of a cadet taking leave from the deputy headmaster's office, I'm half-relieved and half-disappointed when the male nods his dismissal and starts toward his desk without a backward glance at either of us.

Tye holds the door open for me, my stomach clenching as I step out onto the landing and face the downward stairs. My limbs still feel like partially boiled noodles, and the thought of the climb is as appealing as dealing with Tye just now. Or Han.

"You look well ridden," Tye drawls.

With my foot halfway down a step, I jerk so violently that my balance falters, and I hop about like a dimwit to find my balance. My gaze locks on Tye, but the hard lines of his beautiful face give away nothing. My hand closes on the railing in a bone-white grip, my nostrils flaring. "Was that a statement of fact or a threat?"

"Could it not be both?" Tye cocks his head, looking eerily like a tiger examining his prey. "I could report you."

Heat rises through me, my blood quickening. I open my mouth to curse the bastard, but force myself to take the high road before I make a bad situation worse. Tye does have every reason in the world to hate me just now—every reason in his version of the world, at least. "If your mission was to show me how threatening a place on the team feels, I assure you that you've accomplished it several times over in the past sun cycle."

Tye's hands shift in his pockets, and he continues down the stairs at a pace that makes me jog just to keep up, avoiding looking at his smoothly sculpted muscles. With his back to me, the resemblance to my old laughing, feline quint mate is too painful to bear. "The difference is that Prowess has defined every step of my life, past and future. For you, it's another cord to twist to your liking."

I grab the top of Tye's arm as we clear the next landing, the feel of his coiled muscles beneath my fingers excruciatingly familiar. His white sleeveless shirt is damp, the pine-and-citrus scent mixing with the rain, which also hangs in fine beads from his hair. For once, he's left his red uniform jacket somewhere, and this close, even for a moment, the warmth of his body brushes against my skin. "If by my *liking* you mean keeping the Academy safe, then yes."

Tye snorts, turning on me with a flatness to his emerald eyes that chills my blood. "I feel safer already."

My free hand closes into a fist, and I take a slow breath to cool my simmering blood. There is one thing I've not done to repair this void between us, and I owe that to us both. A last-ditch effort that should have been the first. "Tye, I'm sorry."

"No, you are not." Emerald eyes flash. "And in case no one ever told you, you are a terrible liar, Lera."

"I'm sorry that I hurt you." Full truth there—though, cruel as Tye is being, it might not be true much longer.

Tye's nostrils flare, pain flashing in his eyes before ice crystals grip his irises. "I was no more than collateral damage in your plans." He tips his head back, taking a few moments to breathe before looking back at me, his voice collected once more. "If the deputy headmaster decided to take his conversation over your performance into the southern territories, it was plainly done with mutual consent. So, don't worry, Leralynn—I won't throw River to the wolves. That's your style, not mine."

My teeth grind together. "Thank you."

"Don't bother. I'm doing it for River." Tye jerks his arm free from my hold and continues down the step. "As for you, you want to be on the Prowess team? Well, welcome. Now you get to discover what that means in Han's world."

Covering the rest of the steps in speedy silence, Tye and I exit the keep into what's now turned into a pounding sheet of rain, the sky so dark gray that it might as well be evening. The water soaks my uniform and hair at once, which at least has the advantage of washing River's scent off me. The courtyard is empty, save for a few scurrying servants braving the rain to complete their tasks. And Han. Waiting under the cover of the arena's scaffolding, he stands with his arms crossed, his eyes boring into me with a butcher's evaluation.

"That stunt you pulled in Briar's class was unacceptable," Han says by way of greeting. My gut churns as always at the sight of him. The wrongness of him. "Especially with only three days until the opening ceremonies."

My pulse taps a beat to match the pounding rain, my bunched muscles tingling with energy. "Sir—"

Han's backhand strikes my face with a vicious casualness, and I stumble back, wiping a trickle of blood now snaking from the corner of my mouth.

Through the sheet of rain, I mark Tye standing easy a few paces away, hands still in his pockets as his soaked white shirt molds to his chest and cut abdomen.

"You want to stay on the team?" Han kicks the ground, sending chunks of muddy earth into the air and splattering against my uniform. "Then beg for it. On your knees."

For a heartbeat, I think he's jesting, but one look at his hard blue-gray eyes tells me the man means every word. Not out of vengeance or mindless fury, but sheer calculation—as if I were a dog whose nose he intends to rub in a carpet mess. My gut clenches, my pride clashing against my mission. Before I can decide, however, Tye grabs the back of my shirt and forces me down to the ground with iron strength, not stopping until my knees and then my face are ground into the mud. His lips brush my ear as grit slides into my mouth and eyes.

"Do it," Tye demands. "Beg or quit. Choose, Leralynn."

Something inside me snaps, the feel of Tye's hand on my back suddenly more despicable than Han's presence. I shared myself with this bastard—my body and my soul—and now he's grinding both into the mud as if I'm a bug under his shoe. I don't deserve this. No one does. And maybe that's the point, the final period at the sentence's end. We are done, Tye and I. From this moment and forever.

Everything inside me coils, and it's all I can do to keep from turning and driving my fist right into his jaw. Except the bastard isn't worth it. I need to stay on the Prowess team for reasons that have nothing to do with him. And now, never will.

"Please, Master Han." I raise my face from the mud only so far as to ensure my words carry, shouting through the pounding rain. "Forgive my impertinence at the mock exams earlier and permit me to stay."

My heart pounds as Han's boots close with my face, Tye still gripping my shirt.

"Kiss them." Han sticks the dirty toe beneath my nose, shredding my dignity a bit deeper with every breath.

For a moment, my fingers grip the mud, itching to flip the man onto his back, but I overrule them, pressing my lips against the dirty leather.

Han snorts. "Animals. All alike at the core." Stepping back, he straightens his rain-drenched tunic. "Good enough. Tyelor, run her for two hours on the arena steps to encourage a change in attitude, and we will consider the matter closed."

Tye's grip on me releases as Han walks away, and I am on my feet in a moment, a handful of dirt I'd pulled into my palm flying directly into Tye's nose. The caked mud lands with a sticky *thwap*, covering his freckles and one sharp cheekbone.

"I hope you enjoyed the show." My voice is so cold, I barely recognize it. "It would be a shame to have wasted the opportunity."

"You're welcome." Tye rolls back on his heels, the pounding rain already washing his face clean. Despite the attempt at nonchalance, his jaw is tight, the muscles vibrating along the side of his face. His voice drops, and I wonder if he didn't feel it too, that moment when the bridge between us cracked and fell into a cold abyss. "Had you let your mouth run, the afternoon would have been a great deal more painful."

"Noted." I jerk my chin at the arena steps. "You heard our master. Lead the way."

"Stars damn it, lass." Closing the distance, Tye grabs my arm, his lips pulling back from his teeth. "You could have walked away. No one is forcing you to stay on the team—but if you choose to, you play by Han's rules. Believe me, you are fortunate to have been reminded of this by me rather than by him."

"Oh, so that's why you ground my face into the mud?—To protect me from the fierce Prowess coach? I should be thanking you on my knees, no doubt."

"Lera—"

I yank my arm away just as lightning cracks the dark sky, outlining the keep's jutting tower in eerie detail. "One—don't touch me. Two— I'm not out here to talk."

"Don't be an idiot, Lera. You barely walked down the keep's dry steps. Run these, and you'll break your neck." Tye shakes his head, soaked red hair flying. "Just wait here. If Han cared enough, he'd have stayed."

Turning my back to the male, I hop onto the first of the impossibly long row of benches letting the cold rain keep me anchored. I don't want Tye's favors. Or words. Or anything to do with him. My wet boots pound the wooden steps, the slippery surface taking all my concentration. Overhead, thunder claps its hands as if urging me to move faster.

"Leralynn." Running up with soul-deadening ease beside me, Tye shouts over the rain. "Stop before you hurt yourself."

I run higher, the *pelt pelt pelt* of my boots hitting wet wood echoing through my bones. Faster. Inside me, the cords of magic flail in their shackles, the occasional escaping lash of power sending out sparks, which sizzle and die in the rain.

The next time lightning strikes, it silhouettes Tye's lithe form snatching for me at the top tier of the arena's wooden bleachers.

"Go to hell!" I jerk away before Tye's hand can connect, my boot catching a patch of slippery wood. My breath stops. My knee gives way, my body weight pulling me down to my right shoulder—except there is only air there. With a swallowed yell, I fall from the top of the arena bleachers to the earth below.

"Tiga!" Tye's shout follows me down, the last syllable hitting just as my back lands on the wet ground, my arms slapping out on instinct to dispel some of the force.

The deafening thud ripples through my whole frame, the world blurring through stinging rain and shock.

For a moment, all I can do is gasp for air. As my lungs slowly refill, I assess the damage. Between the soft earth, my immortal body, and a head full of good fortune, I'm more dazed than hurt. As I blink myself back to awareness, I see Tye vaulting from the top of the bleachers to land beside me in a crouch, his emerald eyes fevered with a terror that my cotton-filled mind doesn't share.

"No," Tye whispers, his hands on my shoulders. "Not again. Please."

"Get off me." I shove him away, noting distantly that his lithe body gives easily beneath my push, the male coming to rest on his knees in a puddle. His shoulders shake, his breath as ragged and fast as the streams of water running down his cheeks.

In another world, I'd ask after him. In this one, I pull myself slowly to my feet and trudge away without a backward glance.

14

Zake

Standing by the window of a servants' corridor inside Great Falls Academy's keep, Zake—an invisible servants' master inspecting his underlings' pitiful work—watched the arena through the sheet of falling rain.

The stars truly had a wicked sense of humor. Every coin of golden fortune that had hit his palm in the past year had had a layer of muck on the other side, while the puddles of dung he'd stepped in had jewels beneath. The present situation was a perfect example.

Never in his life had Zake—the man destined for immortality's kiss, the lord of the only estate daring to stand sentinel at Mystwood's edge—imagined himself donning the rags of servitude now covering his muscled body. And yet, the disguised post turned out to brim with the one power that evened out all battlefields: information. Which Zake had gathered more of in the last hour than Owalin had in the past year.

First, the wench who'd led Zake on for years, abusing his kindness and generosity to steal his birthright from right underneath his nose, was here. Flaunting her—*his*—immortality as she scurried about like one of Han's silly little racing pets. Second, and perhaps even more interesting, no one but Zake seemed aware of this fact. Even Han himself seemed to believe that both Leralynn and the redheaded male currently kneeling in the mud, of all things, were human.

Even without seeing the male's pointed ears and ethereal beauty, Zake well remembered the bastard's face from when he and his friends had shown up at Zake's estate and robbed him blind. Given how that day had gone, Zake recalled the friends less clearly, but no matter. This in itself was interesting enough.

Initially, Zack had considered going to Owalin to discover just how much the revelation of Han's incompetence was worth to the Night Guard leader. But that was an amateur move, something an underling who licked the immortals' boots would do. Leralynn and that male beside her had some kind of magic that veiled the eyes and minds of everyone but him—and Zake would learn the how and the why of it before bartering such information, showing Owalin that Zack was no less than a peer.

But that would come later. Before Owalin or anyone else got their paws on Leralynn, Zake needed to have a private conversation with the girl to whom he'd opened his home and heart before she'd ripped it to shreds. They'd have words of reckoning. Of forgiveness, perhaps, if she repented truly and accepted the punishment due. And then, she'd tell him everything.

Knowledge was power. By the time the Night Guard was ready to descend upon the scurrying Academy mice, Zake alone would hold all the keys.

Tilting his head, he watched Leralynn stumble through the rain for a few more moments before turning away with a chuckle. So many times, he'd cursed the stars for the girl's betrayal, and yet here that very betrayal was, bearing gifts.

Zake licked his lips, savoring the soon-to-come time when he'd get the wench alone.

15

Lera

Ta da daaa da daaa da dadaa!

The exhilarating call of the trumpet burst from the Academy gates, summoning a party of liveried servants racing to greet yet another royal arrival, a lapis-blue carriage with gold accents drawn by six pure-white horses. Another high-value target for the Night Guard's picking. With the opening ceremonies for the Prowess Trials officially happening tomorrow afternoon, today is about greetings and logistics for the royals.

For the cadets, today is about the start of exams.

Arisha and I join the stream of students heading from breakfast straight toward the arena, all silent or murmuring quietly instead of the usual loud chatter. Even with each cadet presenting on only a single, randomly chosen question, the sheer number of students ensures the gambit will run for days on end—a side attraction for the visitors to enjoy between bouts of athletics. While a mere option for our royal guests, attendance at the first exam session this morning is mandatory for all students. Those who know they're not facing exams today are visibly relieved, some even carrying books and notes under their arms so they can study surreptitiously during the exams.

Thanks to River, I'm near last on the list—though, despite Arisha's urging, I've not bothered to eat anything this morning anyway. Even with each spare moment between Han's training sessions spent in intense tutoring under either Arisha's or River's watchful eye, my chances of passing the exams are one in two at best.

Ta da daaa da daaa da dadaa! Ta da daaa da daaa da dadaa!

I push Arisha from the path of a harried-looking young man with a basket of wet towels and bottles of chilled wine rushing to greet their royal highnesses of whatever kingdom is now arriving in a cloud of dust and whinnying. Some royals themselves, having settled into their rooms and changed out of travel clothes, have now joined the crowd in the courtyard, milling about in colorful groups or drifting into the arena for the morning's entertainment. Their fashions represent every corner of the kingdom, from stunningly simple silk gowns and jeweled tiaras to elaborately embroidered robes with headdresses to match. One beautiful, olive-skinned noble wears what looks like an actual snake coiled around her neck, which she strokes and coos at lovingly. Three enormous peacock feathers jut out of her chignon, waving pleasantly in the summer breeze.

Another set of servants nearly bowls us over, carrying goblets and fruit and messages of personal greeting toward the keep from the headmaster. In the distance, a man with wiry dark hair appears to be yelling at yet another group of new servants, and though I can't make out the yeller's face, the way the crew seems to cringe away tells me enough of his personality.

When the yeller sticks his thumbs into his belt in a way that reminds me too much of Zake, I turn my back to the group. The mix of nerves, training, and waiting has done little good for my nightmares, and now I'm seeing the man's image even when I'm awake. *Stop it,* I order my mind. In addition to there being no reason for Zake to step foot into Great Falls, the man I saw wore a servant's uniform, not a lord's coat. *There are plenty of real threats to go around without adding imagined ones to the mix.*

"Are you all right?" Arisha asks. Her chances of being tested this morning are high, barring any unforeseen disruption, but unlike the other students, she seems cool and collected, even excited. Though I know she tries to hide it for my sake.

Shaking off the illusion, I rub my face and conjure a smile before Arisha can worry. "Do we really need all these people every time the gate opens? You'd think it would be more efficient to guide the guests to the wine than chase them with the bottles."

"Protocol." Arisha fidgets in her pretty cap-sleeved dress, a light blue linen—which I envy just now. The red-and-gold uniform of the Prowess team is smoldering hot, the high standing neckline and thick sash around the waist doing nothing to ward off the sweltering sun. The only one possibly worse off is Coal, who refuses to let go of his signature black just to accommodate the weather.

I stop a frown before it touches my face. Coal, who has been doing nightly patrols, reported the same thing we've seen for two months now —the forest is quiet. Too quiet.

"Look over there," Arisha says, pointing with her chin toward a small group gathered in the shade of the towering arena wall.

As I turn, my gaze lands on a familiar muscled back that draws the attention of every female—and several males—on the Academy grounds. Unruly red hair shining in the bright sun, Tye stands beside Katita and an older man who—as the portrait in every Academy classroom informs me—is none other than His Majesty, King Zenith of Ckridel. Not that I need the portrait to tell me—his thick white hair is perfectly coiffed under a tasteful gold crown, his turquoise eyes and patrician features a thicker, more masculine version of Katita's. A team of five guards stands at a respectful distance, their sharp attention raking every blade of grass in their charge's vicinity.

His hands articulating in the air, King Zenith seems to be telling Tye an animated story. The tall male bends down to listen, only to lean back with a full-chested laugh a moment later, the king clapping his shoulder—clearly a bit dazzled by Tye's beauty, as most people are when they first meet him. Tye's smile fades, however, when the king points behind him, his hand beckoning ...*me.*

Summoning a polite smile that I hope communicates something other than my desire to be most anywhere else, I approach the group.

"Ah, and here is another gold-and-red uniform I've not yet had the pleasure of meeting." King Zenith smiles welcomingly as I approach. "And who would you be, my dear?"

"Leralynn of Osprey, Father," Katita answers for me before I have a chance to complete my bow. "Who won't be wearing that uniform too much longer if she keeps standing out here." The princess's sugar-sweet voice drops as if filling me in on a secret. "Didn't you see the new exam schedule?—You are in the first batch. In fact—we'll all come with you for moral support."

My stomach drops. Throwing manners to the wind, I turn my back on the king himself and rush to the board listing the testing roster.

Sure enough, my name is there, right at the front of the list, where it wasn't only an hour ago. The change is written in River's own hand. What the bloody hell happened?

My heart hammers. I was supposed to have two days until facing the exams—three if things stretched longer than expected. Which all had a fighting chance of giving me enough time to protect the Academy before being expelled from it. Now... Panic makes it impossible to think clearly. I look around for Arisha, only to catch sight of her back disappearing into the arena, taking her place in the stands as she's supposed to. The bell atop the keep tolls the hour.

"Aren't you going in?" Katita asks innocently, her father, Tye, and the king's bodyguards all closing around me. "Arriving late is an automatic fail."

Mouth dry, I walk around to one of the arena's several entrances without bidding the group goodbye and start toward the dais set up in the center. The sand crunches under my feet, the sun shimmering off it in waves. Cadets and groups of chatting visitors cover the benches in patches of color and slowly quieting conversation, glancing at me with mild interest. In the distance, another familiar trumpet call announces a new arrival at the gates.

Yes, after months of work, I'm about to get kicked out of the Academy without anyone even noticing. A sideshow to entertain the early arrivals. To ensure I'm off the Prowess team before the opening ceremonies even start.

I take the stairs toward the platform in the center of the arena on shaking legs, a surreal haze over my eyes.

"Lady Leralynn, you are running late." River's voice comes to me hollowly from the dais, as if sounding through a tunnel. Looking up, I find the male standing beside a large slate just like the one we practiced on in Master Briar's room. His face is somber, his gray eyes unreadable steel as he points to the table laden with questions that have the power to end me. "Over here, please. Select your question and let us get the exam started, please. We've over two hundred students to hear from still."

Somehow, I make my way toward River, my gaze begging his for an explanation and finding none. It's all I can do to keep my hands from shaking as I reach to draw my question.

The paper crinkles beneath my fingers, the ink swimming before me as I stare at the neat handwriting outlining the question. Mathematics. Something about baking supplies that could be in a different language for how much I understand of it. I may as well forfeit now.

Taking the paper from my hands, River clears his throat and announces the problem to the watching audience. There is a catapult, he tells them. A wall. A required calculation.

The very question I pulled in Briar's class, the numbers changed slightly. The question that River worked through with me in excruciating detail after the disastrous practice exam.

And one that has nothing to do with the words penned on the slip of paper I pulled.

My gaze lifts, traveling up from River's chest to his chiseled chin and penetrating eyes, and somehow, without his saying a word, I understand. Without the ability to delay my exam time, he's taken a different route to help me stay with my mission. One that may get us both thrown out of the Academy, but not yet. Not when such dirty laundry would tarnish Great Falls' reputation.

The gratitude and relief rushing through me is nearly enough to rattle my balance.

Taking the allotted time, I make notes on the offered sheet, ensuring my calculations will seem smooth when I go up to the large slate and show my work to the predatory eyes watching from the stands. Eyes that, for once, are about to see a competent girl striding across the stage.

16

Lera

*A*s the last grains of sand on the large hourglass mark the end of my preparation time, I square my shoulders and walk to the center of the platform, turning to bow my salute to the audience.

The arena has gone silent but for the whistle of wind through the bleachers and a whispering rustle of conversation. The half-empty stands suddenly feeling crowded for the scrutiny they exude. The cadets—all two hundred of them—crowd the top benches, chalks and slates poised on their laps to practice along with the show. In the front row, Katita sits primly beside her father, Tye lounging with his long legs extended on the princess's other side. Behind them, most of the rest of the Prowess team is gathered as well, a space forming between the sea of red-and-gold uniforms and a gathering of Fothom Kingdom athletes clad in blue silks farther up. Even here, the swarm of servants is ever present, rushing between the benches to refill wine goblets before disappearing back out the far exits, the large head servant I saw earlier berating them as they pass.

As before, my stomach clenches at the sight of that wiry dark hair and towering body, even though my logical mind knows that the man who once tormented me cannot possibly be here at the Academy. Then

81

the servant turns, the light catching the scar crossing his face, and my heart stops beating altogether.

Zake.

My breath quickens, my feet taking an instinctive step away from the dais even as my hands clutch my work slate. Images flash before my eyes at once. A stable. The scent of hay and wine and ripe sweat. The *whoosh* of a belt cutting the air. *No.* With desperate gasps, I focus on the here and now. On the wood floor beneath my feet and the Academy's flapping flag waving above the keep. I have to be here. Have to think.

Through the haze of rushing blood and rising bile, I focus on the facts. Zake knows me from before the Academy, from before I put the amulet around my neck. Which means the amulet's magic will not work on him. One quick glance, one twist of Zake's head toward the stage, and he will know me at once.

And then the bastard can call a whole mob to descend upon me. Given that Zake believes I stole his chance at immortality, he'd do it from pure spite.

Quickly as I can, I step back off the dais, returning to the shadow of the preparation space.

"Lady Leralynn," River says with a tone suggesting this isn't the first time he's calling my name. "It is time to present your answer."

Performance anxiety? Tye mouths to me from the front row, his cutting smile fading when I just stare back at him, eyes wide.

Stars, the males. Zake met them only briefly a year ago, when the quint magic called River, Tye, Shade, and Coal to cross the Mystwood forest to collect me. How much does Zake remember of them?

"Lady Leralynn, your answer, please." River raises his voice, a tinge of worry behind the frustration.

River. Zake must have seen River by now. That he's not raised a fuss about it must mean Zake failed to recognize River on sight, letting the amulet's magic spin its veil. Not surprising, given that Coal and Tye played the most prominent roles in the initial encounter. Still, would Zake's recollection change if he saw River and me together, the combination spurring his memory? Fear pulsates through me—for myself, for the mortal realm, for my males, whose veiled minds Zake could rip apart if he said the right words. The sounds of Shade's and Coal's agonizing screams when I'd tried to tell them the truth echo through my mind again and again. Truth that Zake can throw at them by accident, even if he doesn't get it into his head to sic a fae-hating mob after us before we know it.

Stars. My thoughts race, desperately seeking options. But there are none. If I go up on that stage, Zake will find me. See me. Expose me. And then—

I can't defend the mortals from a gallows. More to the truth of it, I can't let him harm my males, the mortal world be damned.

"Cadet. Now," River's voice snaps in warning, but I've not even time to mouth an apology.

Clamping my hands over my face as if holding in bile, I turn my back to the spectators and race for the nearest exit, the chuckles echoing from the stands whispering at my heels. I little care. I need to get away from the arena. Out of sight before Zake's gaze touches my face.

17

Tye

Performance anxiety? Tye mouthed to Lera as she stood clutching her exam ticket, her wide brown eyes and anxious scent giving him a grim satisfaction. A few more moments, and the lass would choke under pressure. And then she would be gone from Tye's Academy. From Tye's team. From Tye's soul.

She had to be, because Tye had woken up in a cold sweat every night since he'd watched Lera fall from the bleachers. Since he'd lost his last chance with the lass.

Leralynn isn't Tiga. Leralynn isn't Tiga.

The words Tye had been repeating to himself over and over still did nothing to ease the tight band around his chest. The heart-shredding pain that ripped through Tye every time his gaze strayed to the lass was as alive as ever. Which was cosmically unjust.

At least Lera refused to speak to him now, after the night encounter with Han's wrath. Tye shook his head—now *that* was a stupid reason to get upset, showing just how little the lass understood of competitive athletics. What exactly had she expected that day with Han? The man was a bastard, but he was a bastard who tuned the Prowess Team's performance to scalpel-sharp precision. Training under Han was an

85

agreement—put up with his cruelty for a competitive advantage, or don't.

Everyone on the team understood that. Except Leralynn. Which was her problem, not his.

So why did Tye feel like he'd made the greatest mistake of his life in letting her walk away from him?

"The wench is making a fool of herself," Katita purred into Tye's ear, watching Lera's jerking motions with the interest of a house cat following a stray rodent.

"Dinna call her that." The ire in Tye's voice made his accent thicker, but the intent of the words was clear enough to make Katita clamp her mouth shut with a frown. Tye refused to look at her, to answer the confusion lining her coldly pretty face. Because he couldn't explain it to himself either. Lera didn't matter. Or, more accurately, Lera needed to stop mattering. And quickly.

Even as Tye waited to savor Lera's failure, he couldn't look away from her. Couldn't stop himself from watching each and every one of her movements. The nervousness with which she'd chosen her ticket had given way to a relief that had made Tye growl unhappily—until the anxiety returned and all was well with the world. Lera deserved the coming humiliation and failure for betraying his trust, for forcing her way onto a team she felt no loyalty to. She—

A shiver raced down Tye's spine as the breeze carrying the girl's scent suddenly became heavy, laden with a terror that was absent only moments ago. On the stage before him, Lera was backing away, her eyes wide and heart beating so quickly that Tye could see it pulsing on the side of her neck.

Twisting around, he followed Lera's gaze toward one of the arena's exits, where a large mustached man spoke with a pair of serving maids. Wiry brown hair, a scar down his face, and a familiar cruel set to his shoulders. Even without being able to place the man, Tye knew he wanted to kill him.

No, hurt him first, then kill him. Because… A small burning along his chest and neck disrupted his thoughts. Tye was a cadet and a competitor in the Prowess Trials. He wasn't here to start fights with strangers.

That man hurt Tiga. The ridiculous thought fought its way through the burning, filling Tye's being with a protective instinct that made him want to tear the world to pieces. Except the notion was absurd. How could Tye think that bastard had hurt Tiga if he didn't know who the man was at all?

The man shifted his weight slightly, and Lera's fear morphed to a primal terror that punched Tye's chest.

Lera was cowering away from the dais now, clamping her hands over her face as if trying to keep her breakfast contained. Except she wasn't. She was running for her life.

"Where are you going?" Katita's hand closed on Tye's wrist, her gaze a mix of annoyance and genuine concern. Which made Tye realize that he was on his feet, his hands clenched into fists.

Katita pouted at him. The princess was pretty, but her looks did nothing for Tye. Never had. Just as her touch meant nothing now.

"Sit down," Katita hissed, her grip on him tightening. "The schedule is shifting. They can call your name any time, Tye, and if you aren't here, your scores will be forfeited."

Tye yanked away his hand, the exchange with the princess having cost him the sight of the man and Lera both. For the first time in his life, he couldn't have cared less about the Prowess Trials.

18

Lera

Rushing out of the arena, I see the keep rising before me and set a course for the grand structure, its thick stone walls beckoning with the promise of safety. My heart races, the courtyard streaking by in blurs of color. If Zake sees me, he'll hurt me. He'll hurt my males. Somewhere around me, a bell is tolling the time while a flock of birds exchanges news across the sky. But all I truly hear is my own panting breath, the soft pounding of my boots on the grassy earth.

The library door swings open with a familiar ring of bells that sounds too loud as I rush by the bookcases, barely registering Gavriel's surprised frown before I'm out the back door. Into the next corridor, then another. Not stopping until I'm in the wide hallway somewhere deep within the keep, only torchlight lighting the carpeted floor. My heaving shoulders press against the stone wall. As I catch my breath, my gaze lands on the slightly open door of a large utility closet. Even better. Slipping into the shelf-lined darkness, I finally sink to the floor amid buckets and brooms and stacks of candles and cradle my head in my arms, the scent of dust and wax filling my nose.

My body trembles, the mere memory of Zake's image having the power to reduce me to a shaking puddle.

Safe. You are safe.

Forcing my breath to slow, I push what wits I still have to focus. To catalog the facts and dangers. Somehow, Zake is here, posing as a head servant. And while he may have failed to recognize River, whom he only met briefly, and wouldn't mark Shade, whom he only met in wolf form, Tye and Coal he'd remember.

Tye, whom I left sitting there on the front bench of the arena.

Looking around at the brooms and shelves and candlesticks, I curse myself. At the very least, I should have stayed in the library with Gavriel and worked out a way to get messages to Coal and Arisha. To find a way to protect Tye.

And instead, I fell right into the trap Coal warned me about, my terrified mind making all the wrong choices. Which I need to start correcting quickly. I try to swallow, though my mouth is too dry for it, my heart pounding against my ribs.

Get up. Do something, you coward.

Forcing my legs to move, I climb to my feet. Grip the door handle. Take another breath. Finally, and much too slowly, I ease open the closet door, the headmasters of old watching me from their portraits along the candlelit corridor.

"Pity the fae gave you immortality instead of brains." Zake's rough voice grabs me by the throat.

Striding down the long hallway, the man looks as big as a mountain, his dark hair and weather-beaten face surreally familiar this close. The *tap tap tap* of his boots on the stone floor echoes through the hall, paralyzing my body and mind. A nightmare. Maybe this is a nightmare.

But no—that scent of hay and acrid sweat, sharper now through my immortal senses, is too real. Unable to move, I shrink against the wall, my breath coming quickly enough to make me dizzy.

"Did you imagine you could outrun me, Leralynn?" Zake demands, the high-necked brown servant's uniform on him at utter odds with his commanding swagger. "Did you think there would be no price to pay for your betrayal?"

"Touch me, and I'll scream," I whisper into the thick air. "I can yell loudly enough to summon the guards."

"Oh, I'm certain you can." Zake's lips pull back, showing yellow teeth. "You've always had a decent set of lungs on you. But you'll call no one, lest I tell the blind idiots here they have a fae in their midst. *Several,* in fact."

Ice slides down my spine. *Several.* So Zake's marked at least one of the males as well. And the lack of surprise on his face now, the casual satisfaction… *Stars.* The bastard didn't just recognize me at the arena—he knows I've been at the Academy for some time now. Knows and has kept it quiet. Waiting for his chance to strike at me when I'm alone—and I just gave it to him on a platter.

"What do you want?" I whisper. There has to be something if Zake has waited.

Halting a pace away from me, Zake opens the door of the same utility closet I thought my sanctuary moments earlier. "Get in, wench."

I shake my head, the only thing I seem able to make my body do.

Fae. You're fae, my mind whispers. *Stronger than him, faster than him.* But it does no good. My limbs may as well be filled with sand.

With an annoyed grunt, Zake snatches the front of my dress uniform and shoves me into the small room. Taking a lit candle from one of the hallway's many holders, he joins me a moment later, shutting the door behind him. The scents of wax and dust fill my lungs again, but only for a moment before morphing to something else entirely. Hay. A stable. A man's stale breath.

My whole body begins to shake, a faint ringing in my ears making Zake's voice sound low and distant, coming at me from all directions at once. Every fiber in my body tenses with the knowledge that there is no escape. Not from his temper. Never.

"I gave you everything, Leralynn." Zake's words hang thick with anger. "Home. Food. Protection. I indulged your wavering mind, waited for years and years for the maidenhead that I earned. I offered you a future so far beyond your sorry strain that you should have been begging to lick my boots and my cock. And what did you do instead?" Zake's hand grips the nape of my neck, squeezing the muscles painfully. "You betrayed me. Stole from me."

"No." The words come in a pitiful voice that feels like it belongs to someone else. Every breath brings hay and manure, the slow clomp of boots down the aisle, creaking stable hinges. I try to stop breathing altogether, but dizziness descends quickly. I'm alone, as I've always been. A worthless orphan who would have starved if not for Zake's charity. Who might starve still. "I didn't steal anything," I breathe, desperate for the man to believe me. Not that truth is much of a defense. My hands rise toward my ears, shielding my head for all the good it will do. Zake is too strong to defend against, even if I was stupid enough to try. "I never steal."

"You fooled those fae messengers that I'd waited my whole life for into handing my birthright over to you." Zake's voice thunders, and he takes several calming breaths before speaking again. "I will punish you for that first. Take it quietly, and I shall grant you a second chance you don't deserve. Explain how you did it—conning both the fae into thinking you were me and the dimwits here into believing you a human lady—and I'll let you go. We'll consider the books closed. The debts paid. A better deal than you deserve."

I can't move. Can't escape, no matter how much I try to tell myself that things are different now. Because they aren't.

His hand still on my neck, Zake twists me around to press my face into the wall. The sound of his belt pulling free of the loops fills my ears, mixing with the small puffs of his breath and the blood racing in my ears. The acrid scent of the man's sweat wraps around my throat. Choking me. The stone walls and dusty supply shelves around me have disappeared entirely, making way for a narrow wooden stall, its back wall hard against my skin. One of the boards is unfinished, its rough surface leaving splinters in my cheek. Hay crackles under my bare feet, which are nipped red with cold. I've outgrown my old boots, and Zake hasn't spent the money on a new pair.

With the flick of a knife, Zake nicks the top of my tunic, splitting the fabric open down my back. I have time for a single breath before the whistle of leather cuts the air, the sound slicing into my gut even before the strap lands on my shoulders, cutting right across the spine.

Pain explodes across my back, and I buck despite knowing it's a mistake.

"You know better," Zake barks into my ear. "Be still. Stubbornness and disrespect will only make it worse for you."

Another lash cuts my skin. A third.

I can feel my insides growing small and cold. Silent. My mind traveling to a different place as always. A babbling stream, a mossy bank—

"What did you give them, wench?" Zake demands.

"Nothing." My words are choked, my heart racing so fast that my head swims. I can already tell from the sound of Zake's voice and the first strikes that this will be the worst beating yet. That I will spend a week unable to move, blood turning my pee red, the brush of a shirt against my skin a torture. But I will move anyway, saddling Zake's horses and mucking his stalls because if I don't, he'll make it worse still.

"Don't lie to me, damn you. What did you give the fae for the immortality I was due?"

"There are fae somewhere handing out immortality?" A familiar male voice enters the conversation, the slight tinge of amusement in it hiding a simmering fury. When my head turns toward the sound, I see a large emerald-eyed male, unruly red hair falling over his face as he steps inside the small stable Zake holds me in.

My eyes widen. Over my racing heart, the stable morphs back to the large closet it is, clearing the way for a yet more frightening present. Zake knows Tye is fae, while Tye himself does not. And the amulet burned into Tye's flesh is ready to kill him to keep the secret.

"Run, Tye," I yell even as the belt lands again. "Go. Now!"

19

Lera

*I*nstead of heeding my order, Tye prowls toward Zake.

My heart pounds. Gathering my body together is an effort of will, my limbs shaking with the mix of pain and fear. "Tye, please." I make the words sound strong, though I know that the moment Tye is gone, Zake will hurt me worse than ever. "Go."

Tye's hand circles into a fist, his sharply angled face pale, his eyes glinting with murder.

"I wouldn't do that," Zake says, his knife back in his hand, the blade now pressing against the base of my ear. "Touch me, and I'll sever the wench's pointed little ear. What do you think the dimwits here will make of it? How will the mobs sway when they realize you two fae have been hiding among them all this time?"

Tye stumbles at Zake's words, his eyes glazing for one horrible moment.

"Fortunately, I am a man of business," Zake drawls. "Tell me, you fae bastard, how much is your secret worth to you?"

"What the bloody hell?" Tye says thickly, his hands rising to his ears before he shakes himself like a tiger trying to dislodge a bur from his coat. "What did you say?"

"I said, I'm a hair's breadth away from telling the whole Academy

95

you two are fae," Zake snaps, his patience clearly at an end. "How difficult is it—wait." Zake's voice changes. "Do *you* know you are fae?"

Despite the knife at my ear and the pounding fear rushing through my blood, my body coils, my elbow striking back to land a blind thud into Zake's ribs. A distant burning sensation envelops the side of my head, something hot snaking down my neck as Zake stumbles backward. Twisting around, I lock my gaze on Tye's, his face tight with pain beneath the amulet's assault. He raises his hands to his ears as if to block some terrible sound.

"Tye, go," I yell. Plead.

Zake grabs for the front of my ripped tunic, the cloth coming loose in his hand and leaving me bare to the waist. As I gasp, the man shoves me back into the wall, my hurt back striking the stone. My heart pounds against my ribs, letting in all the ghosts of our pasts. My breaths come so fast that the closet swims in front of me.

With a growl too primal to be human, Tye lunges for Zake's throat.

"Down, fae dog!" Zake's words drop the male to his knees with a shout of pain, a streak of blood now snaking from Tye's ear. Zake barks a laugh. "I know what this is. It's the stars' own repayment for when you came to my stable. You remember that? Remember shoving me down in my own home? The corrupt magic inside you knows I'm right, doesn't it? Recoils from the truth. Call a fallen fae a fae and—"

Tye's pained whimper sounds like a kitten, lighting every nerve in my body.

Before my mind can protest, I close my hand into a fist and strike Zake's mouth with every ounce of strength in my immortal body. It's no contest. Teeth and flesh give way beneath my unforgiving knuckles.

Zake stumbles back with a cry, blood flowing from his broken mouth. His eyes widen, the self-confident rage in them changing to confusion. Fear. His nostrils flare, his balance wavering as he recovers himself.

Then he blinks, wiping the back of his hand against his injured mouth as his dark eyes settle on me. Furious. Vengeful. Sadistic enough to make a new wave of paralysis slam through me. "You dare strike me?" The man's voice is thick with blood, shaking with rage. "You owe me your life, you piece of filth. Without me, you'd have died on the street or worse, sold your maidenhead for a piece of moldy bread and then—"

"And then you'd have found some other poor soul to whip

instead." The words spill from me in a torrent of truth as I watch Tye whimper and rock on the floor, clutching his head. Suddenly, it's not just my pain at stake, but Tye's and that—*that*—springs open the shackles of fear Zake has held me in my whole damn life. My gaze flashes up at him, my anger growing like a storm, spilling across my face.

I am immortal. I am a warrior. And the bastard before me is about to learn what that means.

"You think you did me a favor?" I say, my voice steel. I step forward, Zake retreating on bewildered instinct. Something shifts in his eyes. A predator who suddenly realizes he's become the prey. The once-threatening scar across his face is now just a sign of human weakness, just like the blood still pouring from his mouth. Blood I put there. "You kept me in a prison of fear."

"I was building your character. Work ethic. No one wanted you!" Zake's palms and shoulders come up to protect his head, though I've not raised a hand again. Not yet. He gasps. "I took you in. That has to count for something, Lera."

"Oh, it does." I take another step toward him. Darkness swirls inside me, the pain and fear of my paralyzing nightmares gathering into an energy that dims the world. My eyes burn as magic pushes against its shackles, testing and probing and—

The candles stowed on the shelves flare up at once, the closet alight with hundreds of tiny lights and racing shadows.

Zake screams, and drops to his knees, the stench of urine suddenly filling the space. "Lera, please. I did my best with you. I waited for you. I would have given you everything. My estate. My name. I raised you the best I knew how—"

"Shut your mouth." Standing over him, I wrap my hand around his fragile throat, his whimpering so at odds with the insurmountable male who's haunted my nightmares that I have to blink several times to assure myself of reality. "You want to know the price of immortality, Zake? It was death. And I'm going to help you pay it right now."

"Right now wouldn't be convenient." Coal's low voice sounds from the open door, and I whirl, bringing Zake staggering with me. From the warrior's relaxed stance, leaning on the doorframe, I've a feeling he's been standing there for some time. Then I see the sparking purple gleam in his eyes, and I know he has.

Behind him, Rabbit—Gavriel must have sent him to find Coal after

I sprinted through the library—stands panting, his hands still on his thighs.

My gaze meets Coal's, and he nods once, just for me, as if reading all the conclusions my mind is racing to. Then, with the warrior's signature casualness, the male juts his chin toward Zake, who still writhes in my steel grip. "Can this filth's death wait until he tells us what the hell he is doing here, and who else he brought along to his party?"

20

Lera

With Coal and Zake gone, Rabbit trailing after them, I turn toward Tye, almost afraid of what I might find. The male kneels on the floor, shoulders heaving under his sweat-soaked golden shirt, head hanging low as if in prayer. Blood has dried in dark reddish-brown trails down his jaw and neck, the sight making my own blood freeze in my veins.

"Tye?"

He doesn't respond, and I notice for the first time a fine tremor shaking his whole body.

I go to him and kneel by his side—hardly caring that I'm naked from the waist up, that the last time we spoke, it was to spit vitriol at each other. All I care about is if he's okay, if it's still Tye's soul in there. Taking his rough cheeks in my hands, I pull his head up—and gasp. His emerald eyes hook mine so deeply, I couldn't look away if I wanted to. They're bloodshot, fiercely lucid, and swimming with tears.

"Forgive me," he rasps.

"Why—?"

"Forgive me, Lilac Girl."

"What—" My words catch, my heart skipping a beat. The name

Tye used to call me in Lunos teases my skin, pulsating with meaning. "What did you just call me?"

With a shake of his head, he dislodges my hands, hesitates, then takes them so tightly in his that my knuckles crack.

"I remembered," Tye whispers. "And I've been trying to work out why you did it, fought Zake to protect me. I certainly deserved none of it."

I bite my lip against sudden tears, my body flooding with a relief that's almost too much to bear. Too much to believe. With everything that just happened, it's very possible that the only way for the amulet to have overpowered Tye's memories would have been to kill him. My heart quickens in delayed fear of how close we might have come to that.

Tye's chin drops to his chest again. "I remember everything. Remember wanting the cadet I thought you were, remember watching you fall off those bleachers, remember choosing the Prowess Trials over your word." Each of his whispered words makes him flinch. "I remember it all, Lera. And I'll bear any punishment you can think of."

"Tye." I swallow, my heart aching for him. For us. When the male refuses to lift his eyes off the floor, I take his face again, tracing his cheekbones, the square angle of his jaw. "The magic—"

"I should have fought harder!" Tye shakes his head, his red hair flying violently from side to side. Tears glisten on his cheeks, catching the flickers of torchlight in the hallway. "I failed you, Lilac Girl. And it nearly cost us all."

I wipe his tears away with the back of my hand, the immortal male beneath my touch shuddering at each caress.

Tye looks at me, and at last, I see the faintest glimmer of a smile in his beautiful eyes.

Before he can withdraw again, I throw my arms around his warm shoulders, burying myself in his pine-and-citrus scent and velvety strength. The pounding of his heart against his ribs is so powerful, I feel each beat vibrate through my own body. Once. Twice. Then the male's strong arms wrap tightly around me, crushing me against him.

"I'm not letting you go, Lilac Girl." The whispered words ruffle my hair, tickling the back of my neck. "Ever."

◆

"Mearrrow!" Leaping off the top of a bookshelf, Minion catches himself on Tye's bare shoulder—the male's tunic now covering me—and scrambles up his flesh. Several of Gavriel's treasured books, which the cat launched off, fall to the library floor in a cascade of slithering booms that make Rabbit tuck himself deeper into a corner.

Twisting lithely, Tye grabs the orange kitten by the scruff of his neck and holds him at arm's length before him, the small bundle of fur hissing and clawing the air with demonic intent.

"I'll kill him," he says—the first words he's uttered since I pulled him to his feet in that dusty closet and half dragged him here.

"Would you?" Gavriel asks, warm brown eyes looking hopeful. "It would be a great service to humanity indeed."

"No!" Arisha lunges for her beast, her braids and glasses bouncing along with her.

Bringing the still-hanging kitten close to his face with one long sculpted arm, Tye locks green gazes with the sharp-clawed monster and growls, the noise rumbling from deep down inside his wide chest.

Minion's air clawing stops at once, the tiny kitten suddenly meowing piously and licking his own nose with a tiny pink tongue.

"Not the cat," Tye says, setting Minion back atop Gavriel's books. "Coal."

"You can try," I mutter, nearly laughing when I hear the warrior's own words come out of my mouth. But laughing would be too much work. Everything hurts. My back. My ear. My heart. And that's all before I can even get started parsing out the disastrous mess that we still have to deal with.

"He should have fought," Tye mutters. "The bastard should have interfered sooner."

"The gentle soul that Coal is?" I put my hand on Tye's cheek, the light stubble scratching my skin. My voice softens. "Coal knew a great deal about what was happening in that closet. I think... I think I needed someone to trust in me more than I trusted in myself just then."

Tye turns to me, meeting my eyes—reluctantly, it seems. The emerald green in his penetrating gaze is as beautiful as his hard body, each line honed to a deadly perfection. If I thought the male was ethereal back in Lunos, under Han's harsh tutelage, he's a predator incarnate. "So if you forgive Coal, do you think you might eventually—"

"Tye." I raise my bow. "There is nothing to forgive. Not anymore."

Tye shakes his head, his shoulders hunching, the four parallel scratches Minion left on his skin beading with tiny drops of blood. Around us, the library quiets, Gavriel setting his teacup gently on the porcelain. "You did it all," Tye says. "Everything. And I tried to trip you every step of the way."

"Not *every* step." Sitting on a chair a few paces away, Arisha strokes the impertinently purring Minion. "And then there were all those times that involved no standing of any kind. I'm rather certain Lera enjoyed those."

"Why weren't they standing?" Rabbit asks, brown eyes wide.

"I'm trying to apologize, if you two don't mind." Tye swings his face around to glare at Arisha, his tight brow narrowing. "Wait. Does Braids know—"

"It's a little late to ask now, don't you think?" says Arisha.

I push Tye into a wooden chair and climb onto his lap before he can protest, looping my arms around his neck. Feeling his heart pound beneath me, I press my forehead to his. Absorb his delicious heat, the silver flecks in his eyes. "We'll just give it time, okay?" I say.

He smiles with just a hint of the old Tye and angles his mouth toward mine.

"I like your ears," a small voice says from the corner. Tye stiffens against my lips as Rabbit's words register. "Is it true that they can hear everything?"

Pulling out of Tye's embrace, I share a concerned gaze with the male before turning my head to Gavriel, whose frown mirrors the dread starting in the pit of my own belly. Coal's memory returned without destroying his disguise, but things are changing. "You can see Tye's ears, Rabbit?"

"Uh-huh."

"I can't." Gavriel shakes his head. "Tyelor looks no different to me than he always has. Though I'm more used to seeing the young man fully clothed."

Rabbit shrugs, as if the bit of news is utterly unimportant to him. "I've always seen them. But it seemed not so smart to say so. Since no one else seemed to see. Not even Master Shade and he, you *know*... woof." Rabbit makes his hands into claws.

Tye squeezes my shoulders, then walks over to crouch beside the skinny boy, Minion following in his wake like a little furry honor guard.

"What would have happened if you said something, do you think?" Tye asks the boy, his gentle voice at utter odds with his great size.

Rabbit's chin lowers. "I'd be thrown out, and I have nowhere to go."

Tye shakes his head, and I suddenly see the little boy he used to be, both in the veil-spun memories and his own past. The damn veil amulets didn't just spin disguises—they exploited every pain to their advantage.

"Headmaster Sage was going to put me out," Rabbit whispers. "Before you came and everyone thought Commander River was the deputy headmaster. But then River said I could stay. And everyone listened to him. Please don't tell River who he is."

My chest tightens.

Tye shakes his head. "Won't happen, Rabbit. I won't let it, all right?"

"Rabbit." I crouch beside the boy as well, my knee brushing Tye's. "Can you see Han's ears?"

"Sure," says Rabbit. "But he looks human."

"That's because he is." Walking into the library, Coal surveys us with a grim face, his blond bun uncharacteristically mussed, the streaks of blood on his hands clearly not his. "I'd say I'm sorry to break up this feelings fest, but I'm not in the least."

"A pleasure to have you join us as always," Arisha mutters.

Coal gives her a dark look, then surveys us all, his blue eyes heralding back reality even before he speaks. "*Master Zake* proved to be rather cooperative once we started a conversation. Han is a shifter, with human as his animal form. The long and short of it is that the Night Guard and their minions—which includes many of the new serving staff—have us surrounded. The attack will happen during the closing ceremonies to the Prowess Trials, when everyone is in the arena for the awards ceremony."

"You were right all along, Lilac Girl," says Tye. "I—"

"You need to get back out to the exams like a good little athlete," I say, disbelieving my own words. Ignoring Tye's vigorously shaking head, pull his golden uniform shirt off my back, stuffing it into his hands. "I'm off the team now, maybe even out of the Academy if I can't find a way around it, so you will be the only one able to stay close to the royals. Looks like you'll be getting your glory days spinning around a bar after all."

"Lera—" Tye says.

"She is right." Coal hands me his own blood-crusted shirt to replace Tye's, his suddenly bare, rippling torso making Arisha look away with an eye roll. "Go, Tye. Plus, I think the mortal wants to yell at me just now, and you are in our way."

Sliding the uniform over his muscular body, Tye pats Rabbit's shoulder and leaves, his green gaze holding mine until the door finally shuts behind him.

With Tye gone, Coal leans his shoulder against a bookcase and cocks one brow. "Yes, I stood idly by and watched while that human stain tried to make mincemeat out of you—and vice versa, " the male says evenly. "And no, you won't be getting an apology. But if you'd like to take a swing at me over it, now would be the most opportune time for it."

Brilliant.

I snort. "On the contrary, Coal. Given how wonderfully it all worked out, I think I'll simply keep it in reserve to use in your own nightmares." My brow rises to match his, heat flooding my sex in spite of myself. "But not now. I just want to make sure I've the time to enjoy it."

"You've an evil streak to match Minion's." With a shake of his blond head, Coal snatches me into his arms, his lips hovering a breath away from mine. His teeth flash, the blue in his eyes blazing. "You scared the hell out of me, mortal, so don't mind me if I take a moment to account for all the pieces of you."

An exaggerated barfing noise sounds at the other end of the room, quickly followed by Arisha and Gavriel herding Rabbit from the library.

Coal runs his hands down my sides with more pressure than necessary and up my back, under his shirt, hesitating on the raised welts left by Zake's belt. I suppress a flinch, looking him clear in the eyes, daring him to say something.

"Anything missing?"

"All there," he says roughly.

Before the last of the silver door bells finishes its chiming, Coal's strong hands slide down to grip my backside. Lifting me easily to his eye level, he plunges his mouth over mine, the primal need echoing through the bond between us, making me worry for the fate of Gavriel's precious library.

PART II: PROWESS TRIALS

1

———

Lera

Tye's calloused hands slide slowly along my bare arms as he extends them over my head, pressing me into the bedsheet. The male's pine-and-citrus scent flickers over me, as full of mischievous promise as his sparkling emerald gaze. Powerful muscles flex beneath warm skin, his naked body a study in sculpture, as a small purr-like sound rumbles from his chest.

My heart quickens in response, my breath short and shallow as a small blaze of need pools low in my belly. The contrast of Tye's hot heavy body atop me and the cool sheets beneath my bare back makes the tingling along my skin even starker. More intoxicating.

With Tye's veil surrendering to his will and my own amulet lying discarded on the writing desk, the mating bond I've missed for so, so long overwhelms every fiber inside me. My mate. Here. Touching me. The sheer bliss of the moment is almost too much to bear.

Beyond the window, the sun is just starting to peek over the horizon, brushing the pines and oaks in gentle warmth while a stray hawk bids the world good morning. Sneaking into the bedchamber, another ray of sunlight illuminates a streak along the stone floor, cutting over Tye's discarded Prowess uniform to open the shadows along his chiseled muscles. I arch my back, pushing myself into Tye's hardness, my bare, aching breasts falling open.

Tye's eyes follow my nipples. "Stars, I've missed you," he drawls quietly, sneaking the words beneath Arisha's soft snores on the other side of the bedchamber. Tye's naturally musical voice is even more songlike now with his guard down. "So verra much."

"You know you are talking to my chest, right?"

"Oh, aye." Gripping my wrists more tightly, Tye runs his nose along the swell of my right breast, taking the nipple into his warm mouth.

I gasp, the zing from my bunching nipple rushing straight to my dripping sex. Heat spills into my blood, my pulse and breath catching as waves of sensation grip the backs of my thighs. My breasts. My already undulating mound. When I collide with Tye's engorged cock, the shaft so large and hard that I can feel it throbbing against my skin, my mouth waters with the need to take it into my mouth.

His hands still pinning my wrists, Tye circles my nipple with his tongue, ruthlessly flicking the tip.

It's all I can do to swallow a groan, my lower half moving hungrily up and down, seeking contact. My hands curl against the sheets, the mattress whining in a steady rhythm of my—

"Would you two find a different place for that?" Sitting up in bed with a groan of frustration, Arisha pats the table beside her until she finds her glasses. "I'm mortal, not deaf."

My breath freezes, heat blazing in my cheeks. When I try to yank the covers over us, however, I discover Tye's grip on my wrists is as insistent as ever.

Raising his head toward Arisha, the male grins, his sharp features and sudden dimples making him unfairly beautiful. "You might enjoy watching, braids." His tongue rolls over his teeth with feline indulgence. "Never know until you try."

"No. Noooo nooo no." Arisha's words trip over themselves, and I attempt and fail to knee Tye's naked backside from where I lie beneath him. Despite having just donned her glasses, Arisha pulls the covers over her head. "I hate you, Tyelor."

Tye's grin widens, his red hair flopping over his face in a way he knows is irresistible—which just makes him more annoying. "Impossible. Really, braids, I don't see why you'd want to deny yourself the pleasure of looking at—ow!" Releasing my wrists, Tye rubs the spot on his neck where I just bit him—third try's a charm—and glares at me. "What was that for?"

"You seriously don't know?"

"Never mind." Tye tips his head toward the pile of blanket that is Arisha. "You can pretend you don't want to look at me, but you can still enjoy Lilac Girl, you know. I think we all agree that *she* looks ethereal and shouldn't wear clothes. Ever."

"Put on some clothes, for stars' sake," Coal's gravelly voice sounds from the doorway. Bouncing a red apple in the palm of his hand, he invites himself into the chamber and surveys the place as if he owns it. Blond hair already pulled neatly into a bun, Coal is dressed in loose black pants and a sleeveless leather jerkin that shows off the corded muscles twining beneath his skin. His blue eyes and chiseled face—the square jaw and strong cheekbones devastatingly enticing—are alarmingly tight.

As Coal goes to close the door, Shade's wolf pushes past the warrior and trots inside, his long gray tail lifted in victory. I've seen more of the wolf than of Shade's fae form lately, which must be leaving the male utterly bewildered whenever he returns to his normal body.

"Have you ever heard of knocking?" Shoving Tye away, I snatch the blanket around myself while the naked male stretches lazily and sprawls into a sunny spot.

"I heard your bed creaking half a hallway away, so I knew you, at least, were here." Twisting around, Coal launches his apple at Arisha's bed, nodding to himself when the mound of bedcovers squeals in indignation. "Both of you. Good."

"Rrrrrrr." With a growl deep in his chest, Shade leaps from the floor in one giant stride, his golden eye entirely focused on the circular fruit now rolling across Arisha's covers.

"Shade, *no.*" My words land together with Shade's paws on Arisha's coverlet, the wolf's powerful legs pushing against the girl for leverage as he scampers for the elusive apple. A heartbeat later, Shade shoves the tangle of Arisha and bedding to the floor, and—in a flash of salivating canines—makes the final pounce for the fruit. Mission accomplished, the wolf settles on the warm spot Arisha occupied moments ago to noisily munch his kill, the *thump thump thump* of his tail on the mattress adding the final flourish of insult to the morning.

With one hand covering my mouth and the other holding on to the sheet, I rush to my friend's side. "Arisha, I am so, so sorry."

"You bloody immature, idiotic…immortals," Arisha says, extricating her head from the mess like a vicious hatchling and glaring around the room, a halo of frizzy brown hair rising around her. "Can you not—"

"River is awake and catching up quickly." Ignoring Arisha's sputtering, Coal leans his shoulders against the wall and looks at me meaningfully. "That's what I came to say. It seems, you said nothing to him yesterday after you ran from the exams?"

The temperature in the room plummets at Coal's words, the sudden tightness in my spine apparently evident enough that even Tye makes no remarks when I drop my sheet to start pulling on clothes.

"He was busy yesterday," I say.

Coal raises an unimpressed brow. "When I mentioned that you were assaulted by a servant named Zake after fleeing the arena, I thought he was going to combust on the spot." His blue eyes pierce me so sharply, it's all I can do not to squirm like a pinned beetle. "In case you forgot, mortal, we need River on our side. Hundreds of human lives depend on it."

Trust Coal to know exactly where to put the knife—and then twist it. "I think I preferred you without your memories," I mutter. At least then, my failures had a smaller audience. In the month of being on my own, I'd forgotten that the males' support came with a healthy dose of oversight. That no matter how much they claim otherwise, I'm yet to prove myself as a warrior—my one year of being immortal stacking up poorly against their centuries of elite training and fighting. With the initial shock of the memories' return wearing off, the decisions I've made—or avoided making—are now unfurling, warts and all.

The worst part is that Coal's right. Guilt scratches along my skin as the last tingles of denial yield to a wave of nausea.

River *was* wrapped up all day, first with cadet examinations and then meetings with various royal delegations—but he sent messages with Rabbit three times, asking me to meet him whenever he could snatch a few minutes to himself. To explain why I ran off during exams. To tell him whether I was all right.

"I didn't know what to say to him." I pour myself water from a pitcher in an attempt to settle my stomach. It doesn't work, for my stomach or my mind. But it's the truth. River has done so much for me —spending hours tutoring me and even going so far as to rig the exams to ensure I could remain at the Academy through the Prowess Trials—

and I ran off on him. My heart squeezes as I remember his face when I fled the stage. Shock, worry—hurt. Working up a way to explain my behavior, much less Zake's identity, without triggering River's amulet had been a mountain too high for my overwhelmed mind to conquer. "I couldn't think yesterday."

Hopping off Arisha's bed, the wolf trots over to lean his weight against me, his golden eyes narrowing at Coal.

"And you figured saying nothing would do the trick?" says Coal.

Shade snaps his teeth at him.

"I figured I'd have a clearer mind in the morning." I rub my hands over my face. "How upset is River?"

Snatching my shoes off the floor, Coal tosses them into my hands. "You are about to discover that for yourself. And you've lost the chance to do it on your own terms."

2

Lera

*C*oal is right—the discussion with River doesn't happen on my terms. In fact, even calling it a *discussion with River* turns out to be a stretch.

Standing with my arms folded over my chest, I follow Sage's pacing back and forth across the plush carpet of his new office while River, Coal, and Tye listen on in tense silence. After summoning us with all haste, Sage and River then kept us waiting so long that Tye's stomach now growls loudly enough to be heard across the courtyard. I almost envy the male's hunger—though River has yet to say anything, one gaze from his flat, storm-gray eyes ties my insides into knots that barely tolerate air, much less food.

"This claim of yours, Lady Leralynn, that you were attacked after you left the examination arena… It does seem rather convenient, if I may speak frankly." Headmaster Sage's gold chains rattle against each other as he walks, his bald pate shining in the pale morning light. River stands silently in the background in his crisp red jacket, dark hair neatly combed, sternly breathtaking—and utterly unreadable. "An attempt to shift everyone's attention away from your actions toward someone else's."

"I did not find Zake's assault convenient at all, sir," I tell Sage, my red dress brushing my ankles as I shift my weight. My face is hot, my hands gripping my arms. I little care what lies Sage wants to twist my words into, but River's heavy silence is something else entirely. "Without Coal and Tye's intervention, I might not be standing here."

At this, River's jaw tightens dangerously, the first sign that he's anything but a deputy headmaster watching a student be interrogated. Without moving so much as an inch, he's suddenly stolen all the air in the room, his broad back and shoulders all but vibrating with tension. And fury. At what he is hearing. At *how* he is hearing of it.

Feeling my throat tighten, I force myself to focus on the room around me lest I lose control of my emotions with River, Coal, and Tye all watching. I've held on for this long, navigating the Academy and an invisible enemy on my own, and I'll be damned if I drop the reins now.

Sage's office, once at the top of the keep tower, now sprawls over an entire first-floor suite. With wide easy steps, comfortable leather chairs, and fine wines, cheeses, and scones overflowing their platters, the space is set up as a receiving room. As with the arena, flags representing each of the ten kingdoms decorate the wood-paneled walls, while a grand iron candelabra—a mini replica of the one dominating the Great Hall —hangs from the high ceiling in imitation of starlight.

A room meant to entertain kings—the most powerful of whom is currently standing by Sage's side. Ironically, Sage is as unaware of this fact as the king himself.

Leaning against the wall, Coal turns his face toward the headmaster in a single clean movement that somehow manages to seem lethal. "Given that I took the attacker into custody and questioned him myself, I'd say Leralynn's *claim* is valid."

Ignoring Coal, Sage opens his palms toward me in a poor imitation of a concerned headmaster. "Lady Leralynn, is it possible you simply stumbled into a servant who misunderstood your intentions? This, sadly, is not the first time I find you in the middle of a creative mess and—for your sake—I want to urge you to put flights of fancy behind you before you land yourself in flames you can no longer escape."

"There was no misunderstanding," I tell Sage, my gaze shifting to River in hopes I'll find something new in the strong planes of his face. But the male is looking out the window, seeming for all the world to be watching two servants sweep the courtyard. "A man named Zake attacked me yesterday. We fought. I won."

"Why did you not come to me with this yesterday, Lady Leralynn?"

River asks suddenly, addressing me directly for the first time this morning. The full force of his gray gaze and deep voice make my heart race. "Certainly something this serious should have been brought to my attention before now. Not to mention any possible explanation for the unacceptable choice of behavior you made at the examinations." His words ring with righteous authority, but his eyes tell a different story. *I shattered my own moral code for you, and you threw it back in my face.*

"I—" I cut off, wanting to scream in frustration. I finally have River's attention, and I'm as much at a loss for words as I was yesterday. Anything I say that he might possibly believe will only trigger his amulet, and any half-truths will only fan his flames higher.

"With due respect to everyone," Coal interrupts in a voice that's anything but respectful, "but who the hell cares? Leralynn is uninjured, and the attacker is in custody. Right now, the greater problem is the attack this Zake claims is being planned for the closing ceremonies of the Prowess Trials. Can we worry less about who said what how, and more about how to evacuate ten kingdoms' worth of royals from the Academy grounds?"

"Are you insane?" Sage turns from Coal to River. "Is he insane?" Without waiting for a response, Sage wheels back toward Coal, starts to take a step toward him, and then wisely thinks better of it. "We've no reason to believe this prisoner. And even if he were telling the truth— which is highly unlikely—the Academy fortress is infinitely safer than an open road." Sage straightens his tunic, mastering himself and lowering his voice from its high wheedling pitch. "In all truth, we've nothing but a chain of he-said-she-said several times removed from the original source."

"The headmaster is right," says River, his gaze never leaving me. Though said quietly, the male's words carry more power than all of Sage's posturing combined. "Bring the prisoner here, Coal. We will ask him ourselves."

Blood drains from my face. Even if Zake doesn't remember River —and thus doesn't see him as fae—he will certainly tell River what I am. That can't happen, not until River gets his memories back. He will never forgive my lie otherwise.

I swallow, not knowing where to look.

River's too-keen gaze bores into me. "Would there be some problem with our hearing Master Zake's account, Lady Leralynn?"

"Master Zake is unconscious," says Coal. The wave of relief

rushing through me nearly pushes me off my feet. The blond warrior shrugs with immortal nonchalance, his perfect face expressionless. "I may have been overeager in my questioning. My apologies for the inconvenience."

"I see." River's jaw tightens, his cold gray gaze raking Coal before cutting back to me. "In that case, I believe there is nothing more for us to discuss, Lady Leralynn." The male offers me a small, too-formal bow. "Given your forfeit of yesterday's examination, you are no longer an Academy student. Please be on your way this morning."

"Yes." Sage's little eyes light up like candles, his excited words clinging to River's before I can process them fully. "Commander River is quite correct! Lady Leralynn, for security reasons, we must limit the Academy guests to only official students, competitors, and their families. I thank you for your understanding and patronage. A guard escort will oversee your departure at once."

3

<hr>

Lera

$\mathcal{M}$y mouth dries. Caught up in Zake's attack and the return of Tye's memories, I'd given no consideration to little things like Academy rules. Rules that River broke for me once and has no intention of compromising again.

My gaze darts around the room, finding Coal tense against the wall, his blue eyes clouded with thoughts that no doubt parallel my own. As he stands with his hands behind his back, River's chiseled face holds a mix of pain and resolve that's thick as a rock wall. Sage bounces on his toes, all but vibrating with glee. And Tye…

Sprawled on one of Sage's leather chairs, his starched Prowess uniform jacket folded carefully over one arm, Tye pours himself a glass of the most expensive wine in the room. As all eyes settle on him, he pops a piece of cheese into his mouth and salutes me with the crystal goblet in his hand. "Right. If you are all done talking. Will you marry me, Lera?"

"What?" I hear the word and am fairly sure I'm the one who said it.

Tye swallows his cheese. "I asked you to marry me. Say yes."

"Yes?" I shake myself the same way Shade's wolf does to dislodge a fly. "What—"

"The initial yes was sufficient." Taking another sip of wine, Tye turns to the headmaster. "It appears Lady Leralynn is now a 'family member of a Prowess competitor.' Unless you'd like both of us gone from the competition, the lass stays where she is. Or in my bedchamber. That would be preferable, actually."

For the first time since meeting Sage, I find us both equally slack-jawed while River blinks wide-eyed in a fair imitation of Arisha. Tye winks at me, his green eyes sparkling with feline self-satisfaction.

Putting down his glass, he rises smoothly to his feet and holds his hand out to me. "Shall we go, Lilac Girl? I am opening the Prowess Trials with an exhibition in a few hours' time, and you can watch me get ready."

Squeezing the male's strong, callused hand, I finally find the spine I seemed to have lost last night. "I'll join you in a bit," I tell Tye, turning to face River head-on. "I hope to have a word with Commander River in private first, if he's amenable."

Matching River's straight back and powerful stride, I follow him out of Sage's office into the same wide candlelit hallway I fled to yesterday, the portraits of headmasters and kings judging my every step. Yesterday, this false refuge led me right into Zake's trap. I hope today's foray will end better. I will *make* it end better.

"I should have come to you yesterday," I tell River without waiting for his questions. "I owed you an explanation. Keeping the attack from you was wrong. And I'm sorry."

River turns and grips my face, then my arms, his cheeks ablaze. "Are you all right, Leralynn?" he demands. "Are you hurt?" The unbridled fear in his eyes ricochets through my body, shaking me to my core. It's everything he was hiding in Sage's office and more. "Did that bastard—"

"He landed a few blows. Then I remembered I knew how to fight, but River—"

"Thank the stars." River exhales, and hope fills my chest. Then he pulls away so quickly, I stumble. Ire saturates his woodsy scent, his broad chest, every sculpted angle of his face, rising between us as thick and impenetrable as any wall. "Why, Leralynn?" River asks. "You knew that the only thing that could drive me more insane with worry than watching you run off the exam stage would be the silence that answered each of those queries. Knew what it would do to me to hear —secondhand—that you were attacked. What have I done to earn so little of your trust?"

"I—"

"Have you any regard for me at all?"

Swallowing, I lay my hand on River's corded arm, the muscles hard as steel beneath the heavy woolen jacket, but he flinches away. My mouth is dry, the words I'd hoped would miraculously appear refusing to cooperate. "I don't know where to start. Whatever you think happened in the past day—"

"Stop." River takes a step back, his quiet voice a punch in the gut. "I don't want an explanation."

I blink. A dozen yards down the hallway, a servant carrying firewood ducks out of one of the many passages and scurries into another. Somewhere above us, a carpenter bangs his hammer. All normal sights and sounds for a conversation that is anything but. "You don't?"

"No." Shaking his head, River clasps his hands firmly behind his back. "I can't do this anymore."

"Do what?" I ask.

"Be with you." River's voice lowers to a near whisper, his storm-filled eyes fighting with all their might to conceal the vulnerability sparkling inside. "And before you say anything, I'm well aware that Tye's proposal was simply a way to keep you in the Academy. And no, he isn't the reason I need to walk away. It boils down to trust, Leralynn. I can't be with someone who will not trust me when things truly matter. Whom I cannot trust in return."

I clench my nails into my palms, the only thing I can do to keep myself from reaching for him again. "I trust you, River."

"No. No, you don't." A muscle tics along River's jaw. "I only learned that you were in a fight this morning. From Coal. Because you couldn't confide in me until you were all gathered together, and confident and patched up."

River's words are an eerie echo of my own thoughts this morning, though he speaks them as if they are a bad thing. As if he himself doesn't wear strength and composure the way other people don clothes. After months and months of forging my own path, maybe I don't want to prance around naked. Maybe I have a right not to.

"It was a bad day, River." I can hear my voice stiffening. "I was *attacked*. Cut me some—"

"You weren't attacked, you were in a *fight*," River snaps back at me, his control wavering. Without moving, he seems to grow taller above me, making me fight the urge to step back. "As you are on a regular basis. I'm not daft, so don't make me pretend to be. You and I both know that your sudden departure from the arena yesterday wasn't caused by panic over the exam question. Moreover, if you had actually feared for your safety, you'd have stayed right where you were—in plain sight of a dozen guards and a pace away from me. But you didn't. Which all means you weren't running *from* the arena, but rather *to* a place. You left because there was somewhere—or someone—you needed to see. And lo and behold, then you clash with the one man who has information on the very attack you've been worried about."

Damn it. "I know how it looks," I say, keeping a firm grip on my voice, despite my racing pulse. "But you are wrong."

"Am I? Where exactly do the lies start and stop?" River stops as a servant rushes past with a clattering tray of empty wine bottles, then continues in a harsh murmur. "Every time I think we've made it to a new level of trust, vaulted over a barrier that I'm certain is the last, I discover you're playing me still. You told me that learning to read mattered greatly to you, and I believed you and helped. But then you claimed that staying on the Prowess team was more vital than anything. I violated every rule and regulation, every bit of my own code, to let you stay by the royals as you asked. Except the Prowess Team turned out to little matter after all—you were already on your next solo mission targeting a Night Guard ally you told me nothing about. You know what I think happened? I think you saw Zake, recognized him, and decided to go after him on your own then and there, instead of telling me the truth."

"No." My heart thumps. I step forward, though it means having to tip my head back to keep River's gaze. "I wasn't looking for a fight, I swear, River. I was trying to avoid one. I was trying to protect you."

"From what?" He waits for an answer that I can't give, then snorts softly. "Let me guess, you can't tell me. But you'd like me to trust you that it was important. To convince myself that you haven't been lying to me with every breath for months and months."

I open my mouth to shove back against the accusation—but this time when River holds out his hand to stop me, the finality of his words hits my soul like a shard of ice. "I love you, Leralynn. I probably always will. But I can't be with you. You and I, we're done."

4

River

River's gut twisted as he turned to walk in the opposite direction from Leralynn, the portraits in the hallway looking on with morbid satisfaction. *Yes,* the painted frowns said, *you fell in love with and bedded a student—that pain filling your soul now is just the punishment you deserve.*

The portraits weren't wrong—but that didn't make walking away from Lera hurt any less. Finding an open window, River braced his hands on the windowsill and drew in desperate breaths. His chest was tight, his eyes stinging in the bright sun. Now that he'd stopped walking, he couldn't move, his hands gripping the aged wood so tightly that his knuckles blanched. Try as he might, his mind refused to think of anything but Lera's musical laugh, the way she twined her auburn braid around her finger when she was thinking, how perfectly she fit into his arms when he pressed her soft body against his.

But River couldn't be with her. Lera's lies left him no choice. If she still wouldn't trust him with the truth after everything he'd done, then that was that. The end. It had to be. And now that he thought about it, when he'd told her he loved her, she never said as much back.

River pushed himself away from the window, straightening his jacket in time to nod courteously to a passing pair of guards. The deputy headmaster did not get to sulk, no matter how much his heart ached. The Academy deserved better from its leader. He had to look the part whether he felt it or not.

River realized he'd walked himself to the dungeon only as he was already checking the ledger to see where Coal had left Lera's attacker. He pressed the page flat, his breath quickening again. He was here to check if this Zake might have awoken. If he had more information about the alleged impending assault.

Ensuring firsthand that the bastard who'd attacked Leralynn was paying justly had nothing to do with River's actions. It didn't.

Pulling open the heavy door to the lowest level, River inhaled the stench of urine and fear mixing with the mossy stone. His footsteps scraped dully against the steep stone steps as he wound his way down, bracing himself for whatever he was about to hear.

"—the mountain." The prisoner's voice, coming from his cell around the bend, was thick with panic, rising to a whine before deteriorating to sputtering mutters. "They're in a mountain, that's all I know. Owalin blindfolded me. Fae. You bloody fae."

"Talking to yourself, Zake?" River called.

"No." Stepping out of the shadow, Coal looked River up and down with impassive blue eyes, probably assessing whether River intended to give him trouble or not. "He's talking to me. If you can call these insane ramblings talk. We have a name, but little else. Zake's been provided with few details of the attack itself."

"Perhaps because there isn't going to be one," River said with a raised brow, though his heart hammered his ribs. Unlike River himself, Coal had been there when Lera was attacked, and that made River want to thank the man and slug him in equal measure.

"If you believe that, you're even more Sage's puppet than I thought."

River swallowed a hot retort and turned toward Zake's cell to avoid Coal's annoyingly placid face. "Rumors of the prisoner's unconsciousness seem to have been resolved," he said. "Is there anything else Leralynn is having you lie about?"

"River, Zake the prisoner. Zake, Deputy Headmaster River," Coal said, blithely ignoring River's question without even a twitch of an eyebrow. "I don't believe you two have met." Jerking his chin toward the door, Coal stepped neatly around River. "I'm heading out to see about locating this dark mountain lair. Excuse me."

For a second, River could only stare at Coal's back, what the man *hadn't* said replaying in his head like a deranged type of drum.

Yes, not only had Leralynn been lying to River—Coal has been in on it. A flash of pain seized his gut before he could suppress it.

It doesn't matter. Whom Lera chose to confide in wasn't his concern. Not anymore.

Turning back to the prisoner, River took in the man's appearance. His coarse brown curls were plastered to his head with blood and sweat. In the drab uniform of a head servant, with missing teeth and a swollen-shut eye, Zake was nonetheless using the metal bars to stand as tall as his body allowed. A man plainly used to being in charge and obeyed. As Zake's good eye focused on River, his back straightened further, a spark of confidence racing through him.

"Commander River! Finally!" For a moment, River thought the man might look familiar, though he couldn't place from where. "Please forgive the disguise. I'll have you know that I'm not only the lord and master of the greatest estate this side of Mystwood, but the leader of the fae inquisition movement that—"

"You assaulted Lady Leralynn." River's voice was too calm by half. "Is there a reason I shouldn't castrate you right here?"

"*Lady* Leralynn?" Zake spat on the floor. "Is that her latest set of lies? I assure you, Leralynn is no more a lady than I am."

River's hand twitched at his side before he could stop it.

"More to the immediate point, I've information you need. That you can have." Zake's manicured but now filthy fingers played nervously on the bars. "I know about the fae's plans. All of them. But I require—"

"Master Zake—" River held up his hand, silencing the babbling. "Have you evidence of even a single fae near the Academy? Not deductions or theories— but hard facts?"

"What in stars' name do you mean? You were talking to one not two minutes past." Zake pointed to the door Coal left through moments earlier, his voice rising to fill the dungeon. "Did you not see his ears? And Leralynn's? That bitch is a lying whore who—"

River caught his own swinging fist a moment before it could shatter whatever bits of nose and sanity Zake had left, slamming his knuckles into the metal bars instead. On another day, perhaps, he could have patiently sifted through the prisoner's twists of lucidness and insanity. But not today. Not now.

It was difficult to believe Coal had listened to or believed anything the dimwitted man said. But then again, two days ago, River would never have imagined himself capable of sabotaging the Academy's exams to let a student cheat. On that note, two days ago, Tye would have happily gutted Leralynn, and here he was today, proposing. One strange behavior was an anomaly. Two could be a coincidence. But three? Could Leralynn possibly hold that kind of sway over men's minds? Or was magic involved after all?

River backed away from the bars, heading for the door.

"Commander!" Zake called to River's retreating back. "Wait."

River didn't turn around.

He found the captain of the Academy's guard as soon as he left the dungeon. "Spread orders that no face- or head-concealing garments may be worn inside the Academy or the Prowess arena," he ordered. "I don't care what the fashion, I want everyone visible."

"Yes, sir." The captain obeyed quickly, turning to convey River's order. "Anything else?"

River ran a hand through his hair. "Shuffle all guard shifts. Randomly. I want no predictability as to which man is where and when. The servants too."

The captain's eyes widened in protest, but River walked off before the strange order could be questioned. With only hours remaining until the opening ceremonies, he would spare no effort to ensure the guests' and students' safety, no matter how much it inconvenienced the guards. This arrangement would reduce efficiency, but if there were any more imposters like the prisoner, any plans and routines they might rely on would be disrupted. It was something.

It was also the last proactive decision River got to make, with the morning rolling into the natural chaos of final royal arrivals.

Within a quarter hour of walking out of the keep, River was too busy to think, much less plan. No, an exception could not be made to allow the Yulti king to house his dozen traveling concubines in separate suites in the keep. Yes, the same honor guard of veteran soldiers had to meet and escort all royals around the grounds, even if said royals tried to wave the extra security off. No, Lady Gertrude could not wear her snake garb if it covered her face and ears, no matter how lucky the snake was.

With Lady Gertrude's shrill discontent still echoing in his ears, the sight of an Academy instructor chatting away with a man in a deep-hooded cloak sent a streak of irrational fury through River's veins.

Reining himself into a dignified gait, River set course for where Han and his companion huddled in the shadow beneath the arena's wooden risers, their voices low in a discussion that was plainly meant to be private. Well, if Han couldn't be bothered to respect River's orders concerning concealing garments, River felt few qualms about interrupting—or stepping away from the path where the bleacher's setup carried the men's quiet voices. At least River presumed the bleachers were to blame for the magnification, because there was no other reason his ears should have picked up a discussion happening twenty yards away.

"What are you doing here?" Han asked, his black hair and crisp red Prowess uniform hugging corded muscle. Even in the shadows, the Prowess trainer's strange pale eyes flashed bright with anger.

"I've learned that a certain stain of a human got himself arrested." The hooded figure's equally quiet voice was rich with confidence. And unfamiliar. "We can't allow—"

"Zake lost his mind along with a good deal of blood." Han crossed his arms, his attention split between his companion and a high flip Tyelor was practicing above the horizontal bar, one final pass before guests flooded into the arena and Sage announced the commencement of the Prowess Trials. "No one believes his ramblings."

Zake? What did Leralynn's attacker have to do with anything? His chest tightening, River changed course to position himself behind the central stage, the annoyance over Han's companion's hood giving way to more pressing questions. Bending low to pretend interest in a wooden support strut, River focused on the quiet words.

The hooded figure grabbed Han's wrist. "You knew the idiot was arrested?"

"It makes no difference."

"That isn't your decision," the stranger hissed. "I've indulged your little side hobby long enough. I won't be taking a risk to let you race your bloody hamsters."

"Humans," Han corrected, sending a shiver along River's spine. This was the second time the word "human" had been uttered in this conversation as if it were a curse word—as if its speakers were anything but. "Same brain, but more muscle. And a third of them aren't even here yet. This is simply an opening exhibition."

The stranger released Han's wrist with a noise of disgust and turned away, Han turning back to his athletes with an unreadable expression.

Quietly straightening from his crouch, River followed in the hooded man's steps as he left the arena through the far exit. Something wasn't right. Well, many things were not right. And River was done watching and waiting and arguing with people who were either too greedy to think straight or too deeply conniving to tell the truth. From now on, River intended to keep his own counsel. Ask his own questions.

Dogging the hooded man into the thick band of forest that hid the Academy's wall from view, River finally decided to drop stealth for the sake of efficiency. They were far enough away now that any confrontation would keep clear of cadets and their guests, which was the best River had time for just now. Raising his head, River added his voice to the wind. "A moment of your time, sir."

No answer, just a red cloak flashing in between brilliant green branches.

River's brows twitched together, his senses peaking as he picked up his pace, his boots kicking up the scent of mossy earth. Soft oak branches brushed River's face as he hurried through them, his lungs and heart taking on a familiar steady rhythm. River might be wearing the stiff woolen coat appropriate for a deputy headmaster, but he was much more than that—and the stranger would learn it one way or the other. "Sir. Remove your hood."

The man quickened his pace, heading deeper into the trees. A mistake given that the forest led nowhere but to a wall, though the man might not realize it.

Caw caw.

A pair of crows caught River's attention for a moment, the birds unusual in this part of the Academy. Looking away from the man's swishing red cloak, River blinked as more and more flapping wings landed on the branches. A hawk. A trio of vultures. An eagle with a bright white head and sharp yellow beak.

Caw caw. Caw caw.

What in stars' light? Shaking himself, River hurried after the fleeing figure, his pulse now rising with each step. The birds didn't belong. Just as this man did not.

The tall stone wall came into view through the trees, and the figure slowed his pace, giving River just enough time to reach him. Gripping the man's shoulder, feeling hard muscle beneath his thick cloak, he spun him around.

"Who are—" River's voice tripped.

The stranger's hood had fallen to his shoulders, revealing silvery-blond hair pulled back into a braid, magnetic blue eyes, and a pale ageless face that was not of this world. His ears came to points. When he smiled, his canines did too.

"Commander Owalin of the Night Guard, at your service," the male said in a voice that sent ice trickling down River's spine.

Owalin. The same name Zake had babbled to Coal in the dungeons.

Reining in his pounding heart, River stood his ground as he met the male's pale, haunting gaze. "What do the fae want with my Academy?"

"I'm afraid it is no longer your Academy, Deputy Headmaster River." Something flicked in the man's hand just as one of the crows launched itself from the nearby branch and flew straight for River's face.

River's forearm rose on instinct to ward off the bird, which tore into his jacket with razor-sharp talons. Woolen threads snapped and— and River gasped at the fire exploding along his chest. The world flickered for a moment as he looked down, surprised to find Owalin pulling a long blade out of his flesh, his own vivid red blood streaking its length.

As River went to swing for the male, branches rustled overhead and someone cracked a blow across River's temple from behind. This time, when the world wavered, the darkness remained. All River recalled as he fell flat to the ground was Owalin's voice addressing one of the crows. "Our human idiot got himself arrested and will be babbling shortly if he's not doing so already. Find Krum. There has been a change of plans."

The *caw caw* of the bird's answering call followed River into oblivion.

5

———————

Lera

"Thank you all for coming to the first Prowess Trials to be held at the Great Falls Academy," Sage's pleased voice booms over the filled arena stands.

Hundreds of people in every manner of finery fill the raised benches, guards and servants patrolling the walkways to ensure everyone who matters has goblets of wine to ward off the heat. Some personal servants stand over their masters in the bleachers with parasols; others flutter elaborately painted fans. Overhead, flocks of birds wheel over the arena, perhaps attracted by the afternoon sun sparkling off the sand. A dozen yards in front of me, teams of Prowess athletes in every color parade around the arena, each kingdom celebrating its own with music and cheers.

The clamor of clapping hands and raised voices flying into the air is both deafeningly loud and incomplete to my immortal ears, Coal and River both noticeably absent. Coal disappeared earlier on a fool's errand to singlehandedly find the Night Guard's lair, while River...

I don't know where he went, just that he wanted to be away from me.

We are done.

My fingers curl around my belly, my chest tight as the words repeat

133

themselves over and over in my mind, burning me each and every time. *We are done. We are done.*

All because I made a mistake. Didn't speak to him on a schedule he thought I should. What would River think if he knew all the other decisions I've made over the past months—some good, some not. All of them mine.

"He couldn't have meant it." Arisha touches my thigh, her hand snaking out of a hideous yellow gown that makes her resemble a frizzy sunflower. She sweeps her distracted blue gaze over the crowd. "And once he gets his memory back—ah, stop it! I can barely see over the fur in my mouth."

"What—oh." I frown down at Shade's wolf, his black muzzle burrowed into my midsection as if looking for treats, his raised tail whacking Arisha in the face with every wag. I'd have expected the male to have shifted into fae form well before now, but here we are. Still in wolf form. Too long in wolf form. Grabbing the scruff of Shade's neck, I try and fail to drag him to a more convenient location, the people around me shimmying away despite the tight seating.

I shift myself to provide some blockage for the tail, my voice bitter despite my best efforts. "Once they get their memory back—do we know *how* they get their memory back exactly? Or anything about these wards we're supposed to be repairing? Because right now, the best plan I've got is to sit on my rear, waiting for something bad to happen."

My own words remind me to survey the filled stands, though I find nothing out of the ordinary but the number of birds and royals. And their sheer breadth of dazzling fashions, from a huge woman in a shapeless black sheath with what looks like an actual bowl of fruit on her head, to a whole family of laughing blonde girls, at least six strong, wearing matching gowns of pink tulle, their thin father cowering in the middle.

But all pale in comparison to Tye, bouncing on the balls of his feet at the arena's edge, his emerald eyes alight. With a special gold athletic uniform hugging his muscled frame and his fiery hair catching the sunlight, the male exudes a confidence that rivals River's striding across a throne room—a fact not lost on the many, many eyes watching the male's every graceful move unblinkingly.

"Actually, we do know something." Arisha moves closer to me so only I can hear her, her freckled cheeks bunched in thought—I have to use my foot to get Shade's hind end to swing out wide enough to let her in. "Coal got Zake to admit that this Owalin and his Night Guard minions have been messing with the magical wards, which isn't really new information, but that proves they have *someone* who knows how to manipulate them. If we find who ever that is—"

"Then maybe this *someone* might also have insight into lifting River's and Shade's veils." I rub my face. "Or at least information on how to patch up the magical leak we'd come here to patch."

"Information that he'll no doubt be more than happy to share," Arisha says with a crestfallen wince. "I imagine Coal will need to…you know."

I squeeze her leg. "We'll deal with interrogation when we have someone to interrogate," I say, right as another round of applause draws my attention back to the stage. With the last of the ten parading teams clearing the sands, a set of men dressed in black carry a horizontal bar into the middle of the arena while Tye—whose exhibition round is to officially open the trials—dunks his hands into a bucket of chalk. As he slaps his hands together, working the chalk deep into his callused creases, bits of powder rise into the air like snowflakes, settling on his muscular thighs.

The music stops. Tye's muscles bunch in preparation for the run. In the hanging silence, the creaking of benches and calls of overhead birds are a distant irrelevance.

Caw caw.

A gong sounds.

Tye leaps forward, his powerful legs propelling his body with a feline grace. Each step a practiced, measured precision, the male hits his launch point with ease and leaps into the air. Grabbing the high bar smoothly, Tye's taut body swings around it in a blur of color and muscle. Beautiful. Powerful. Breath-stopping.

Reaching the zenith of his spin, Tye releases the bar and flies like a pike into the air, twisting in defiance of gravity and the stars themselves before catching the bar again as if nothing of great consequence just happened.

Applause rages through the stands—and not a few disgruntled mutters from the other teams. But even they can't help staring in jealous admiration. Tye deserves this light gathering around him, I realize. Has earned this moment over and over for centuries, despite having it ripped from him by those in power. If this one good thing comes from our voyage to the mortal world, perhaps that's worth it.

On the bar, Tye picks up speed and flies into the air again, his body tucking into a tight ball. Streams of silk lace he must have hidden in his uniform release from their bonds and trail the male through the air. Red and gold and blue, all flapping like standards in the wind, the *whoosh whoosh whoosh* of cloth cutting air loud in the breath-held silence of the arena.

Though I know it's impossible from several benches away, I'm sure I can smell Tye's pine-and-citrus scent, the exhilaration pulsating from him an intoxicating wine that makes my core blaze. The magic inside me rouses, bubbling and reaching to freedom, the cords of power clamoring jealously for their turn beneath the sun's rays.

I blink over the flood of sensation, the sounds around me suddenly distant, unable to compete with the inferno inside my own body. The bench beneath me is hard, the wood slightly uneven, the silk of my scarlet cool against my skin except for where the sun has heated the fabric. The people around me stink of rose perfume mixed with unfamiliar spices.

Shade whines, the lupine call forcing itself into my swimming consciousness. That and the call of strange birds flocking around us. More than before.

Caw caw.

The crowd suddenly gasps, then breaks into shouts of delight and applause.

"Lera. Lera!" Arisha grabs my arm hard enough to hurt, while around us, the crowd grows rabid with excitement, many on their feet, the children jumping for a better view. "Look."

Forcing my gaze back to Tye, I feel my eyes widen. The colorful silk ribbons flowing around him are now alight with flame. As the male spins faster and faster still, the fiery rings follow in his wake like blazing hoops, which the crowd thinks are all part of the show.

Except I know they aren't. And if Tye has access to—

I gasp, the shackles holding my magic suddenly springing open almost painfully, my body flooding with what's been gathering just beneath the surface. My heart races, the small breeze suddenly too hot, my dress too constricting. "He did it." I snatch Arisha's wrist, my words coming in pants over the effort of keeping the sudden tsunami of magic at bay. "Owalin released the magic's shackles."

"No." Arisha shakes her head violently. "No, it's too early. Zake told Coal it wouldn't be until the end and it's only—"

"An inconvenient change of plans, then." I force my breathing to tamp down. "I feel it, Arisha. And that's not part of Tye's show either."

"Neither is that, is it?"

The note of panic in Arisha's voice has me on my feet before I see where she's pointing, my eyes just catching a glint of metal in Han's hands. His pale gaze trained on the circles of fire following Tye, the Prowess coach's handsome face is set with grim realization. The mortals might imagine the flame a part of the show, but he has worked out the truth—and is meeting it with murder.

He lets the knife slip fully into his palm, confident that no one will notice it with all eyes on his star athlete.

"Tye!' I yell with all my might as I surge forward, shoving my way down to the arena through the two rows of spectators before me. "Tye, look out!" I shout again, stepping on royal feet and fingers with equal disregard. "Tye!"

My words drown beneath the crowd's cheers and the sudden synchronized call of birds settling one by one on the flagpoles around the arena. Crows. Vultures. A pair of hawks.

I'm still five paces away when Tye releases the bar, offering a final airborne twist as he marks his landing.

Han draws back his throwing blade, the metal giving a final wink in the sunlight as he launches it at my mate.

My heart stops, my stomach clenching in horror. With no more time, I throw myself forward, rushing to get between a grinning triumphant Tye and the weapon flying toward his heart. Too far. I'm still too far, no matter how my flesh stretches forward. But I still try. Still press forward as if I can conquer time and distance and—and suddenly, I can.

Not with my body, but with magic, which shoots forward with all the desperation in my soul.

And not a shred of control.

6

River

_D_istant music and applause penetrated River's haze as he opened his eyes. For a moment, he didn't know where he was. All he saw were shifting green leaves etched in bright light. Sunbeams streaked through sudden gaps, making him throw a hand up to cover his eyes.

A mistake.

Pain stabbed the side of his chest and echoed dully inside his skull, making him gasp for breath. Blinking, he inhaled the forest air and nearly choked on the sudden bouquet of sensations, his nose—always sensitive—now able to tell the very earthworms apart from the wet ground they lived in.

Alive. Not only was River alive, but he felt as vibrant as he'd only ever felt in Leralynn's company—which was ironic on all counts. Especially the fact that his blood was still leaking into the earth, slowly but unhindered.

Sitting up, River ripped open his shirt to stare at the stab wound that should have, by all rights, killed a man. He could still feel the knife sliding into his flesh and hitting his rib, the blade fortunately diverting into thick muscle. Even with no vital organs touched, in those last moments of consciousness, River had been certain the wound was fatal. Obviously, he'd been wrong. A mistake of surprise and pain.

Rubbing a bit of prickling burning on his sternum, River removed his outer coat, the pain along his side making him grit his teeth. In the distance, more applause sounded, enough to make him think the Prowess Trial opening exhibition had begun. He'd been out for some time, then. Two hours at least. Two hours since the fae named Owalin left him for dead.

Tearing off his shirt, River ripped the cloth into a set of long strips and wrapped the wound, pulling as tight as the bandages would go. The world flickered around the edges, stabs of pain shooting along his skin. But he was moving, breathing, thinking. That had to be enough. Climbing to his feet, he pulled his coat back on, taking time to do up all the buttons. He was still a commander, the Academy's safety his obligation. That meant everyone from the guard to the royals needed to see him as alive and strong. In control.

In control of what?

River's memory flickered, the attack once more replaying before his eyes. Owalin had certainly been fae, and there seemed to be at least one other immortal with him. Talking about a change of plans.

Plans—that could only mean one thing. An attack on the Academy, just as Leralynn and Coal had warned the Night Guard would try. The bastard in the dungeon had claimed the same. Except he'd claimed other things too. Including that Leralynn wasn't who she claimed to be. Not a lady. Not even a human.

Fae. Zake claimed Leralynn was fae, just as Owalin was. Which was absurd. Had to be. Otherwise, it meant that Leralynn had been lying to River with every breath since the very beginning. That nothing between them had ever been real.

No, of course Leralynn was human. River would have seen through such lies. Leralynn was simply a brave, kind, beautiful woman who spoke to his soul but did not hear his own soul speaking back. She wasn't Diana, and it was unfair to them both to continue a charade built on illusion. River needed to stop acting like a schoolboy moping over a woman when there were immortals likely to storm the Academy at any moment.

He needed to get to the arena, separate the royals throughout the Academy, add an extra detail of guards on each family. Not just the royals, he needed to have Leralynn—to have *everyone*—scatter while his guards checked each and every soul. While River interrogated Han.

Sage would protest the interruption of his precious opening ceremonies, and that was fine. River wouldn't let the headmaster's greed get in the way of people's lives, no matter what the high-ranking bastard did to him afterward.

Holding on to the trees, River tightened his jaw and started toward the arena as quickly as he could, discovering that his body was more cooperative than he had any right to expect. Over the steady hum of pain, his muscles vibrated with a powerful energy he couldn't explain, except feeling that it somehow came from the earth. And that it longed for the one person whom River *really* needed to stop thinking about.

Exiting the tree line, River squinted in the bright midday sun, gathered himself, and broke into a stiff lope across the rippling green grounds toward the Academy's stone buildings—and the vast wooden monstrosity rising above them. Pain haunted his every step, but he pushed it to a small place in the back of his mind, praying to all the stars that Owalin would just wait to enact his plan until River could warn the guards. Until they could make some semblance of a plan.

He stepped into the arena, momentarily blinded by the sun reflecting off the white sand, and quickly scanned for any signs of trouble. All seemed well—more than well. Sage must be beside himself with delight. The crowd was screaming and clapping, every face lit with joy, as Tyelor spun around the horizontal bar. The never-shy athlete had somehow managed to light the silk lacing streaming from him on fire, the flames following him through the air as—

As Leralynn ruthlessly shoved her way to the stage, stepping on and over people as if they mattered nothing, her face set in a harsh snarl.

A wave of confusion washed over River, the power that had been pulsing inside him since he awoke roaring into a blaze just as Lera extended her hands and…set the whole arena on fire.

7

Lera

Flames erupt around me, the trembling ground sending people toppling from their seats. Wooden benches crackle, screams of pain and fear rising into the air. The birds take to the sky as the warm breeze fans the orange tongues that hop along like blazing rabbits.

Surreal horror floods my blood. I close my hand around Shade's fur as I struggle to get the magic back under control. I did this. Me. I became the very monster I wanted to protect the Academy from.

In the middle of the arena, Tye is getting up from where the shaking ground threw him off his feet. He looks dazed, shaking his head to clear it from the impact. A trickle of blood runs down his forehead, but he's alive. The relief rushing through me cools the rampaging cords of magic. The male's emerald eyes flash around the stands in dawning horror—before the panicking crowd blocks him from my sight.

"Great Hall! Every one to the Great Hall! This way!" The shouts are echoed by servants and guards across the arena as the sea of bewildered spectators and competitors rushes to get away from the flames.

"Lera!" Arisha's voice hits me in the back. "Lera, we need to go."

I don't want to move. I can't. Not with the reality of what I've just done raging around me. *Stars.* After worrying about the Night Guard's plans to wreak havoc in the Academy, I've done half the work for them.

Shade's teeth close harshly around my arm, dragging me toward the arena's bottlenecked exit. I see Arisha's yellow dress flashing amidst the stampede of bodies racing for the safety of the stone-walled keep, her face blanched with terror. When our eyes meet, my friend flinches away, holding up her hands as if to ward off some assault she thinks I'll launch.

My throat closes.

The flood of people parts around me—around Shade's growling wolf—before converging again into a grand stream. I've just gathered the courage to chase after my friend when a child's high-pitched scream spins me to where Rabbit stands in the middle of the flaming benches, his skinny limbs frozen and shaking like his namesake. Guard after guard rushes past, none bothering to help the lowly boy when there are kings to be protected.

"Rabbit!" Mind spinning, I start toward the boy, searching for a path through the flames. "Rabbit, I'm coming."

Shade blocks my path, his body vibrating with a warning growl, every coarse gray hair standing on end. As if I don't know the danger. As if the danger even matters. My heart pounds, smoke filling my lungs each time I take a breath. White-hot flames lick down the wooden benches toward us from every side. "I need to get to him," I scream at the wolf. "Move!"

Yellow eyes flash. *No.*

Rabbit howls.

I push forward toward him, shoving Shade with all my strength. I didn't save this boy from Katita's brutish cousins just to let him die in a fire I started, that I could have prevented if I'd just been more prepared.

Shade snaps his teeth at me, nothing of the male I know behind the furious golden eyes, and I swallow a sob. Salivating fangs reflect the fire, the hackles on the wolf's neck rising like a rooster's comb. Retreating one step from me, Shade's horrendous growl leaves no doubt of his demand that I stay the hell away.

I stop, my chest heaving.

Shade cocks his head for a moment. Then, with a powerful lupine stride, he turns and leaps over the flames toward Rabbit's whimpering calls.

I wait only a heartbeat before following—only to be shoved aside by a pair of rushing men, the stench of sweaty panic trailing in their wake. Someone steps on my long red gown, sending me tumbling to my knees. I've just recovered my footing when Rik and Puckler barrel by, knocking me aside into the blue-clad team from Fothom, which is trying to stay together as they move. Realizing I'm not one of their own, the shouting athletes bump me away to be swept up into the crowd building at the arena's main exit, crushing together as if by a slowly tightening clamp. Without Shade's wolf at my side, no one is keeping clear any longer.

Setting my jaw, I aim for where Shade is dragging Rabbit toward the open safety of the arena's sand, my fists set to forge my way through the cascade of bodies. One step. Two.

Then an iron-hard arm sweeps around me from behind, a familiar woodsy scent filling my lungs.

"River?"

"Come with me." The male's cold demand is that much starker for the blazing inferno rising around us.

I shake my head, pressing against his implacable hold. "Rabbit and—"

"That wasn't a request." Holding my body against his hard chest with one arm, River drags me out of the arena and across the courtyard toward the keep, his towering body parting the sea of people easily. I shout and twist, craning my neck to try to make eye contact with him, but all I can see is his hard jaw, the pulse beating steadily in the side of his corded neck.

He bellows orders to the guards as he goes—to check around the arena's exits for anyone injured in the stampede, to let the arena's structure burn down and focus on ensuring the fire has no chance to jump elsewhere. The guards look askance at me, but River may as well be carrying a sack of grain for all the attention he pays me.

My heart pounds against my ribs. There is nothing I can say to make him understand why I can't just leave. That I'm responsible for this and can't just run for cover.

Baring my teeth, I try a new tactic, elbowing the male with all my strength.

River grunts and lets go with surprising speed.

I've no time to contemplate my success as I shove my way back toward the arena and the flames roaring within. Black smoke billows so high into the cloudless blue sky that all of Great Falls will be able to see it.

My mind is moving too quickly for conscious thought, just repeating a litany of dread over and over. *I did this. I have to make sure no one is in there. I did this.*

I reach the arena door. Heat slaps my face, scorching my lungs when I make the mistake of inhaling. Inside me, magic rallies, ready to make up in force what it lacks in direction or plan.

Feet pound the earth behind me. This time when River grabs hold, he twists my arm ruthlessly behind my back.

Pain grips my shoulder, and I bite back a cry. River's breath is hard and furious on the back of my neck, his grip unyielding. My words and curses fall on ears so deaf that a shiver runs along my spine. Forcing me away from the mayhem in the courtyard, the large male marches me toward the green border of the reflection garden—and a small side door of the keep. It's low and wooden, half hidden behind a huge flowering rhododendron.

I barely catch sight of Arisha's horrid dress amidst the crowd before the flow of bodies shoves her along again. This time, my friend doesn't seem to mark me at all, whether by chance or design.

"Arisha!" My voice is lost beneath the panicked screams and thundering shouts of the guards. Before I can call her name again, River throws open a side door and shoves me into the keep.

I stumble, blinking against the sudden dimness. We're in a large marble-floored corridor with portraits decorating the walls. The same corridor where River broke up with me just this morning, though far down on its opposite end. The same one I took when trying to escape Zake. Nothing good has happened in the corridor yet. "What are you doing, River?" I demand.

River quickly surveys the space, his usually perfect uniform now streaked with patches of dirt and soot, his dark hair standing up in sweat-soaked strands. The chiseled lines of the warrior's handsome face are unyielding as stone. Finding what he was looking for—a narrow door so blended into the fine gilded wallpaper that I wouldn't have known it was there—River yanks it open. "Get inside."

I stay where I am.

River moves toward me, his intent to shove me clear.

"Stop it." Slapping the bastard's hand away, I step into the narrow opening to find myself in what appears to be a dank staircase.

River follows at my heels, pulling the door closed behind him. As my eyes adjust, I see that we're on a landing no bigger than two paces across. The male's bulk takes up most of the space. Most of the air. The scent of smoke, blood, and ire cling to his clothes. The first two are merely the scents of a frenzied rush from a burning structure; the last one makes my insides twist in dread.

River's nostrils flare as he twists me around. Between the sunlight drifting in through strategically positioned slits in the wall—the ugly utilitarian things being too small to be called windows—and my immortal sight, the anger in River's gray eyes is as plain as day.

"Why, Leralynn?" He spits the words, his deep voice echoing against the curved stone walls, his body unfurling for full effect. *Stars,* River is truly using his height to intimidate me, to force me back a step, though there's nowhere to go. His broad chest heaves, his beautiful face jagged with fury.

An utterly different male from the one I saw this morning—the one who said he loved me even as he severed me from his life.

"Why what? You are the one who forced me in here, so maybe you tell me why," I hiss back, indignation raising my blood to a simmering heat. I can't do this now, can't be in the same space with the male whose very presence rips into my soul, making me unable to think. And I especially can't be here while innocent people are choking, their skin blistering with burns because I couldn't keep my magic in check for ten bloody seconds after getting it back. I need to be out there helping, doing something to correct this. I shake my head at River. "Better yet, don't tell me anything. You and I are done, remember? So stay out of my way."

"I know what you are," River snaps, a flash of pain crossing his gray eyes. "Stop lying."

A crashing sound comes from above us, turning River's attention up the steps before I can say anything. Footsteps echo from the walls, a chorus of voices rising in a growing rumble.

"What's happening?"

"Fire."

"Earthquake."

"The islanders are attacking. I warned you this was a trap—"

"My arm! Someone help! My arm!"

"I see they finally got the Great Hall unlocked." River's teeth flash once in the dim light, then he's pushing past me and up the stairs with the stride of a male who knows exactly where he's heading. "I need to check on them. You stay here."

Ignoring him, I turn right back around and shove at the door.

It doesn't budge, the engaged lock clattering at me mockingly. River locked me in. My jaw clenches, murder flooding my mind as I stalk up the stairs after him, the muffled noises growing louder with each winding step.

Taking the final turn of the spiral stairs, I expect to step into a populated room—only to discover myself in a plain, white-walled antechamber, the stone floor worn with years of servants' boots and spills. Unlike the landing below, the musky room is spacious enough for a dozen people to stand comfortably.

A shelf large enough to hold a half-dozen platters is built into the wall next to a single door, the space beside it sporting a series of narrow slits at an average man's eye level. Seeing River stoop down to peer into one, I realize the peepholes were intended for just that—a master butler quietly examining the needs of his masters on the other side, sending out foodstuffs and drinks as the situation calls.

Pulling away from his viewing spot, River glares at me. "I told you to stay downstairs."

Ignoring the male, I brace my hand on the stone and peer into the lowest slit. The mezzanine overlooking the Great Hall beneath sprawls before me, the great space right by where River and I once danced now hosting overflow tables and chairs to supplement the seating. The servants' antechamber appears to be several steps above the mezzanine floor to afford the best view possible, just as the acoustics carry the sounds from the large chamber the best they can. Clearly, River chose this particular location for a reason.

With the clever positioning of the peepholes, I mark people pouring into the hall itself in heedless droves of royals and guests, cadets and servants. Most are covered in ash-streaked sweat, some with blood. Most of the children are crying—though the ones who aren't worry me more, their numb, wide-eyed silence a clear sign of shock.

I make a move toward the door, desperate to be out there helping, but River's steely hand closes over my arm. "Don't even think about it," he murmurs, eyes still on the crowd.

I twist my arm out of his hold with a sudden burst of fury. "You want to tell me what in star's name is going on with you?"

"You think I'm the one who owes you an explanation?" Pulling away from his observations of the Great Hall, River stands to his full, formidable height and levels me with his gaze.

My back tightens, the sting from the verbal lashing rousing my own ire. "You just dragged me across the Academy and locked me in here. Of all the times to indulge in mood swings, River—"

"I dragged you across the Academy from a fire, Leralynn." River towers over me, his voice grim. Shoulders spread, penetrating gaze intent on my face, the male looks every inch the lethal warrior. Beside his powerful thigh, his hand opens and closes as if the energy and tension coursing through his hard muscle needs some way to escape. It's a testament to the male's mastery of himself that the whole keep isn't shaking now, his body controlling its magic with the very instinct I still lack. "A fire that you set. With magic. How long have you been a member of the Night Guard, *Lady* Leralynn of Osprey?"

8

———————

Lera

I stare dumbly at River. The ice slithering over my skin morphs to a prickling heat.

My mouth is dry, my heart knocking against my ribs, echoing through the small chamber. "Have you lost your mind?" I enunciate each word as if speaking to someone slow of thought. "I'm the one who's been telling you nonstop that you have a problem with the Night Guard. Why would I be working with the very people I've been openly trying to stop?"

A low growl escapes beneath River's breath. "I saw you. Right before the arena went up in flames."

"Doing what?" My voice rises, drowning out the clamor in the Great Hall below.

"Doing magic." River's fingers flex at his side, his voice never rising above a dangerous murmur. "You were angry. You extended your hands. You set the fire."

"I was trying to stop Han from murdering Tye in cold blood!" My nostrils flare, drawing in the musk of the antechamber with every breath. "Maybe if you'd been paying attention to that bastard instead of trotting around doing Sage's job for him, you could have stopped that little problem before it happened."

151

I've struck a nerve. River leans over me, his teeth flashing as he speaks. "Then you don't deny setting the fire?"

I rise on the balls of my feet, forcing him to lean back, taking up the air between us as effectively as he did. "By accident, not by Night Guard order."

The male steps back, his face paler than it was moments ago, the sudden silence in the room as loud as thunder. "So Zake told me the truth. You *are* fae."

River hadn't believed Coal's claim and had gone to talk to Zake himself. I exhale in a sharp puff, my thoughts tearing between gratitude that none of Zake's words set off River's amulet and annoyance at which highlights the pompous immortal ass decided to focus on. "How do you talk to Zake and walk away thinking that *I'm* the fae you need to worry about? Or did the impending Night Guard attack not bloody come up?"

River flips his wrist, sliding a knife from his sleeve into his palm. "Show me your true self, fae." He spits the last word like a slur.

"You're pulling a knife on me?" I shove River in the chest and am as surprised as the male himself when he stumbles back into the wall behind him. Blood rushes loudly in my ears, the whole antechamber feeling hot as blazing furnace. "Do you actually think, with any shred of logic, that I'm working with the Night Guard?"

"I think you're working toward your own end, and always have been." River snarls and pushes himself off the wall to regain his coiled fighting stance. I can't believe we've come to this, facing each other like two enemies on a battlefield. "I said, let me see you."

Before I have time to second-guess it, I reach to the back of my neck and snap open the clasp. The dreaded relic clatters to the stone floor with a high-pitched *ting*, a weight lifting off my senses at once. Despite everything—the fire, River, Zake—my body can't help but pause to savor its first breaths with both the amulet and the mortal world's wards gone. Power thrums through my veins. Deep inside my core, my freed mating bond pulses along with my heart—a bond River's veil will not let him feel. The one he wouldn't want, even if it were offered. "Happy now?" I ask.

River doesn't answer.

Standing frozen for the first time since I've met him, the male simply looks at me, his beautiful face laid bare. His gaze drinks in my face and ears and body with a reverence usually reserved for the stars alone. The first breath he draws into his lungs makes his chest expand against his coat, his clean scent overpowering all others in the space, even headier now with my amulet off. Bringing his fingers to his lips, River exhales slowly, the wonder that colored his face only moments ago melting into something different. Regret.

"River?" I reach a hand toward him.

"No." His eyes shutter, and he steps back quickly, the knife in his free hand shifting to a different grip. "Don't touch me."

I flinch, letting my hand drop to my side. An ache twisting deep in my soul creeps out into my newly sensitive body, magnifying each small way River's rejection cuts into my flesh. My chin shifts to point at the weapon in his grip. "You want to kill me?" I ask.

"Want? Stars, no." The strong, smooth planes of the male's face are drawn so tight that I can see the small muscles twitching along his jaw and the shimmer of silver pooling along his lower lids. He swallows, his throat bobbing. "But you've the power and will to set an arena full of innocent people on fire, Leralynn," River says quietly. "And every tale you spin is a lie. I've tried everything I could, but there are no more chances. No more risks I can take with so many people's lives at stake."

The tears welling in River's eyes spill quietly onto his chiseled face now, making my throat ache with tears of my own. Then his words— and the knife still in his hand—register, leaving me too shocked to move.

"I have to stop you," says River.

My heart pounds, pain branching through my chest and limbs, seizing my air. Because...because maybe River is right. I am dangerous. Not from malevolence—but from sheer, bloody incompetence. From the moment I shattered that rune tablet that made the males absorb the veil amulets, to my ongoing failures to make any progress in securing the wards or even convincing Sage to stop the trials, to now outright setting the arena on fire—it's all been me. I'm the common denominator. I glance at the wall separating us from the Great Hall, echoing louder now with the frightened voices of parents and children seeking each other out, whimpering in fear and pain. I did all that too. I lost control of magic despite knowing it returned—all while River contains his own power on instinct. Even Tye, who was in the midst of an acrobatic stunt when the wards faltered, kept his flames moving as precisely as scalpel cuts.

River takes another step toward me, and despite his soft voice and damp cheeks, every muscle in his body vibrates with tension. The warrior inside him knows that a prey's instinct to fight for her life can wake at any instant—no matter how docile she seems.

Except I have no intention of fighting. Not because I can't—a few choice words to River's amulet will have him howling in pain so great, he'll turn the knife on himself before slipping it across my throat—but because such victory would hurt more than defeat. Because no matter what my mate does, I can't bear to turn the amulet's magic against him. I can't hurt my mate.

My eyes widen. *I can't hurt my mate.*

And I don't think River can actually hurt me either.

The veil magic's vise-tight grip on my males' memories has survived everything it's encountered but one: the male's belief that my life's in peril.

Coal's memory returned when he tried to defend me against the nightmare-born qoru he thought was real. Tye overpowered the amulet's magic only when struggling to get to me in the midst of Zake's attack. Even the short-lived clarity Shade had in the forest came on the heels of my being stabbed, his magic—and memory—surfacing to protect me.

Excitement wakens my body, the magic prickling my blood as my thoughts fit the facts together. If the one thing stronger than the amulet's magic is my mate's drive to protect me, then said mate has to believe my life is in danger first.

Swallowing, I raise my chin, exposing my neck. "You're right, River. You need to take my life. Now."

The male's dark brows pull together, his gray gaze surveying my body as if expecting to find balls of blazing magic hovering above my hands. "You want me to kill you?"

"I need you to try. Sounds like splitting hairs, I know but..." I swallow a curse as River's frown deepens suspiciously and he shifts away from me. *Life in danger,* I remind myself, *and trust the bond.*

"You were right," I say, trying to make my voice hard, to make his attack easier. "I'm dangerous. I set the fire to the arena. I've been lying to you since the day I stepped onto the Academy grounds."

No response.

"I am working for the Night Guard," I say suddenly. "You were right. I'm working for the Night Guard. You can't afford to take any chances with me. "

River shakes his head, confusion flitting across his gaze. "I'm fairly certain that now you *are* lying."

I grind my teeth together. *Fine.* "I've used magic to manipulate your mind. How else do you explain how little you care that I'm coupling with you and Coal and Shade and Tye all at once? Putting me down is the only responsible thing to do. You know it is."

"Put you down?" He takes a step forward, his eyes wide. "Are you insane?"

"You're the one who said you needed to stop me," I remind him.

He throws up his arms. "I was going to arrest you and put you in the dungeon, not butcher you. Who do you think I am?"

"I'd love to tell you, believe me," I mutter, my thoughts racing at my miscalculation. River isn't trying to take my life; he's trying to take my freedom—and that won't do at all.

"You know what, never mind. We'll do this a different way." Reaching through the slit of my tattered red dress to the blade I've strapped to my thigh, I pull out steel. Not the balanced throwing knife Han took from me when he fought Coal, but a decent enough blade pilfered with Tye's aid from the armory. Sharp. Deadly.

River's gaze sharpens, the male dropping at once into a fighting crouch, his hands up defensively. It would almost be comical, this powerful immortal warrior thinking me a threat, if the situation weren't quite so dire.

"No need for that," I assure him, forcing air into my suddenly tight lungs. Twisting the knife toward my chest, I beg the stars to help me avoid severing anything too important when I do what I must. River needs to *believe* I'm about to die, but I'd prefer to stay as far away from actual demise as I can.

"Leralynn?" River says, a note of panic making my name sound breathless.

Coal's lessons sound in my head in a voice ever too calm for the deathly facts being imparted about vital organs. My stomach squeezes, pushing bile up my throat.

"Leralynn." Now River's voice takes on a note of command, as if he hadn't been the one to pull a weapon on me just moments earlier. "What are you doing?"

"Trusting you." Without waiting for the end of my own sentence, I plunge the knife down toward my ribs.

9

River

*R*iver leapt with a speed he did not think himself capable of, slamming Leralynn's hand against the wall. The knife clattered harmlessly to the floor. His side burned, the wound a distant pulse against the gravity of what had almost happened.

Kicking away the knife, River gripped Lera's waist and hoisted her up against the stone, bringing their faces level. Her sweet scent washed over him, tinted with the harsh metallic shimmer of fight and fear.

Lera's chest heaved, beads of sweat glimmering at her temples as she struggled to get to the knife despite the futility of the effort. One deep look at the desperation in her chocolate eyes, and River knew that she'd not been toying with him. She *had* been trying to plunge the knife into her own flesh, though it scared her spitless. A desperate last-chance move toward an end River could not begin to guess. And it drove him insane.

Leralynn's lilac scent wrapped around River as his lips pulled back into an infuriated snarl that felt more animal than human. His breath came in short, shallow bursts that grew more desperate the longer he looked at her. Really, really looked.

The ears, he saw those first. Delicate elongated points that made River hard from a single glance. Leralynn's face was her own, yet somehow even more beautiful, the bones slightly elongated, sculpted into ethereal perfection, the skin satin smooth, almost pearlescent. The girl's hair had strayed from her braid and cascaded over her bare shoulders in locks of thick auburn that River's fingers longed to bury themselves in. Leralynn's strapless dress had slid down in the tussle, showing the tops of lush breasts peeking above the red silk.

And then there was something else, a shimmer of power that River felt rather than saw. Just as he felt a power inside himself rouse to it in response. Waking his body to fuller sensations. To strength. To need.

River inhaled again, the girl's lilac scent making the blood in his veins rise to a simmer. Especially when he could tell that the female was drinking him in as well, her gaze resting so intensely on his features that, despite what he'd just done, he knew she wasn't giving up on him. "Why don't you hate me?" he demanded.

"Because I love you," Leralynn whispered.

River's heart clapped like thunder, dizziness threatening the edges of his vision. Watching those words cross her perfect fae lips was a surreal kind of torture, hardening every muscle in his body.

Her nostrils flared delicately as if she could smell the bead of moisture River knew was at the end of his engorged cock—the bloody thing having a mind of its own. Her lips parted, the scent of her own reciprocal arousal flaring even as River held her against the wall. Which only made his cock pulse harder, drowning out the pain in his side.

"River—" Leralynn's musical voice was husky, her hands wrapping around his neck.

"Quiet." The order came in a snarl that echoed the chaos the girl was wreaking inside him. River was going to kill her for turning that blade on herself. Was going to bundle her up like a package and throw her somewhere she could harm no one, least of all herself. He was going to … He was going to kiss her, stars damn it.

River pressed his mouth against Leralynn's, her lips parting hungrily to let him inside. She was warm, the tips of her elongated canines sharp little points that sent zings of sensation from River's tongue all the way to his straining cock, making his senses swim.

River's tongue swept through her lips, softly at first, then deeper. Harder. Pillaging the mouth that Leralynn yielded to him freely while his mind finally quieted, this moment between them existing beyond time. As if the pull of some undeniable magic had taken his soul hostage.

Pulling his head away for breath, River stared into Lera's face as he held her up against that wall. Her lips were pink and swollen, her skin flushed. Without the necklace on, her brown eyes were only deeper and more intoxicating, threatening to drown him whole. His entire body trembled with longing, the heady taste of her having triggered a new level of desire that made his hips press forward of their own accord, grinding against her mound.

When Lera moaned softly, it was all River could do to keep from howling with desire. Yes, more. He wanted—needed—more. And from the girl's dilated eyes and tight grip on his shoulders, so did she.

Lera's nails dug into River's coat, and he stepped forward roughly, hoisting the girl's legs around his hips, even as his wound gave a screaming blaze of protest. The pain made him waver for a moment before his cock took over his common sense, Leralynn's body feeling too perfect around his to change anything.

Yes, with her thighs wrapped around him, River couldn't care less how much his wound hurt. Couldn't care about fires, or fae, or the end of the world itself. And when he slid his hand beneath her dress to find her shift soaked with the same thick arousal that coursed through him, there was no more thought to spare for anything.

Swiping the hem of Lera's shift out of the way, River ran his hand between her wet folds, her hips pushing into his touch in desperate command. When his fingers reached her apex, the small bud already swollen and ready, he felt the growl rumble through his chest. Baring his teeth, he ran the tip of his finger over the sensitive nub, the flesh smooth and engorged enough to make Leralynn's small body shudder beneath his touch.

"Stars." Lera's desperate gasp was sadistically delicious, echoing in River's core as he jerked open his buttons.

Positioning the head of his hard cock at her entrance, River sheathed himself inside her in a single stroke. The girl moaned, tightening her legs around his hips like a vise. With one hand beneath Lera's silky backside, River paused for a heartbeat to let the girl adjust to the intrusion, tracing the hood of her swollen apex with his free hand.

"More," Lera growled, her tight channel gripping River, magnifying the throbbing in his shaft until it echoed through his body.

She bit her lip, her breath coming in small pants as she jerked against him, her brown eyes flashing as she tried to slide herself along River's cock. Trying to make him start pumping.

River bared his teeth, making her wait an extra heartbeat just to gather the reins of control. Then he started thrusting, the strokes deep and powerful, his cock pounding out its own rhythm.

Lera buried her face in River's shoulder, muffling her moans as River drove into her, shoving her toward the release he could smell coming. One of her hands tangled sharply in his hair, making him gasp and pump harder. Arousal dripped from her filled sex, slicking his hands. Her body trembled, strong and vulnerable with him inside her, where he could feel each of her responses. The pleasure at each thrust, the frustration as he pulled out, teasing her bud for just a moment before impaling her again.

Yes, there was no hiding for Leralynn now. Not anymore. And River was going to make as much clear to them both before they finished. He was going to command her body and soul, giving them both the reckoning they needed.

10

Lera

The coarse wool of River's coat scratches against my cheek as I press my face into his powerful shoulder, clinging to him tightly as his hips slam against mine at a furious, spine-tingling pace. Drawing a shaking breath, I fill my sharpened fae senses with River's woodsy scent. With my amulet off for the first time in his presence—the mating bond writhing through my veins at full force—River has become overwhelming, tipping my hunger for him into a frenzy.

As the thick head of his cock slides over my ridges, the escalating crescendo of sensation rises and rises, stops just short of pushing me over the edge. Again. I grit my teeth.

Thrust. Thrust. Thrust.

Outside these walls, Academy life is moving on. Servants curse as they discover the door to this stairway locked and find another way around to bring refreshments into the Great Hall. Each rattle of the lock downstairs prods my arousal, making my toes curl. I press my face into River's neck to more effectively muffle my moans...and sink my teeth into his skin. Tasting him—and prodding him to give me what I want.

River roars and pounds harder, clutching my bottom so tightly I know I'll have bruises.

His engorged shaft fills me with sensation that shoots from my sex to my aching breasts, the bunched nipples rubbing against the smooth silk of my dress. As if reading my mind, River shifts to hold me with one hand and uses the other to pull down the front of my dress until my breasts tumble free. He scrapes his palm over one aching nipple, back and forth, making me gasp and press into him.

So, so close. *Stars.* I'm a breath away from begging. More. I need more. Faster.

And the bastard knows it.

From the pulsing of his cock inside me, it is of a similar opinion.

Pulling back, River drives into me again, sending molten waves of pleasure through my sex. My hands tingle, my nails raking over the woolen coat covering the male's powerful back.

Forcing my head from his neck, River takes my mouth even as he continues to massage my breasts and thrust inside me. Deep and hard, pillaging me at the top and bottom until I can do nothing but take what he gives me. Which should annoy me, but magnifies every sensation instead. The moisture flowing from me, my body's ultimate betrayal to my mind, leaves no doubt of the effect River is having on me. And… and maybe that's all right.

As River's tongue makes another powerful sweep of my mouth, I yield it to him. Let myself focus on the connection, the slide of him inside me that fills a void. *You can have my truths, River. You can have all of me.* My eyes sting with the realization of how much I missed this. The trust. The openness. The mating that makes my body sing in response to River's masterful thrusts.

River scrapes the top of his teeth along my lip, leaving a trail of tingling pain that morphs to hot pleasure. A moment later, the finger River used to tease the sides of my apex rubs a firm circle directly over it. "Now, Lera," he orders.

My body clenches, the wave of pleasure rising inside me rippling from my apex. More and more, until each muscle clenches in a mix of uncontrollable pleasure and ache that makes me spasm around River's great cock with dizzying intensity. The world flickers, the spasming waves raking my core over and over and over until I hang like a limp doll in the male's arms.

My head is swimming as the room solidifies once again around me, the worried buzz of servants returning below, my breath coming short and fast. A bead of sweat snakes its way down my neck before dripping impertinently between my breasts. For the first time, I feel the cold stone of the wall against my back. Feel the male's hot, powerful hips that I still grip with my thighs. His callused hand beneath my naked backside.

His cock still in me. Still throbbing.

My eyes widen.

River grins wickedly, flashing his teeth.

In the next heartbeat, the male pulls out and thrusts into me again, his slicked finger entering my back hole at the same moment. The dual sensation rushes through me like an explosion, magnifying everything that came before it. I gasp desperately, over and over, falling into the abyss of pleasure without any choice of my own.

River groans. As I feel his warmth spill inside me, the last of my strength drains away. My sex pulses with the clenching aftershocks, the little shots of energy along my nerves that make me shake in the male's arms, and we lower to the ground together, my head on River's chest.

Stars. Oh bloody stars.

I rise and prop myself over River, tracing his strong jaw, the hint of stubble scratching my skin. The words I need to say to him again tingle my tongue. Maybe now he'll really hear them. "I love you, River."

The corners of the male's mouth lift, his gray eyes dancing with a fevered pleasure that seems to come as much from my words as the release he just found. Bringing up his hand, River traces his thumb along the pointed tip of my left ear.

"Leralynn." He swallows, his jaw tightening for an instant, before returning with visible effort to focus on me alone. "I love you too. I could never stop. No matter—" He swallows again, his eyes closing for a moment. Now that we are no longer in the midst of fevered action, the male's skin looks pale.

And is getting more so with every heartbeat.

"River?" My stomach clenches. "River, what's wrong?"

He shakes himself and gives me that reassuring calm look that I know he's perfected over the centuries. "Aside from the fact that we are concealing ourselves in a servants' passage while half the Academy is up in flames and a small army of immortal warriors are likely scheming an attack against Great Falls?" He gives me a crooked smile that doesn't quite touch his beautiful gray eyes despite a hell of a lot of effort. "Aside from that, my lady, all's well."

No, no, it isn't.

Pulling away, I survey River with my gaze—and find a large wet stain saturating the breast of his woolen coat. Red, coppery, and growing before my eyes. That blood I smelled on him earlier and dismissed as nothing of consequence. "Just how badly are you injured, River?" I demand.

"A deep scratch, nothing more," he says—and doubles over in pain.

11

Lera

"River!" Wrapping my arm around the male's waist, I ease him to sit on the stone floor. "What—no, forget what. Where?"

River fumbles with the buttons on his coat.

Pushing his hands aside, I work the polished metal pieces through the thick fabric, easing the royal red jacket off River's muscled shoulders. My jaw tightens when, instead of being covered with a shirt, I discover the male's hard, bare torso wrapped in self-made bandages. Bandages completely soaked through with fresh red blood. "You knew!" I hiss at him, seeing my own furious expression reflected in his gray eyes. "You knew you were injured. Badly."

"I was there when it happened, so yes." River clenches his teeth, his skin growing cooler and clammier with each passing heartbeat. He rubs his hands over his face. "The prisoner, I went to talk to him this morning. And then I met the fae named Owalin. That didn't end as well as I'd hoped."

River discovered Night Guard fae on Academy grounds, got stabbed, and then, seeing me set the arena ablaze, drew his own conclusions. And came to stop me, injury or not. Unfortunately, since none of our encounter successfully endangered my life, River is still beneath the amulet's veil spell.

I inhale the smell of his blood and snarl. "I understand why you went after me, but why did you think coupling while stabbed was a good idea?"

"Truth be known, I wasn't thinking much at the time. *Agh.*" River grunts in pain as I peel away soggy bandages to behold a freely bleeding gash along River's right pectoral. From the way its draining, I'm fairly certain the gash is newly reopened.

I should have stopped this. I should have smelled the blood on River and taken him to Shade immediately. But my instincts were too distracted by the male himself—his anger, his rejection of me. I can feel my mind wanting to spiral into darkness, to cover my head with my hands and wait until this is all over.

As if in ironic response, the magic inside me surges, the cord of Shade's healing power sensing a chance to escape into the world.

I tamp it down. Hard.

Healing is far more dangerous than fire, requiring not just precision and control, but also the knowledge of internal structures that I couldn't draw on a chalk slate, much less in my mind. With River's wound along his chest so close to his heart, a misplaced slice of magic would leave him dead as easily as healed. And after what I just did to the arena, I've no desire to bring my magic anywhere near so much as a candle—and certainly not a mate. I've done enough damage.

But blood pools beneath River now, thick and shiny, making my mind numb with panic. I press into the stone floor as I breathe through the magic's roaring, until the silver power is a tiny trickle along my hand. My heart pounds. "For an epic military commander, you are an utter idiot."

One brow on River's face rises in acknowledgment. Even pale and hollowed out with pain, the male is beautiful. Unjustly so.

Placing my palm over the bleeding wound, I let the magic dribble inside as if filling the gash with drops of melted wax. River flinches at each dab, his face growing even paler, but makes no move to pull away or ask me to stop as the flesh knits together with agonizing slowness. I don't know how Shade can bear it, to hurt the people he loves when he heals them.

"Very convenient." River smiles faintly as I pull away, his wound raw but no longer leaking life blood. "Thank you."

I shake my head. "I only stopped the bleeding. We need to get a healer here. Shade." Ripping the hem of my dress, I wrap it tightly over the wound as a backup to my handiwork. River winces as I pull tightly on the fabric. "Will you be all right while I get him?"

Bracing a hand on the wall, he climbs to his feet. "I need my jacket. Can't go out looking like this. And not to the infirmary either. No one can know I'm hurt. We must prepare for an attack, and I can't lead the Academy from a sickbed."

"You can't do it from a deathbed either. So—" I cut off as the steady din of noise coming from the Great Hall changes subtly. River's suddenly alert gaze tells me he's heard the difference as well.

Squeezing his shoulder once, I scramble to the slit near the door and look out. The mezzanine looks as it did before, the Great Hall below it now fully crowded with guests enjoying the spread of food and wine the servants trotted out while River and I were occupied. On the whole, Sage's most honored guests look relatively unscathed—I count a half-dozen kings surrounded by their families, looking only a bit disgruntled and soot tarnished. Relief thuds through me that perhaps my tally of injured—or worse—won't be as great as I feared.

With another quick scan, I confirm that Coal, Tye, and Shade are nowhere in their ranks and some of my relief fades into worry again. Are any of my other males hurt? Did my fire… *Stars.* Of all things to feel nauseated over just now, anxiety over the elite warriors' reaction when they discover my incompetence lying behind the fire shouldn't make the list. But it does.

A section of the hall is partitioned off, the Academy's healers—with the notable absence of Shade—tending to the wounded. And then there is… I frown at the large crow soaring above the anxious crowd, flapping its wings as it settles on the mezzanine rail, its iridescent feathers reflecting the chandelier light. More birds join the first, soaring in through the open balcony doors.

Caw caw. The birds' calls echo from the walls, their taloned feet settling on perches as the people in the Great Hall quiet with thickening unease. Something doesn't feel right to them. Not to me either.

River curses, staring toward the stairs. "I need to get to the guards. Those birds—"

A flash of light piercing through the view ports halts River in his tracks. Blinking sight back into my eyes, I gasp as bird after bird shifts into a fae warrior. Four. Eight. A dozen. More. Immortals of every size and age land smoothly in a crouch on the Great Hall floor, swords and bows at the ready, as magic crackles through the air in waves of power. With their sleek black armor, pointed ears, and smoothly beautiful faces, they make a terrifying sight, sending panic speeding through the guests and servants.

Their screams and shouts echoing against the high raftered ceiling, the humans stampede for the Great Hall's door, crushing against it as they did in the arena—but this time, the door doesn't open. Cries of pain sound from those in the front.

Through it all, my immortal ears pick up a deep, calm voice from somewhere in the middle of the crowd.

"Your attention, please," the speaker says, making no effort to be heard above the pandemonium.

No one seems to hear the voice, the strongest of the men now trying to shoulder open the hall door, which must be barred on the other side—or else held shut with magic.

"I said, be quiet," the voice repeats almost kindly, the words drowning amidst the humans' shouts.

"Leralynn." The note of horror in River's voice has me searching the Great Hall for the source—to discover small bits of fire dancing along the thick ropes connecting a man-sized iron candelabra to the hall's high ceiling. The rope strands crackle as they are consumed, snap by snap by snap.

My chest squeezes around my ribs. But I can do nothing but watch, paralyzed, as the last of the tether holding the grand metal construction snaps in two, releasing it from the ceiling. Guests scatter from the candelabra's path, the thick iron bands nonetheless crushing two men who couldn't get out of the way in time. The crack of bones sends bile up my throat.

The cry of the victims' agony proves as effective at getting the hall's attention as the fall of the candelabra itself.

Striding over to the wreckage, a tall fae male in long blood-red robes kicks debris out of his path. His long white-blond hair twists down the back of his head in an elaborate braid, highlighting a high forehead and blue eyes nearly as piercing as Coal's—and far more terrifying in their detached enjoyment of the scene before him. In the sunlight streaming through the windows, the male's jewel-decorated ears are a plain sign of his immortality. As are the sparks of fire dancing like fireflies along his hands.

"Silence," the male orders—this time with immediate results.

"Better. If a few shouts of agony are needed each time I demand your attention, it will be a small price to pay." He stops in front of a cowering young Yulti girl, studies her as if having spotted an exotic creature in the woods, and then continues walking through the crowd until he stands on the steps leading to the mezzanine. "Now then, allow me to introduce myself. I am Owalin, your future continental emperor." Owalin waits several heartbeats to let the news settle before smiling benevolently. "I will be dismissing you from the Great Hall by kingdoms—just as soon as each throne is signed over to me."

1 2

"He can't be serious," I whisper, hot blood thudding through my temples.

Every bone in my body wants to rush out there and attack the male we came here to stop, standing in the open, so close I can see his long, delicately painted fingernails.

"He's putting on a damn good show of it if he isn't." River touches my arm. "Whatever rash thoughts just stampeded through your mind, rein them in before you get yourself and many more killed."

"But he—"

"Owalin has hostages, Leralynn. Any threat to his position, and they die. He's not covered the windows yet because he *wants* everyone on the outside to know what's going on, and the death that will happen should anyone try a rescue. He may not know you and I are watching, but he is wagering that *someone* is."

In the Great Hall below, Owalin walks around in a small circle, his red robe swishing gracefully against the marble floor, the hostages moving out of his path. I now count two dozen immortals and as many allied humans—all still in the uniform of Academy servants—stationed around the Great Hall. Fifty captors to about three hundred hostages, six of them kings, whose gazes now jump between each other and their own families. The stench of terror and triumph saturates the air so greatly that it manages to snake through the cracks into the musty antechamber holding River and me.

Pulling a knife from his boot, River sticks it into the crack beneath the door, jamming it shut.

I nod. With the servants' passage designed to blend into the decor, the fae now patrolling the mezzanine have paid it no mind as yet—and if they do, finding it locked should further deter investigation, except perhaps to have a bowman keep watch to ensure no one enters.

Not that anyone stupid enough to come through here is likely to survive the encounter on the mezzanine.

"Any ideas?" I ask River.

He holds up a finger to silence me, his attention firmly on the view port. A commander surveying the battlefield with calm intensity. A situation I'd feel much better about if said commander was not still unsteady on his feet from a half-healed wound.

Flinging his cloak behind his shoulders, Owalin straightens the cuff links on his black silk shirt, the small movement mesmerizing the hostages into deeper silence. "Before anyone ponders stupidity, rest assured that you'll discover all exit points from the Great Hall are now locked down, with fae warriors ready to silence any dimwit deciding to test my word. In fact, any sign of disobedience or rebellion will be punished with the archers on the mezzanine selecting a target at random." Owalin snaps his fingers, and an arrow whistles down into the crowd, the tip burying itself in the eye of the man still whimpering beneath the crushing weight of the fallen candelabra. The man screams once, then goes limp, blood pouring down his face while several of the hostages retch onto the floor.

Owalin wrinkles his nose before speaking again. "As you observe, it is in all our interests to get our business done civilly and expeditiously. Unless you force my hand, I've no intention of harming any of my loyal subjects."

I swallow. Fifty captors, at least two dozen of them fae—the others recruited humans. Maybe more than that, if we don't trust Owalin to be disclosing the full extent of his forces. Why should I be surprised? Owalin has been planning this coup—experimenting with magic, bringing in forces from Lunos—for months, possibly years.

"Now then," Owalin continues amicably, "let us get organized. All the royals to the right, please. The lower beasts to the left. Master Han, a bit of help, if you please."

Striding up beside Owalin, Han—whose ears are now as pointed as Owalin's—grabs a girl who looks like a younger version of Katita by the arm and launches her against the frescoed wall, the young princess hitting the painted harp with a muffled cry—a much greater one coming from her father, King Zenith, who rushes toward her.

I press my forehead against the cool stone, hoping my grip on the rough wall will keep River from marking my trembling. I don't know what I was thinking, imagining I could protect the mortal world from the Night Guard.

"Time to go," River tells me, swaying slightly as he pushes himself away from the view port. "There is little more to be learned from here."

Despite the wound no longer bleeding, the male's movements are strained, his corded muscles tight and glistening under a thin sheen of sweat. Bending down, he pulls on his discarded coat, his somewhat glazed eyes already surveying the stairs.

Between the magic, instinct, and sheer bullheadedness, River may be able to keep himself moving—but not for long. Not without help.

"You need to stay put." I grab the male's arm. "I stopped the bleeding, but nothing more. Wait here while I get help."

Pulling my hand gently aside, River shakes his head, his pale, shadowed face set hard as stone. "I have to get down there before someone on either side gets everyone killed," he says, struggling with the red woolen coat.

I open my mouth to argue, then decide better of it and take the coat from him to slide the sleeves over his pale skin, covering the makeshift bandages. I won't be able to hold River here. If the idiot wants a jacket, he can have a jacket. He can have anything so long as we get him to Shade. "We'll go to—" I am about to say the infirmary, but think better of it. "To the library. I'll bring Shade to tend to you there. Agreed?"

A knot in my stomach releases as the male nods. Without waiting for permission, I slip River's free arm around my shoulders, bracing the male as far as he will let me, which is the small landing we entered through. Though the steps keep heading down into the darkness of the keep, River shakes his head.

"This passage is supposed to connect to the kitchens and cellars on the bottom level, but the repairs have blocked off that exit. We can only exit into the main corridor, where we entered."

In other words, River knew there was no place to run when he brought me here. Saying nothing, I snatch up my amulet and snap it back into place while River unlocks the door, both of us listening for the happenings in the corridor beyond. The noise of pounding feet and competing shouts as guards and servants rush about in an attempt to make sense of the mess has River sighing heavily.

His hand closes atop mine as I ready to pull open the door, the warmth of his callused palm seeping through my skin. Caressing me. For a moment, the world stops mattering, the simple touch overshadowing the chaos. Then River takes a deep breath and nods, striding out into the open like the king—or deputy headmaster—he is. Tall. Confident. Unhurried.

And turns the opposite way from where we agreed he'd go.

Stopping sergeant after sergeant midstride, River asks after casualty reports, issues orders for a perimeter guard and staging areas, and swears to flog anyone who so much as thinks about staging a rash assault on the Great Hall. "This isn't a battlefield, it's a hostage taking." River digs his fingers into the arm of a young officer who looks at him with skeptical eyes. "It won't be just your life you forfeit if you rush in there. It will be the lives of the royals and innocents the Night Guard holds."

"So you want us to do nothing?" The young man lifts his chin in defiance.

Wrapping his fingers in the officer's uniform, River slams the man into a nearby tree. "What you do is follow my orders." River's icy voice has the officer's raised arms dropping to his side. "Set up a full perimeter. Get me the plans of every single passage in the Keep. A full account of every person we think is in there. I want to know how many bloody apples they have to eat and how many chairs they have to sit on. And if it is not all in a command room for me by the time I take care of a minor matter, I would not expect you to be wearing an officer's epaulettes again. Am I clear?"

"Trying not to die is not a minor matter, River," I mutter under my breath as the male claps yet another shoulder and issues a fifth order about guard stations. Each man and woman River speaks with continues on with a quieter pace, as if the male's aura of confidence infects their own.

It's not until River personally checks that the flames no longer consume the arena and marks his own frighteningly pallid reflection in one of the keep's mirrors that I succeed in pushing him into the library, the merry jingle of bells at utter odds with the world beyond.

"Gavriel? Arisha?" I call, relieved to see Rabbit curled up safe in a large chair, safe but for a few scratches on his arms—probably from Shade's teeth as he dragged him out—applying himself industriously to a buttered scone. Flaming arena or not, the boy knows his priorities.

Seeing River beside me, Rabbit scrambles away into the stacks.

"Leralynn! Where have you been? Is Arisha with you?" Limping out from a row of bookshelves, Gavriel paces the library floor, limping to his own rambling cadence, his thinning brown hair sticking out in every direction. "First the arena goes up in flames, then Rabbit shows up with Shade, the latter acting so insane that Tye nearly got his throat ripped out before locking the beast in the closet. Meanwhile, Coal returns looking like death incarnate, and the two males rush off looking for you—" Gavriel stops talking, River's presence—and my frantic arm gestures behind him—finally seeming to register. The librarian's eyes widen. Straightening his robes with a flustered yank, he gives the commander a small bow. "Good afternoon, sir. Is there something I might help you with? I have pulled the most authoritative text we have on crisis management theory, which I'm certain would be of great help. If you'd allow me to highlight several passages of—"

"That's quite all right." River settles slowly into a chair while I call for Rabbit and dispatch him—scone and all—to find the other males and Arisha, who I'd expected to be here. Rubbing his face, River turns to Gavriel, the male's gray eyes focusing with effort. "Did you say Shade was in the closet?" River shakes himself as if unsure whether it's his brain or Gavriel's that's gone fuzzy. "If you could send him out, I have need of his assistance."

As if having heard the exchange, a low growl sounds from the back of the library, followed by the sounds of a large body throwing itself against a door.

Grabbing Gavriel's arm, I drag the man to the other side of the room from River. "Are you telling me Shade hasn't shifted and turned the knob in all this time?"

"Yes." Gavriel straightens his glasses. "And I would highly encourage you to keep him in there until he does."

"I don't have time to wait on Shade's pleasure, Gavriel." Somehow, despite the small army of immortals now holding half the continent's royals hostage, we've not one but *two* other disasters trumping the main problem. Stalking toward the growling closet, I take a breath to steady my fraying nerves and pull open the door to two hundred pounds of irritated gray wolf.

Shade's paws land on my shoulders with enough force that I stumble into the bookshelf behind me, Gavriel gasping as precious volumes cascade to the floor. I've barely recovered when the wolf pokes his nose into my midsection, apparently sniffing for injury, before turning away to growl at the newly made mess, lest the ancient tomes get it into their pages to assault us.

Beyond the tall windows on the other side of the library, the courtyard swarms with guards and messengers, the news of the Great Hall attack spreading throughout the already singed Academy. Seeing Tye's mop of red hair rising above the crowd and moving toward us, I let myself savor one stunning moment of relief before returning to the monster at hand. *One quint mate safe. Three to go.*

"Shade." Leaning down to bring my face level with the wolf's, I look into the predator's golden eyes. I don't have time to worry about what River will think of this. *He* doesn't have time. "Shift. Now. River is hurt, and he needs your help." I bite my lip, a small fact I'd forgotten coming to sting me. Despite the return of our magic, Shade's fae form will still be under the amulet's veil, the healer unwitting to his own power.

I draw breath. *Shade is Shade.* He'll work something out. He has to. Because we are out of options. Just as soon as he shifts.

The wolf blinks at me with incomprehension and circles my legs like a land-born shark.

I wait, giving Shade a chance to process my words. To smell the pain and blood saturating River's scent. To feel that gnawing sensation deep in his soul that warns of a quint mate in peril.

Nothing.

Grabbing Shade's muzzle, I force his attention to where River sits in a chair, his hands braced on his knees as if it's all he can do to keep himself upright. Sweat trickles along the strong angle of River's jaw, the veins on his neck thick and pulsing as he watches me in utter confusion. His skin looks gray and clammy, his breathing increasingly labored. If he's alarmed at hearing me call a huge wolf "Shade," then it's buried under a haze of pain. Everything inside me longs to go to him, but I know it isn't me who River needs. "Shade, please. *Please.*"

Shade's gaze finally flickers at River with lupine boredom. Pulling his head out of my grip, he stretches his back, sticking his bushy gray tail high into the air, and…and circles a spot on the carpet before settling down beside me with a contented sigh.

No. *No no no.* My breath catches. "Shade? Shade!"

"You renamed your dog Shade?" River asks, his words slurring slightly. "That's…" He stops, staring toward the library's courtyard-facing window, as if watching people bustle past is suddenly the most important job in the world.

"River?" I ask.

No response, though the male's hands tighten to a white-knuckled grip on the edge of a nearby table. When I repeat his name, River turns his beautiful pain-filled face toward me slowly, his skin ashen as the fog.

"Leralynn, I—" His voice drains away as he sways in his chair, losing his fight for consciousness in midsentence, and slides to the ground.

13

Lera

"River!" My throat tightens as I rush forward. The male is limp as I turn him onto his back, his skin cool and clammy beneath my touch. Even without Shade's knowledge of medicine, I'm all too aware that there is nothing good about River's shallow racing pulse, the subtle change in his woodsy scent. Magic swarms in me, but the rampaging silver cord is as useless as a hammer. "You bastard," I tell River through clenched teeth. "Did you have to stop and chat with every bloody scullery maid on our way here?"

There is no response. Not from River, not from Shade, who watches me with confused curiosity.

"Why isn't Shade shifting?" I demand of Gavriel, who gives me an apologetic shrug of ignorance. "I'll go try to look it up," he says, moving carefully away from the wolf.

My mind races. Grabbing River's spare knife, I slice away the damn coat of his, the rich, tailored cloth falling in useless strips to the ground. I expect to find the wound reopened, but no new blood touches my hands, whatever is killing River is doing so from the inside.

Then I see it. River's wide bare chest rising only on one side as he draws his ragged, labored breaths.

My stomach clenches, nausea washing over me with such force that

Shade is on his feet at once, his warm tongue licking the back of my neck while I wrangle my rebellious insides under control.

"It isn't me who needs help, Shade." Inside me, my magic lashes against its tethers with vicious desperation. It's all I can do to keep myself from grabbing River and letting my wayward magic do something, anything, everything—and destroy whatever chances my mate has to survive.

Breathe, Lera. I force myself to look away from River's deformed chest. *Breathe.*

I'm still kneeling beside River when the merry jingle of bells announces new arrivals, Coal's cursing and metallic scent confirming his presence a moment later. From the way the warrior's ripped black leathers and hair are matted with blood and sweat, I'm guessing his trip outside the walls was no less adventurous than our own disaster.

"The Night Guard set the arena ablaze and now has hostages in the Great—" Coal cuts off as he marks both River's unconscious body and my glowing hand hovering by his shoulder. His voice drops to calm, low command. "Hold your magic, mortal. Tell me what happened."

"He's right, Lilac Girl," Tye says, coming up behind Coal, his green eyes gentle. "You can kill him with that magic as swiftly as help."

"River is doing a damn good job of dying all on his own." Shoving myself away from River, I yield my place to Coal, who rushes in to examine the damage with a warrior's skilled eye. My mouth is dry, my hand tangling in Shade's fur for comfort. My breaths come in shuddering waves. "Shade won't shift to help, and I don't know why. Though the way the day is going, it's probably my fault."

Coal slides his palm along River's chest. "His lung's collapsed. Either air or blood are trapped in there, pressing on it like a sponge."

My throat tightens. I might have done that too, thinking I stopped the bleeding when I just redirected it. Caused more harm than good.

"Nothing about the day is your fault, Lilac Girl," Tye says softly, his voice at odds with the growing pitch of my thought. Tye's once-pristine uniform is covered with rips and soot, a patch of his sleeve ripped open to show blistered, angry flesh. Unlike me, he must have stayed at the arena to help the humans escape the flames—and the haunted sheen to his eyes says not everyone made it out. "But when I find the Night Guard bastard reckless enough to have set flame to a stadium full of innocent athletes and families, I will peel his flesh off in strips."

My heart jolts, the truth skittering away from my tongue. "It may have been an accident." I clear my throat. "I mean, their plan was to attack during closing ceremonies. Why change it?"

"Likely because they learned Zake was captured and babbling," says Coal.

Tye winces as he moves his arm. "I little care why they did it, only that they pay." The male's face softens as he takes in mine. Stepping toward me, the male holds out his palm. "Come here, lass. We—"

GRRRRRRROWW!

Shade, who was pressed against my leg a moment ago, leaps to put himself between Tye and me. The wolf's hackles rise, standing on end like porcupine needles. Pulling back his lips, he reveals a set of salivating canines, the low growl rumbling through his chest carrying promise of a battle to the death.

Tye stops.

Coal scrambles to a crouch, his hands at the ready as he spins toward the sound and puts himself between River and the threat. Shade's muscles tense, his front legs bending slightly in preparation to leap. His gaze fixes on Coal's jugular.

Face lethally calm, Coal flicks his wrist, sliding a knife into his palm. "Get behind me, mortal," he orders with that eerie quiet that sends shards of ice through my blood. "Slowly."

"No." I swallow, my hands coming palms up in an attempt to halt the madness. And it *is* madness. River unconscious. Shade and Coal readying to assault each other. My quint ripping itself to shards when it should be coming together. "Shade isn't doing anything to hurt me, Coal. He isn't going to hurt anyone."

"We agree there," says Coal, moving slowly around the wolf. "Because I am going to hog-tie the fleabag before he gets a chance. And keep him there until the damn bastard shifts." His piercing blue glower turns to Shade. "Forgot what losing a quint mate feels like?" Coals snarls at the wolf, both males' canines reflecting the sunlight. "A few more minutes and you're going to get the reminder of a lifetime."

Behind the squared-off males, River looks far too still and gray, his chest shuddering irregularly as he tries to take in rasping breaths. Panic flutters in my pulse, making my hands shake. *Not like this.* This is not how it's going to end.

"Enough," I yell. I'm as surprised as the males when the room quiets immediately, my pounding heart seeming to echo off the walls.

Without giving myself a chance to reconsider, I extend my hand directly into Shade's salivating maw, his sharp teeth now resting against my delicate wrist. "No one is biting or muzzling anybody," I say, begging the stars that I'm right.

The wolf and Coal growl in twin disapprovals.

Sliding my hand back just enough to curl my finger around Shade's sharp, sharp teeth, I extend my other hand toward Tye, who hesitates only a moment before gripping it and extending his own to Coal.

"We can't connect with a wolf," Coal says.

"We don't have a choice," I answer. "Please, Coal."

The blond warrior's jaw clenches once, his eyes never leaving Shade's as he clasps forearms with both Tye and River. The latter's arm hangs slack in his grip.

14

Lera

*A*fter months apart, the first shock of the quint bond descends on me like a lightning strike, the magic shooting through every nerve and fiber of my being. Burning. Waking. Making each of my senses soar so high that I feel the drop of moisture on the wolf's salivating fangs, smell the leather bindings on each volume of Gavriel's massive library. And the magic itself, the bundle of corded power that coils inside my core, it roars as it leaps toward its mates.

The strands of magic from all five of us crash into each other like lovers intent on coupling with bedroom-wrecking force. Magic thrusting into magic, over and over and over.

Colliding together, but not connecting. Not twining together like they should.

Something is wrong. Something is very wrong.

I can feel the horrid realization pulsing inside the bond, not knowing whether it comes from me or one of the others. I can't speak. Can't move as the cords of our magic tangle and battle, the quint bond that usually syncs our five hearts to beat as one now attacking itself. Threatening to tear my core into bloody bits.

The gentle prickle of Shade's teeth brings back Coal's warning.

The quint connection can't work without Shade's fae form, and he isn't here. Isn't coming.

Now that I know what to look for, I see Shade's silver magic—usually eager to herd all the cords together into a pack—snarling at River's fading power instead. Tye's hand trembles in my grip, his and Coal's faces strained so tightly that veins stand out along their necks as they fight to keep the disjointed magic at bay lest it explode with enough force to destroy the Academy itself. As for River… The quint commander who usually directs the connection with a master's ease is coiling in on himself instead, protecting his wounds instead of inviting the quint's magic to ease them.

Panic floods me, my heart racing as if I were in the midst of combat. With Shade attacking River, and Coal and Tye doing all they can to keep an explosion at bay, I'm the only one left. A weaver who is supposed to be able to tie the cords of magic into knots of great power —and I can't even untangle the strands. *We need to separate,* my soul yells into the bond. *This isn't working. We need to separate.*

Fix it, comes the wordless answer, carried in Coal's strained purple magic. *Fix it. You fix it.*

I can't fix it! And I'm too terrified to try. I'm paralyzed by what could happen if I do. My attempts to fix things today have only had potentially world- and quint-ending consequences. I try to draw a shaking breath but can't make my body move. Just as I can't force the magic to obey my will. Can't reason with Shade's lupine instinct. What does that leave me?

The only thing left to try dawns on me with slow, gut-churning dread. Because the only thing left for me to do is to…stop. Stop coercing. Stop pretending. Stop shielding my failures and accept whatever judgment the males will make. Veils and the lies that followed tore our quint apart—perhaps trust and truth, no matter how bleak, can call Shade back. Except that it's an all-or-nothing game now, with anything I say reaching all the males at once.

This was all my fault, my soul whispers, the tang of my fear and loneliness seeping into the bond between us. *I lost control of my horse and broke the rune tablet that tore us apart. And then I lost control of my magic and set the arena on fire. It was me, not the Night Guard, who got so many people hurt. I hurt River too. I was trying to fix him, and didn't know I was doing more harm than good. I was the weak link all along. Me. And I understand if you don't want to entrust me with so much as a boiling kettle from now on.*

For a moment, I feel silence. Surprise, as Tye and Coal process what I've revealed. Then tightness. Confusion.

Tye's orange magic reaches an inquiring paw towards me.

The wolf's magic snarls, lashing out at the extended cord so violently that Tye and Coal grunt with the effort of keeping the clash contained.

Tye's pulls back before I can tell whether it's understanding or disappointment that wraps his thoughts. Whether I'm digging a deeper hole for myself with every breath.

But even if I am, I have to keep going, have to open the next trapdoor in my soul. *I hurt,* I tell the bond, making myself relive stab after stab of pain that came each time the males gazed at me without recognition these past months. *I tried to seem strong, but it was a bluff.* A drop of wetness I can't control snakes down my cheek. *And I'm afraid,* I add, staring at River's chest, no longer fooling myself into certainty that it will somehow heal. *I'm so afraid that he is going to die because of me.*

I stop, my breathing ragged, my soul's truth bare to judgment. Somewhere in the courtyard, one of the fae is issuing demands, wind magic amplifying his voice to be heard through the Academy grounds. He wants the kings not yet inside the Great Hall to make themselves known. For clerks to fetch parchment and ink for writing. In the backdrop of the demand, the bell tower tolls the time. And in the library, all is silent.

Swallowing, I fill the bond with the one truth I've left. *I love you,* I tell the bond, flooding it with every bit of unfiltered emotion. *I love you, River and Coal, Tye and Shade. And I need you. I need the fae male—not just the wolf. I need the connection that is us.*

The sudden flash of blinding light would have made me shut my eyes if I could blink. But I can't.

With Shade now holding my hand, tall and golden-skinned, black hair loose over broad bare shoulders, his yellow eyes trained fiercely and protectively on mine, a new wave of power washes through the bond at once. Shade is so alive, so longed-for, that the whole room seems to glow with his presence. The magics align in a familiar, perfect harmony that makes us a quint. With the next breath, we share every sensation. Every smell. Every blaze of love flowing through our blood.

It's instinct, not thought, that makes me reach toward the strands, weaving the cords tenderly around one another into a tight, tight braid that shimmers with orange impertinence and earthy power, with strange purple strength and silver healing. I feel River's magic grow in strength as I pull it tighter into the weave, feel his very body start slowly to knit itself closed. A pull of my will, and the cords tighten as one, the greatest tsunami of magic yet shooting along our bond.

The amulet around my neck cracks in two, clattering across the floor.

With the next breath, the veil's snowflake-shaped marking on Shade's chest dissolves like frost from heated glass—and I have a feeling it's not the only one. Tears sting my eyes. No more veils, no more stories, no more lies. The males in my quint stand as the immortal fae they are, the aura of power around them matching their ethereal forms.

The newly made weave connecting our quint collects itself, the tension in it growing and growing until the final wave of power explodes within us, scattering away all thoughts. Suddenly, there is no longer a me. No longer a them. There is only *us*, our hearts beating as a single great force.

All *seven* of us.

My eyes widen as I realize what Shade's wolf has smelled, what—who—he's been defending. The thought sends such a shock through me that I don't realize the quint has separated until I see Coal staring at my belly.

And then he faints.

PART III: THE LAST BELL

1

Lera

Seven.

The library spins around me, books and faces streaking by in confused flashes, and I stumble from the quint to lean my hip against one of Gavriel's sturdy wooden tables. The table's hard edge digs into my backside, giving me something small and concrete to focus on. Which is a good thing. Because if I wasn't paying attention to the table edge, I'd have to think about the seven heartbeats I felt echoing through the quint bond.

Coal's. Tye's. Shade's. River's. Mine. And that of the two tiny hearts beating so very quickly inside my womb.

Around me, the world crawls along in slow motion. Gavriel has his hand to his mouth as he stares at the now-unveiled males. A few paces away, Coal stirs from where he fainted upon realizing the truth and now rises as far as his knees before sinking back down to the floor. His normally tan skin is disturbingly blanched, his blond hair in disarray. Tye stands frozen, his emerald eyes sparkling with a mix of joy and apprehension and too many other emotions to read.

Yet it is Shade and River who capture my attention.

Crouching beside the still-unconscious River, Shade stares at me even as his silver magic flows over River's wound. Golden eyes meet mine with an almost physical intensity.

Wide. Bewildered. Possessive… And filled with the soul-piercing recognition I've missed so desperately over the past months. *Yes,* the magic inside me whispers, tickling my skin from the inside. *Yes. Him. Mate.*

I lick my dry lips. Shade's long black hair hangs around his face, framing high cheekbones, a sharp jaw, and full lips begging to be kissed. With the late-afternoon sun streaming through the window and shaping the muscles of his bare upper body to perfection, the male is as beautiful as he is predatory. And once more mine.

"Shade?" I whisper.

"Cub." The male stretches a shaking hand out toward me. "I'm— the fae I saw in the woods, some part of me knew it was you."

"Your wolf always knew."

Shade rises to one knee, his nostrils flared, seeming for all the world like he's about to carry me off to that stream bank for round two, though there is something haunted in his gaze as well. "Yes. He did. We needed to be with you with every fiber of our being, but only the wolf could make it happen." His jaw tightens. "I—"

River gives a pained groan from the floor, making Shade flinch. With a curse, he leans over his patient again, his magic and focus now fully on his work.

Right. I swallow. I've waited months to feel Shade's arms around me, so I can wait a bit more—especially when River's survival hangs in the balance.

Tye clears his throat. "Well, it does appear we now know why Shade's wolf was more annoying than usual. The wee fleabag must have smelled the pups and decided to take guarding Lera into his own paws." Crossing the room toward me, Tye grips my hips and lifts me easily to sit on a tall writing table. The new setup doesn't quite put our eyes level, but it comes close, the male's pine-and-citrus scent caressing me gently. His sharp, beautiful face is tantalizingly close. In spite of his casual ease, his silver earring glinting jauntily in the sunlight, I can see his freckles in higher relief. The pulse pounding in his throat. "I think this is the Star's greatest gift, Lilac Girl. Or their grandest jest. Probably both—but I'm happy with either."

His words reach me through a fog. Pups. Heartbeats. Inside me.

Panic finally rises up my throat, spurring my breath. I'm pregnant. *Stars.* I'm pregnant and River is unconscious, and the Night Guard hold the mortal world's kings hostage. Magic is loose in the human realm.

"You said it was impossible, Shade," Coal's voice is as full of panic as my own thoughts, the words growing louder with each syllable. Now on his feet, the black-clad warrior has a knife in his hand, his breaths coming faster than I've seen even in battle. Blue eyes blazing, he squares off toward the healer. "That her body wasn't ready. You *said—*"

"Apparently I was wrong," Shade snaps. His golden eyes flash at Coal for a moment before returning to River, a complex weave of silver healing magic now spidering over the commander's skin.

"Who's the pups fa—" Coal starts to ask.

"There isn't a way to know." Shade growls softly. "This would be a good time to revert to your signature silence, Coal."

As he spins away from Shade with a disgusted snort, Coal's hard gaze darts around the library before coming to rest on me—on my stomach. He sheathes his blade and nudges Tye aside to stand between my legs, running his hands over my shoulders, my rib cage, my perfectly flat belly, as if he could feel something in there already. I watch him, his sculpted face narrowed in concentration, his broad shoulders tightened with anxiety. Warmth trails in his touch's wake, his heavily callused palms strangely soothing—though the frantic cast to his sky-blue eyes is anything but. "We need a midwife."

"I'm fairly certain pregnancy doesn't work the way you think it does, Coal," Tye drawls from the chair he's plopped into. "That part doesn't usually come for a wee while. And when it does, well, in my experience, midwives are not the kind of creatures one captures in the shadows at knifepoint."

I'm shocked to feel a laugh bubbling up in my throat and pull Coal's tense mouth down toward mine to squelch it—

"Ahem…" Gavriel's quiet cough is my first reminder that we aren't alone—though how I managed to overlook the librarian's bright red face, I can't begin to imagine. "Allow me to express my congratulations," he says, stuttering through the words. "And oh, do be careful. Things like that can make you lose your wits completely."

It takes me a moment to realize that Gavriel is speaking not about my pregnancy but the broken amulet I don't remember having picked up. Dangling from a leather cord, the two pieces of rune-inscribed stone look dull and harmless, but I can feel confused magic rippling inside.

"Maybe… I'll get Arisha." Without waiting for a response, Gavriel flees his own library, moving more quickly than I'd have thought a limping man could. My mouth is still half-open to call to him—not that I'd know what to say—when the door shuts, the merry bells jingling.

Right. I tuck the broken necklace into my pocket lest one of the humans picks it up.

Pulling away from me with an impatient growl, Coal stalks over to Shade and grabs his shoulder. "She… I mean them… They… Stars take you, *do something*."

"Enough!" With a roar of command, Shade uncoils from his patient, twists and clamps his hand to the front of Coal's neck. The two males lock gazes, Shade's tan skin covered with a thin sheen of sweat, Coal's pale face darkening with fury. With his hand still on Coal's neck, Shade shoves the other warrior against the library wall with enough force to send the nearby books cascading to the floor in a *thump-clatter-thump* cascade that would have Gavriel whimpering if he were here.

"I don't have time to deal with your meltdown, Coal." Shade leans in close enough to Coal's face that there is barely an inch of space between them. Shade is the second-in-command of the quint, but he pulls his authority out so rarely that even Coal flinches from the shifter's low, powerful voice. "Not now, not for a damn good while. So shut up. Go kill something. I don't care what you do, so long as you are not doing it here. Understood?"

The entire library seems to hold its breath as Coal pulls back his lips to flash his canines before looking away. When Coal brushes away Shade's hold, the healer's eyes flash one last time before he lets go.

"I'll go check the area." Coal says, heading toward the library's back entrance as my own mind finally snaps back to function.

Yes, I'm pregnant—but so early in the process that only Shade's wolf could sense the growing lives. The cubs are safe inside me for now, and before I drown in the shock of what this all means for the future, I have the present to deal with. A quint mate to help and a realm to liberate. I have things to do to ensure the pups enter the kind of world I want them to live in.

Seeming to have read the swirling thoughts on my face, Tye has returned to my side now, smoothing my hair back from my temples. Reaching up, I squeeze his shoulder and nod toward Coal's retreating back. "I think he needs company more than I do just now. Or at least a minder."

"Hmmm…" Tye rests his cheek on the top of my head, his breath tickling my hair. "Perhaps I could go after the wee kitten. But only if you give me something first."

"Give?" I turn in Tye's arms to find a breathtaking smile growing over his face. Before I can say another word, he leans down to cover my mouth with his own, the slow leisurely kiss turning my bones to molten lead. When he scrapes his teeth on my bottom lip before pulling out, the tiny sting shoots straight to my sex, making my thighs clench together.

With a grin that says he knows exactly the kind of effect he just had on me, Tye saunters after Coal, his shoulders shaking when I mutter, "Bastard" under my breath.

With Coal and Tye gone, I turn back to Shade, who's still fully occupied with River. While he's still unconscious, the warrior's color is returning, his powerful chest expanding with greater ease. My heart pinches painfully at seeing my beautiful, powerful male so still. I need him to wake up so badly it aches under my skin.

But what if he still doesn't remember you? The tiny voice whispering in the back of my mind is like a shard of ice. We still don't have any proof that what happened to Shade when we joined also happened to River. And I can't imagine how we'll defeat Owalin if it didn't.

"How is he?" I ask Shade through a tight throat.

"He'll be fine once—" Shade cuts off as the silver weave of magic slips along River's skin, muttering curses about working without his instruments.

"I'll fetch them from the infirmary," I say, the ability to contribute something—no matter how small—a comfort in itself.

"No." Shade's attention stays on River.

I frown midway through straightening my dress—for all the good it does to improve the tattered red silk. "I know where they are."

"You aren't going anywhere by yourself, Leralynn." Looking up from River's body, Shade jerks his chin at my midsection. "Not while you are with pups."

"That's ridic—"

"This isn't up for debate."

I stare at him, my pulse beginning to speed. "I was stating a fact, not asking permission," I say with more control than I expected as I start toward the exit.

Pushing away from River, Shade interposes himself between me and the door, his broad, chiseled chest rising before me. He uses every inch of his towering height to his advantage, his fresh earthy scent tinged with anger, his legs tense like a wolf standing his ground.

Beyond the door, raised voices in the courtyard prove that the crisis unfurling there is alive and well. Children cry over missing parents, families and mates calling on their kings, and guards, and stars for help.

I gaze up at Shade, my chest aching. This isn't how the return of our quint was supposed to go. This isn't the way Shade—always the one I could turn to for gentle, steady support—should have returned.

I shake my head, my gaze falling on the book Gavriel was reading before he left to find Arisha. The old pages lie open to a too-familiar drawing of a young fae holding up a sword. Gavriel's prophetic protection. I may not be that, but I am a warrior, for better or worse. And I will fight while I can for the future I want.

"Shade." I put a soft hand on his ridged stomach, the first time I've touched his male form in months—but my voice is anything but gentle. "I've been on my own from the moment we arrived here, surviving— no, more than surviving, protecting your bloody hides. I deserve more respect than this."

Shade's eyes flicker for a moment, but then he pulls away from my touch, steel in his gaze. "You're not on your own now." The hardness of his words matches his eyes. "You deserve protection. You and the pups both."

The *tap tap tap* of my pulse spreads indignation through my body until I can barely think over the roaring in my ears. My jaw tightens, the proverbial line in the sand suddenly forming before my feet. "I'm not a relic or prize broodmare to be protected, Shade. With pups or not, I think and act and make decisions for myself. So stop impersonating a doorjamb and step aside."

Shade's yellow eyes flash. "Try to get past me, and I'll truss you up like a calf."

My hand curls into a fist, my lips pulling back in a snarl. "Magic is loose in the mortal world. The Night Guard are holding hostages in the Great Hall. River is wounded. And you want to argue with me over—"

"I don't want to argue with you about anything!" Shade's nostrils flare as he steps toward me. "And I don't give a bloody damn about what's loose in the mortal world or who is holding who at sword point. And you shouldn't either. Your sole concern now should be—"

I'm as surprised as Shade when I bury my knuckles in his jaw and stalk out of the library into the cool chaos beyond.

2

Lera

It *is* chaos.

Under a sky quickly filling with thick, angry clouds, the smoke still rising from the ruined stadium takes on a queer orange-gray cast. The vast cobblestone yard is covered in white ash and black soot, its hundreds of occupants faring no better—the colorful ceremonial fashions from every corner of the continent have been rendered nearly indistinguishable. The late-afternoon sun has just passed below the rim of stone buildings, deepening the sense of foreboding.

For all that happened in the library since I dragged River there, this milling, frantic mass is a harsh reminder that only moments have passed since Owalin took the Great Hall hostage. A quarter hour at most.

As I skirt the courtyard toward the infirmary, I see that, save for the orders River issued—which account for the well-placed perimeter of guards keeping a large semicircle of clear space in front of the Great Hall entrance—the rest of the courtyard swarms with cadets, competitors, and guests. Family members with loved ones trapped inside shout over each other with demands, sobs, and recommendations of how the situation should be handled.

Standing in the middle of the open semicircle, Headmaster Sage holds a speaking trumpet, sweat running down his pale bald head despite the cool air. If River's presence, even while he's injured, instilled a sense of calm and hope, Sage's has the opposite effect on the crowd, his wheedling, fear-tinged tones only seeming to fuel people's desperation.

Suddenly, a low chuckle booms over the courtyard, seemingly from the roiling gray clouds themselves. It takes me only a moment to spot the tall figure standing on the edge of the mezzanine balcony, looking down upon the mass of people before him as if surveying an unruly garden in need of weeding. His bloodred cloak whips in the growing wind, the raised hood keeping his face in deep shadow.

The entire courtyard falls silent at once, gasps and screams dying into soft weeping and moans of fear. Right near me, a young blond boy with deep tear tracks running down his soot-blackened face watches Owalin with numb terror, neck craned back on his shoulders.

"I have yet to see any clerks with parchment or remaining mortal kings join me in the Great Hall." Owalin's relaxed words echo from the balcony, strands of wind magic magnifying them over the courtyard. "Though I am a generous and fair-minded male, you will discover that I am not one to enjoy repeating myself."

"We are still looking for everyone, sir." Sage holds a speaking trumpet to his lips, coughing wetly before continuing. "But I am Sage, the headmaster of Great Falls Academy. Perhaps you and I can come to an understanding."

"You are useless." Owalin replies. "But that is all right. I believe that with the right motivation, hamsters *can* be taught obedience." He turns toward the enclosed mezzanine behind him. "Get the first one."

Despite the threat, nothing happens for the next several moments, and I continue quickly toward the infirmary, keeping my head down. The Academy—the entire mortal world—needs River to get through this as much as my quint needs him. One look at Sage's sad attempt at leadership makes the truth plain enough. My heart pounds a quick but steady beat as I reach the edge of the courtyard—just in time to hear a terrified wail of pain sound from the Great Hall.

Twisting around, I mark the open shutters on the mezzanine just in time to watch in terror as a uniformed Prowess athlete is shoved headfirst through the window. The young man flies through the air with a scream, his limbs twisting and scrambling for some purchase. The crack of his neck as he lands is as deafening to my immortal ears.

As is the keening howl of a tall, thin man with a crown on his head, trying to get through the guards holding him back.

Stars. A son. That young man was someone's son. My throat tightens.

A tall woman, elegant even in her soot-stained blue gown, screams with grief, bending over the boy's broken body.

The young boy to my left is sobbing now, his mother burying his face in her dress.

Owalin stands calmly through it all, watching with a perverted interest—as if the grieving mother and dead son were a pair of rats caught in a trap. "I have three more children from the royal family of Fothom." Owalin's voice fills the courtyard once more. "Until his majesty of Fothom—who I see flopping like a fish there—joins me, I will be tossing the darlings out at one-hour intervals. We are having a conference of monarchs here, you see, and it's very difficult to do so with half our cadre missing."

He turns to go as the Fothom king fights the guards to get to the Great Hall.

"Wait," Sage shouts into the speaking trumpet. "How do we know you won't kill the kings the way you killed the Fothom king's son?"

"Oh for stars' sake." Owalin sounds exasperated as he turns back. "I am not here to murder kings, but to *work with* them. If I wanted the kings dead, I'd simply have killed them all by now. To demonstrate—"

A flash of sunlight reflecting off an arrowhead in the same mezzanine window makes my heart jump. "Down!" I holler with all my strength just as the bowman looses his arrow.

Sage—not one to be told twice when to hide—throws himself on the ground a moment before the projectile slices the air above his head and lodges itself in a bystander's calf instead.

Owalin chuckles over the screams. "One hour," he calls over tolling bells, now marking the time as five o'clock.

One hour. One hour to heal River. One hour to save another innocent life. Without another breath, I turn to sprint toward the infirmary once more.

"You!" The shove from my left comes with unexpected force before I can take my second step. I stumble from the hatred saturating the word as much as from the power of the shove.

Recovering my footing, I twist around to see a large bald man I vaguely recognize as one of the Academy blacksmiths, Thad. In the remaining silence of the courtyard following Owalin's departure, Thad's shout had echoed loudly, drawing the immediate attention of those nearby.

"What's going on?" I demand.

The man's beefy hand tightens around a mallet in his wide leather tool belt, the heavy metal hammer whispering from its sheath with deadly malice. "You're one of them." He spits a glob onto the ashy cobblestones, his brown eyes hard. "Those fae murderers."

Behind him, more and more people flock toward us, the fear and rancor in their scent shoving itself into my lungs. Many of the foreign royals merely look confused, but the cadets who know me are turning quickly from shell-shocked into furious. I see Rik and Puckler, mouths twisted with fury—and grim satisfaction.

My muscles tighten, my vision narrowing on the crowd, my fae ears picking up their spreading murmurs.

"…evil…disguised as a cadet…"

"…fae filth!"

"I knew there was something off about her…"

It clicks with a sudden, painful jolt, blood draining from my face as I jerk up a hand to trace my pointed ear. The amulet was destroyed—and with it, all the spun illusions the magic created. In the heat of the moment with Shade, storming out from the library into the unfolding disaster, I forgot that the amulet I've grown used to wearing was no longer there—and didn't so much as cover my pointed ears.

Thad takes a step forward, menace riding in his wake.

I tense, feeling magic begin to fill my core. If I thought the full force of my power difficult to control before, it is doubly so now, with my instincts protecting not my life alone. "Easy, Thad," I say, putting up my palms. "Let me explain. Please. There is enough violence without us adding more."

"Kill her!" The woman I saw bent over the fallen athlete's body glares at me now with pulsing hatred, her crown of rich red braids coming undone around her mottled face. "No, cut off her ears first and send them to her friends in the Great Hall. Let them know that what they do to ours, we'll do to theirs."

Voices rise in agreement, Thad hefting the mallet in his hand.

"Friends in the Great Hall? No." I raise my voice, struggling to be heard over the rising chaos. Blood races through my veins, the ground trembling beneath me with a fine warning tremor that has as many people rushing away from me as reaching for their weapons. I swallow. "I'm not with Owalin. I came to protect you, not harm you. I'm on your side."

"She lies!" An older woman who seems to be wearing a live green snake instead of a scarf strides out in front of the crowd and points a long finger at me. "I saw her set fire to the arena, helping Owalin take the hall!"

My stomach drops, all hope that I'll escape this unscathed sinking away with it. Shade was right. I was so stupid—so incredibly stupid to come out here.

"I saw it too! She unleashed a firestorm atop us all. Women. Children. Everyone!" a man shouts from deeper in the crowd, and other voices join his. "My wife is on her deathbed because of this…this creature! I demand justice."

The crowd shifts, the snake and her equally venomous owner both hissing as the calls of "Liar! Liar! Take her!" race across the courtyard. "Justice now! Don't let that *thing* escape!"

A wave of fear rushes through me. I open my mouth to shout that it was an accident, but even I know that nothing of the sort would help.

The crowd advances on me, Thad, the snake lady, and the Fothom queen leading the pack.

I step back to give myself space. Breathing room to think.

It's a mistake. Like the scent of wounded prey in a predator's nose, my retreat sends a renewed energy through the pulsing mob. With each new heartbeat, more people reach down to grab stones, pull daggers, wrap belts around their knuckles.

The air around me tightens.

"Get back. Now." A cold voice that's plainly used to bellowing commands over battlefields blankets the waiting crowd. Men and women part on instinct before Coal, whose rigid muscles and blazing blue eyes leave no room for argument.

The wave of relief is so strong, it nearly makes me dizzy. Tye stalks beside the warrior, stone-cold murder flashing in every sleek angle of his face, his hair nearly bloodred under the growing thunderclouds. Pushing in front of me, he raises his hands in the air and the Academy flag flapping on the top keep bursts into orange flame that sends a rush of sudden silence through the yard.

"Are you all right, mortal?" Coal murmurs, fear flashing in his eyes as he hands me one of the two swords on his back. The feel of solid steel in my hand is as comforting as the male's fierce, metallic-scented presence. And as problematic. What good are we at protecting the mortal world from stray magic and rogue fae if we kill the lot of them in the process?

Coal and Tye's approach has created a wide space between us and the humans, like two sides meeting on a battlefield.

I shift my weight in the shuffling, scraping silence, noting a flash of red up in a mezzanine window. Owalin watching us—watching and probably laughing as the humans waste precious minutes facing off against the wrong enemy. Three ravens circle high overhead, wheeling in the coming storm.

"Now what?" Tye asks us under his breath.

Before Coal or I can respond, a new cry rises amid the human crowd. "Kill them! Kill them all!"

3

Lera

"Halt!" River's commanding voice shackles the entire courtyard in place. "Take a knee. Every damn one of you."

Heart slamming against my ribs, I spin to see the male himself striding from the library's entrance into the courtyard, power trailing around him in a cape of sunlight. River, alive. Walking. As if the past few hours never happened. His sure steps toward the center of the courtyard betray nothing of his brush with death—though it is written all too clearly in Shade's face. The healer walks a few steps behind, making no effort to conceal the predatory fury roaring in his yellow eyes.

Fury that's directed as much at the gathering mob as at me. A trickle of blood snakes from the corner of Shade's mouth where my fist had landed. The male wipes it with the back of his hand.

My chest clenches.

With his short dark hair brushed back, River's pointed ears are exposed in all their immortal glory. If I ran outside without a single thought as to what my appearance would evoke in the Academy, River made his choice deliberately. I almost let out a sob of relief when I see them—proof that this is the real River, *my* River, which means he must have gotten his memories back when the quint joined. I wait for him to look at me, for some sign of love or recognition or union—any of the things I've longed for with my whole being for too many months.

But he keeps his eyes on the mob, no sign of his thoughts visible. Given how sharply the very air in the courtyard is vibrating with tension, holding his entire focus on the humans is probably a good thing—no matter how much I wish River to be holding me instead.

Still bare to the waist, with streaks of dried blood clinging to the taut skin of his ribs and muscled abdomen, he holds himself as if making entrance into a ballroom—the effect of which is lost on no one, least of all the royal families gathered outside. Yes, they see he is fae, but they feel the power of his throne as well—we all do—whether they know it or not.

"*You?*" Wheeling toward River, Thad raises the mallet in his hand. The blacksmith's face is equal parts murderous and terrified, the thin light leaking through the clouds reflecting off his bald head in silver spots. "I knew you were—"

"In charge?" River asks coolly. "Yes. That I am."

"Then I demand justice!" The Fothom queen's keening voice rises to the sky, her finger pointing at me. "Set her aflame as she did us."

"Burn her!" Thad shouts, picking up the idea. "Burn that—"

Thad's words falter, and he grabs his own throat, falling to his knees as a band of Shade's silver magic tightens around his neck. I've never seen Shade use his healing to hurt before, and the terror of it rushes through me just as it ripples through the crowd.

"Shade—"

The male's furious gaze cuts to me, raking my soul with comprehension. He hates it. Hates cutting off a man's air instead of helping him breathe—but he's doing it anyway. Using viciousness to draw the mobs' ire from me to himself. To dilute their calls to drag me to the gallows of justice.

River raises his hand, and the silver band disappears immediately, Shade's obedience to his commander's orders as powerful as the choke hold had been. "Does anyone else need assistance doing as I ask?" River demands.

As if in agreement, thunder suddenly claps overhead, eliciting muffled shrieks from some of the children in the courtyard.

The crowd lowers to their knees. Guards and servants first, then students. Then the royals themselves. I can see the many thoughts crossing their faces, especially those of Academy students and staff—processing that the deputy headmaster, who's kept such a firm, orderly grip on the Academy all this time, is fae. From disbelief to betrayed anger to fear…to rare and slow flickers of comprehension.

River stands still, letting the humans work through their turmoil. To remember that he'd kept them safe for all these months. That he was hard but fair. Trustworthy.

Turning slowly, River squares off against where Coal, Tye, and I stand together, our weapons and magic at the ready.

"Are the three of you hard of hearing or slow of mind?" River asks.

Seriously? My brows rise.

"Looks like River found not only a way back to consciousness, but also a new stick to shove up his ass," Tye mutters, lowering himself to one knee as instructed. A moment later, Coal does the same, squeezing my arm to urge my obedience.

My jaw tenses. With the amulet veil gone and memories returned, I've no intention of cowering before my mate as I did when I feigned being a student. I can't. Lifting my chin, I meet River's hard gray gaze. The wind has picked up, blowing ash into my eyes and whipping my hair across my face, but I don't move to stop it. There's a breathless tension in the courtyard as the kneeling humans watch our silent standoff.

Strong eyes meeting mine, River's shoulders spread with the powerful majesty of an immortal king. His beautiful face, heartbreakingly gray and still only moments ago, yields nothing. He isn't asking for obedience. He is expecting it.

A soft growl tingles the air, and it takes a moment for me to realize the warning tone isn't coming from River but from Shade, kneeling beside the commander. The shifter's nostrils flare in mirror of my own, the bruise I left on his jaw blossoming into a deep red-purple.

Quieting Shade with a glance, River walks toward me until he stands less than a pace away, the entire courtyard silent as the male's hard gray gaze grips my own. His fresh woodsy scent washes over me, nearly making me dizzy, but I refuse to yield. Not now. Not after all these months.

"Leralynn." River's voice softens as he says my name. "Take a knee."

I lift my chin, the breeze catching my hair. "I won't kneel before my mate."

Like a sparked brush fire, my words send a rush of whispers scurrying through the crowd, repeating and morphing as they jump between hundreds of roused humans.

"She called him mate. The arena murderer is his mate."

"…never get justice…"

"…what did you expect of them?"

The wind prickles my skin, turning droplets of rain into shards.

River's face hardens more and more with each whispered denouncement, the mix of regret and resolve in his stormy eyes coalescing into a grand wall. When he speaks again, there is no more softness in his voice.

"I'm not asking as your mate," River says coolly, his voice loud enough to be heard across the Academy. "I'm ordering as your commander. Obey, or find yourself and your righteous indignation keeping each other company in a dungeon cell."

Despite already starting to kneel, I snap back upright at that turn of phrase. Not just a command, but a bloody threat. The sudden rush of blood in my ears drowns out all thought. My lips pull away from my teeth, my canines flashing as another peal of thunder sounds overhead. Pounding against my ribs, my heart is so loud, I wonder how the whole courtyard doesn't feel its fury-filled rhythm. "You wouldn't."

River raises a brow. "Do you truly wish to discover the truth?" he asks steadily. Behind him, Shade shifts his legs, ready to rise and do River's bidding. *Wanting* to. Shade, who had the gall to forbid me to go outside as if I were a trained pet, who is now not altogether upset to watch me get my comeuppance.

My own males, my own mates, looking at me with full recognition —and no warmth, no kindness at all. Who want obedience more than they want me. Even with their memories gone, I never felt as far from them as I feel now.

My throat closes, and suddenly, it's a battle just to keep the stinging in my eyes from becoming a new spectacle for the courtyard. Averting my gaze, I lower myself to one knee beside the males, the slight tightening of River's jaw the only indication that he noticed the change.

Through the veil of stinging pain now gripping my soul, I watch River turn around to survey the kneeling—but now silent—courtyard. "You've no doubt marked by now that I—the man you believed to be the deputy headmaster of this Academy—am an immortal from Lunos, as are my four quint mates. My true name is River—"

"River, King of Slait." Owalin's voice sounds from the mezzanine balcony once again, followed by a slow, mocking clapping that's somehow amplified by the thunder instead of drowned out by it. His hood is thrown back now, and the effect is even more terrifying—silver-blond hair braided tight against his skull, his sharp, elegant face almost skeletal in the storm's strange, vivid light. Even from here, his pale blue eyes shine with satisfaction and curiosity. "Well played, Your Majesty. I'd have pushed the knife deeper if I'd known the details of your heritage."

River turns slowly to the balcony, locking his hands behind his back. Even shirtless and bloody, he makes just as formidable a figure. "Master Owalin. I realize you've control of the Great Hall just now. Is anyone inside injured? On your side or your captives. I'd like the wounded cared for, whoever they are."

"How kind," Owalin replies casually. "But these are my people now, and I will make decisions for their well-being." A smile flickers across his face, falling short of his eyes. "More accurately, I will let them make their own decisions. The fate of each kingdom is in their own royals' hands—follow my orders, and all shall be well. I encourage you to help them see reason quickly, River—in the next forty-seven minutes, preferably, lest I am forced to execute another one of my guests."

Before River can respond, Owalin disappears in a swirl of red.

Letting the pause rest just long enough for the humans to shift their attention from the keep back to where he stands, River nods to the crowd. "Owalin is correct in one aspect—I am the ruler of Slait, one of the three kingdoms in the immortal realm." His voice echoes over the cobblestones, the smoldering remains of the arena silhouetting his tall body. "I regret the necessity of the disguises that my quint and I wore until now, but our original mission was to ensure that your lives continue undisturbed by magical forces. Unfortunately, the Night Guard, who holds many of your loved ones captive now, had other plans."

River pauses, letting the words seep through the bewildered gazes now watching his every move. Letting this new reality slowly settle over them—as long as they believe what he's saying. Even as furious as I am at him, I almost feel a sense of relief, watching the powerful male do what he was supposed to do all those months ago—lead us.

The tension in the air is so fierce, I feel it pressing on my skin, the pressure growing with every passing heartbeat. As it climbs to what feels like a breaking point, River raises his voice again. "The Night Guard, and their leader Owalin, is an enemy of my kingdom, as he is an enemy of yours. I offer you an alliance. Together, we can stand against Owalin and the darkness he brings with him. The situation we face is difficult but not insurmountable, so long as we have a unified front. My quint and I will be in the library awaiting your decision."

Turning on his heel, River motions for the males to rise, but clamps a heavy hand on my shoulder when I start to do the same.

"One matter to attend to before we go," River says, his hard gray eyes gripping me as firmly as his damn hand. "Leralynn of Slait. You lost control of your magic today, an accident that destroyed a vital part of this Academy and endangered hundreds of mortal lives. Am I wrong?"

4

Lera

My stomach clenches, dropping as I realize the male is not letting this go.

"I asked you a question," River snaps, his voice cracking through the air with enough sting to make the watching humans flinch right alongside me.

Behind me, Coal, Shade, and Tye stand silent and motionless. The whole of the courtyard's attention tightens around me like a noose as I kneel before a man who is supposed to wrap me in his arms. I swallow —or try to, my mouth too dry for even such a small feat. As if in jest, the grass I kneel on is soaked with the water that was dragged over the courtyard to douse the flames. The earth's juices seep through the remains of my red dress to chill my knees.

Forcing my face up, I look back at River as if the male and I are having a chat over dinner. As if River has simply taken a jest too far. "If you get into the habit of asking questions to which you already know the answer, you'll find that conversations quickly grow dull."

A tiny chuckle brushes across the crowd, overshadowed by a far larger sense of morbid curiosity, hundreds of people leaning in just a bit closer.

River stares right back, jaw tight, the patches of dried blood on his thickly muscled torso giving him the grisly appearance of a warrior in battle. "Leralynn of Slait, I asked whether it was you who set fire to the arena. Make me repeat myself once more, and I will do so with a lash."

My heart stops. So do all the murmurs and whispers racing through the watching courtyard, the tension in the air shifting to something new. A thick, self-righteous content. They still crave justice for the arena. Vengeance for their pain. They want me to suffer as they did.

And suddenly, I understand. If River doesn't deliver that justice before this temporary cease-fire expires, the mob will take it right back into their own hands.

River thinks he is protecting me. What he doesn't understand is that this, all this, is a thousand times worse for coming from him. I did set the arena aflame, and I'll take whatever punishment I'm due, but not from *him*. Not from my mate, who's just regained his memories, who is supposed to hold me tight and let the stars be damned.

"Do it! Punish her!" someone shouts, the call dying quickly as the iron control River has of the courtyard somehow clamps down on the hundreds of watching humans.

River raises a brow at me, his message gut-clenchingly clear. *I don't want to take this further than I must. But I will. Make no mistake.*

Behind me, a growl that must be Coal's sounds for a moment before River's gaze silences the male with the same cutting efficiency with which he'd raked the courtyard. If Coal thinks the threat real, I'd be a fool to doubt it. My face heats, the humiliation rising inside me giving way to a fear that shakes my body.

"Yes," I say, hurrying to speak before River—whose mouth is already opening—utters another word. "I lost control of my magic. Is that what you want so desperately to hear me say?"

"I want the truth," says River.

"I lost my grip." Ripping my gaze from River's face, I survey the strained, silent faces, all watching and waiting. Giving me a chance to speak.

So I do. Ignoring River, I speak to the people who—unlike the male —have the right to demand an explanation. "As magic rushed into the mortal world, I saw Han readying to throw a knife into my mate's heart.

Into Tye's heart." A shudder runs through me at the memory. "In that moment, I thought about nothing but stopping him. I'd intended for the fire magic to strike Han alone, but the power got away from me."

My chest tightens as I take in the soot and burns marring so many people's skin, my voice wavering. When I speak again, my words are softer, though they still carry as they scrape at my soul. "That is an explanation, not an excuse. No matter the intention, my mistake hurt you—the very people I came here to protect. You are owed more than an apology, but you have it anyway." I swallow, my pounding heart only now realizing how badly it aches to make amends. I brush my gaze over the crowd, not knowing what I'm seeking until I find it. Find the princess who'd once swallowed all her pride to kneel before me for the sake of her people.

Katita's usually perfect blonde hair is in disarray, her beautiful blue-green eyes bloodshot and shadowed despite all the strength she pours into holding herself upright.

"I'm sorry I endangered your people," I say to her alone, my skin so hot that the chill wind feels like shards of ice across my cheeks. "I submit to your judgment."

Katita's eyes widen slightly, surprise, intelligence, responsibility all flashing through her exhausted gaze. When she steps forward, her jaw is set so tightly that I can see the muscle tremble with the effort—but her voice is as regal and clear as ever.

"Leralynn of Slait, you started the arena fire," the princess says, and though she is looking at me, her words are plainly meant for the hundreds of people gathered in the courtyard. "But I see now that this is all you did. The attack on the Great Hall, the actions of the Night Guard who hold my father and sister hostage, they are not your doing. I accept your apology with no reservation."

For a moment, all I can do is stare at Katita, convinced I must have heard her wrong, that something degrading will surely follow—but it does not.

Standing a few paces away from the princess, River shifts his weight, his shoulders loosening the tiniest fraction—the equivalent of a sigh of relief for the male.

"Commander River." Katita lifts her face to look over my shoulder. "On behalf of my people, I consider the arena fire behind us. As for the current crisis—and the news of your origins—I ask that you do as you offered and grant us some space as we decide how best to proceed."

"Of course, Your Highness. We shall be in the library if you have need of us." Turning, River bows to Katita before extending his hand down to help me rise, the callused palm open.

I ignore it. Rising to my feet, I busy myself with dusting off my knees just to avoid having to look at the males.

As River starts leading the males and me back to the library, plainly expecting me to follow like a well-trained dog, it's all I can do to keep my stinging tears from spilling onto my cheeks. The small measure of borrowed dignity stretches hair thin as we pass by the shocked crowd to file into the library entrance, where the familiar bells greet our arrival —and finally snaps in half, along with the fragile hold I have on my feelings.

5

River

*R*iver swayed on his feet, setting his hand against the edge of a table to keep upright, barely registering the other males' retreat to a far corner of the library. The sheer terror ripping through him since the moment he marked the mob closing on Leralynn was only now beginning to recede, leaving him shaking. *Stars.* The trigger on the humans' violence had been featherlight—it was thanks to the stars' own grace that Leralynn walked out of there with nothing bleeding but her pride.

Even though she hated him now.

River swallowed as he watched the girl turn her back to him and stare out the window. What remained of her strapless red dress hugged her curves, the smears of dirt and blood saturating the silky cloth with the same stubborn, unyielding grit that always coursed inside Lera's veins. Her thick auburn hair hung loose past her shoulders, the thick braid she favored wearing on the left side somehow still intact and elegant.

River rubbed his chest. It still hurt to breathe, each inhalation sending a stab of pain through his ribs. Owalin's knife had cut deep— but the self-inflicted wound struck deeper still. The memories that had been flooding his blood ever since he opened his eyes to find Shade's yellow gaze and silver magic gripping him fiercely were enough to bring any male to his knees.

There was something else going on too. Shade had been beside himself when River had regained consciousness, the usually steadfast healer half-crazed at Leralynn's absence from the library. Whatever happened to put the male in that state while River was unconscious, it would need to be dealt with. But not now. Now, River had plenty on his mind just working through everything he remembered.

He had been riding with the others, Leralynn cantering ahead on her mare. And then, then there was a grand explosion in his mind, and he'd forgotten Lera altogether, his soul bottling up his mate's essence in the only way it could—an invented memory of a wife named Diana. Yes, River had tripped and lost himself—but his mate had picked up the quint's standard and carried them all forward, no matter what obstacles life and magic and River himself had set in her path.

Now, with the return of his memories—and the monumental understanding of what Leralynn had accomplished to keep the quint and the Academy safe while the males remained under the amulets' spell—River's first instinct had been to fall to his knees beside her. To tell the female who'd given up everything of herself to protect the quint just how much he valued what she'd done. How much he loved her.

He'd forced her to her knees instead.

Yes, he'd done it to protect her. To control the narrative and separate Lera's accidental fire from the Night Guard's deliberate assault. To keep the mortals from trying to take their hatred for Owalin out on River's mate. But he'd had to hurt her to do it, as he would have had to hurt any member of the quint. She'd set fire to an arena full of people—there wasn't exactly a way to gloss over that.

Yet as much as River's head knew all that, all his soul could see now was the single tear spilling onto Lera's cheek, though her whole body trembled with the effort to keep herself together. Feigning strength that had been exhausted long ago as she'd single-handedly held the quint together, staying the course of their mission when River himself did not.

Pushing away from the table with a soft groan, he stepped toward where Lera still stood by the window. Wrapping his arms around her, he pulled her soft body against his chest even as she struggled, her muscles tense with the anguish he'd inflicted. The girl's soft lilac scent mixed with the salty brush of tears and the light tang of wet earth that still clung to the hem of her dress.

"Let go of me," she snapped, pushing away with all the power in her small, tired body. "I hate you, River."

"I know you do." That made two of them. River held tighter, pressing Lera's face into the groove of his shoulder as he lowered himself into a chair. His healing wound twitched once as he lifted the struggling girl onto his lap, holding her tight. The other males were still hiding in some back aisle until whatever this was blew over—which River thought was a mite unwise, given how the tightening of Leralynn's muscles all but promised that he would need Shade's help again shortly.

As if hearing his thoughts, Leralynn drew her hand back and shoved him with all her might, her position on his lap draining the power—if not intent—from the blow. Well, he deserved that and more. He was well aware that there was no amount of comfort he could offer to undo the pain he'd caused, but he offered it anyway. Spreading one hand along Lera's ribs, he used the other to stroke her back and silky hair while the tears she'd held at bay finally spilled from her eyes, soaking his bare chest. A heartbeat later, sobs racked her small body— sobs she could no more control than she could have stanched the humiliation River inflicted in the courtyard.

"I had to make it real," he said quietly as her breaths finally slowed to strangled hiccups. "People got hurt in that arena. I would have killed them all before letting them lay a finger on you, but short of that, the error had to be acknowledged and paid for. Both to prove that, unlike the Night Guard, we hold ourselves to account—and for the sake of healing everyone's soul. Yours too."

"And you thought you were the right person to dole out punishment?" She turned her face up to him, her large brown eyes brimming with hurt and fury. "That this was how our first meeting with your memories returned should go? You could have found another way, River. Could have found someone else to do it. You chose to be the one wielding the lash. Do you know how much that hurt? "

River felt his face blanch, his chest tightening around his ribs. "No. Leralynn. Of course not. Why would you think…" Taking Leralynn's face in both hands, River traced her cheekbones, strong and beautiful beneath delicate skin. Just like the rest of her. She'd done so much these months, fighting for the mortal world when he himself could not—and was yet so soft and vulnerable around the steel-hard core. "I was trying to hurt you the least I could, not add to it. And I hated every moment of it."

He swallowed, the realization of how Lera had taken his actions burning his own eyes. She was still so young, so new to the fae world. And he was a bastard idiot for not thinking of that. "I'm the quint's commander," he whispered, "Never in three hundred years have I allowed anyone but me to punish one of ours. And when I saw you… When I realized what had to happen… Leralynn, I couldn't step aside, because had it been someone else bringing you to your knees, I'd have ripped out their tongue. Tell me you understand. Please."

Leralynn shifted, her tense body easing just a hair. "You could have given me some…signal."

"I had to make it real, or we risked losing everything—you included." River's voice was soft as he dried a stray tear sliding along Lera's creamy skin. "Plus, you are so bad a liar that even Tye has given up teaching you to cheat at cards."

She snorted. "And you needed to show the mortals that you could control the rabid dog under your command."

River's hands stopped, tightening on her shoulders. "Not a rabid dog, Leralynn," he said, his voice harsher than he intended. "An immortal warrior with more power at her fingertips than any creature the mortal kingdom has laid eyes on. You set an arena ablaze by *accident*, without a moment's thought. A power that would have left most any fae on the ground, too drained to move for days—and yet was little more than a trip hazard to you. Stars, Lera—don't you understand how powerful you are? Because I do. And it scares me spitless."

6

Lera

River's words grip my chest. *Powerful.* Of all the words for River, the king of an entire kingdom, to use to describe me, that was not one I expected. Slipping off the male's lap, I stand between his open thighs, River's face tilting up a bit to keep our gazes locked. "You think I'm powerful?"

River snorts softly, shaking his head. "Stars, Leralynn. How can you not know it by now?"

"But—"

"I could feel your power even when I thought you a cadet," he whispers. "Even when I didn't know who you were, when I could feel nothing of the mating bond, I knew you could eclipse the sun itself if you put your mind to it... Or, well, your emotions." He smiles ruefully. "Just you wait until *you* are responsible for someone who just might destroy the universe by accident."

I wait for River's gaze to slip to my midsection, and when it never does, I realize the reference was for me, not the twins. In fact... My eyes widen, the antics of the courtyard suddenly a distant past. River was unconscious when the rest of us felt the heartbeats. Which means, in addition to waking to discover the mortal world on the verge of war, the male has yet to learn that he's about to be a father.

Lovely.

Drawing myself together, I pull in a long, steadying breath, filling my lungs with the scent of woods and power that comes from the male. *Right. Here goes.* I raise my chin. "River—"

The male puts a callused finger to my lips. "I fell in love with you when I didn't know who you were, Lera," he whispers, his gray eyes flashing with soul-shredding desperation. "With my memories gone, with everything around me screaming that I needed to stay away, I couldn't help myself. You own my soul. Always will."

I catch his wrist, feeling the speeding pulse tapping against the skin. Looking down from above, I can see the tension coiling each of River's muscles, from his impossibly broad, bare shoulders to the hard squares of his abdomen and the rock-hard cords along his thighs. When he swallows, I see the agony lining his eyes, an unbridled terror that what he did in the courtyard—what he had to do in the courtyard—would make me walk away.

"River," I say, my voice gentle. "River, I'm not mad at you. I was, but I'm not anymore. There is something I need to tell you."

He tenses, bracing for a blow. "Please don't," he whispers. "Please don't leave me, Lera."

"No." I catch myself as River flinches. "I mean, no, I'm not going anywhere. In any way. It's something else. And I need to you to stay calm. And not—" *Not faint or go feral or lose all your better sense.*

"Time's up." Shade's voice lashes between River and me as he crosses the library. "Lera and I have unfinished business." I have only a moment to turn and brace myself before the male is in front of me, gripping my shoulders, golden eyes blazing. His muscles are so tight, it looks like he's barely breathed since I left the library fifteen minutes ago. "Pull a stunt like that again, and I will muzzle you."

"Stand down." River is on his feet at once, lips pulled back to reveal his canines.

Standing between the two males, I put a hand on both their chests, shoving River back down into his chair while forcing Shade to take a step back. "I don't need help dealing with this idiot, River," I say, twisting to square off against the shifter, my blood heating. "Speak to me that way again, and I will rip off your balls and feed them to the first hog I find."

"You think it's *me* who is the problem here?" Shade demands.

Leaving River where he is, I pinch Shade's arm right above the elbow and pull him toward the back of the library, Tye and Coal both getting out of my way without a word.

The high-domed ceiling makes it so even the soft rustle of pages turning feels grand and somber. But it also makes it so I can hear every single sound irritatingly magnified—Shade's quick breaths at my back, Gavriel's scratching quill at some private desk in the stacks, tiny squeaks as Arisha's cat, Minion, tortures another mouse. I wonder where Arisha went that Gavriel hadn't found her, what the girl would find more interesting than plotting against Owalin.

A sudden boom of thunder is so loud in the scratching, squeaking silence that I jump, then yank harder on Shade's arm to try to mask it.

The tsunami of emotions battering me with every step turns the edges of my vision dark, the beat of Shade's pulse under my fingers like a tapping against my soul.

This isn't how anything was supposed to go. Like River's performance in the courtyard, it's a bloody mockery of all the times I imagined the return of Shade's memories, the male wrapping his muscled arms around me, his velvet lips brushing against mine. And it's bloody unjust.

Many turns through long narrow aisles later, we reach a reading nook that Arisha showed me once, far in the back corner of the vast library—the closest we can get to privacy, short of going outside. Tall, semicircular shelves surround a space covered in floor cushions, a single curved window cut out in the center of the shelves casting light to read by—though with the coming storm, it might as well be twilight in here.

I shove the male against the wall. "You want to tell me what in the name of all the stars is up with you?" I demand, pressing my fingers into Shade's flesh, my hard tone the only thing I can do to fight against my stinging eyes.

Shade looks down at me, at the grip that I have on his arm, his usually expressive golden gaze as unreadable as River's. His bare chest rises and falls with deep even breaths, every intricate line of muscle casting shadows in the low light, a sheen of sweat glinting on his abdominals despite the swiftly cooling air. Lines of strain spider from the corners of his eyes. If I didn't know better, I'd think he let me shove him against the wall because he needs its support to keep upright. Given that he threatened to *muzzle* me moments ago, however, I am not about to underestimate the male for a moment.

"Well?" I prompt, realizing Shade still has yet to answer my question.

"I remembered who I am," he says.

"And did something go wrong with that process?" Still holding on to Shade's elbow, I press my other hand into his sternum, my canines bared. "Because the Shade I knew was a reasonable and kind male, not a thickheaded coyote who wants to shove, piss, and growl his way to whatever he wants."

Shade's brow twitches at my grip, a hint of irony flashing before it disappears behind that damn mask of cold resolve. "What I am, cub, is a wolf. And a warrior. One who left you unprotected for too many months. That ends now—whether you like it or not. I've told you before, when I have a choice between keeping you happy and keeping you safe, the latter will win every time. I don't give a bloody damn whether you like that answer."

Heat simmers my blood, the tolling bell in the keep's tower reminding me how little time we have before people die. "So I can add my happiness to the long list of things you no longer give a bloody damn about." With an effort that's as grand as squaring off before Coal, I tamp down the streak of violence rushing through me and force myself to try reason. "All right, Shade. Let us play this out. Two dozen Night Guard fae are holding half the continental kings hostage. Magic is free in the mortal world. What exactly do you imagine happening now if you had your way?"

"We go home," says Shade. "Once I'm certain River is stable and we can get you out of here safely."

"You want to abandon them?" The words sound strange on my tongue. "The humans. You want to forget we were here on a mission, that the Night Guard is holding their kings hostage, and sneak out the back door?"

"I don't *want* to abandon anybody," Shade snarls, finally grabbing the hand I have holding his elbow and throwing off my grip. "But I already have. There is no going back on what I've done!" Shade's chest heaves as if he just ran for miles, his tight cheekbones and jaw razor-sharp in the shadows, his long black hair giving his beauty a feral edge. His throat bobs. "I can only try to contain the damage now. To protect you and the pups ahead of all else."

"You—" I stop, something about Shade's words catching inside my chest. Frowning, I study his tight face, the lines that I took for fatigue before now looking more like deep pain. Beneath the taut tanned skin, Shade's muscles are so tense that it's a miracle the male can move at all. I cock my head, gripping his gaze before it can slide away. "What do you mean, what you've already done?"

Shade flinches.

My chest tightens. "What did you do, Shade?"

His head drops, his large shoulder curling slightly around his core. Beyond the window, the rain finally starts, like a bucket being overturned. But through a slim crack in the clouds, a single ray of sunlight sparkles against the silver I now see lining his large eyes. *I don't want to abandon anybody—but I already have.* Shade's words whisper again in my head.

Slowly, carefully, I reach toward his cheek, the stubble there just peeking from his tanned skin.

Shade presses himself farther into the wall, shaking his head slightly.

Ignoring the signal, I lay my palm on his face, letting the tiny shadow of stubble prickle my palm. "Who did you abandon?" I whisper.

He lifts his gaze with as great an effort as I've ever seen from him, golden eyes wide with a mix of vulnerability and sorrow. "You. I abandoned you. For months and months. I left you all alone. You are with cubs, and I left you all alone."

My hand tightens on Shade's chin, and I don't let the male pull away from me. "You had no choice. The magic—"

"My wolf knew!" he yells. "My wolf fought it. Sensed what was happening. If he could do it, I should have as well. I should have fought harder." Shade's voice shakes as he speaks, and when I take a step closer to him, I feel the fine tremor rushing through his body. In all my time with the quint, I've seen Shade angry and worried, stubborn and kind—but this is the first time I've seen him tearing apart with a pain so deep, I don't know how I'm going to reach it.

All this time I was furious with Shade for being a bastard to me, I hadn't realized it was actually himself he was punishing. "It wasn't your fault," I say, enunciating each word. "It was a magical accident. And all four of you were affected the same way."

"It was different for me." He rubs his hands over his face, gripping his hair on the way down. "My wolf knew the truth. And I should have too. But I didn't. I didn't even smell the cubs. And that day in my infirmary, when you were in so much pain and fighting through it, I was too worried about what my own cock wanted to see the truth that was right before my eyes." The ache filling every syllable of his voice spills into the air between us, sharpening the male's earthy scent. With the evening light sculpting his hard muscle, he looks more like a wolf than ever, his yellow eyes intent with a predatory protectiveness that is ready to tear any culprit to shreds.

Ready to tear his own soul to shreds.

"My wolf is furious with me," Shade tells me softly. The delicate flaring of his nostrils draws my gaze, making me aware of just how each one of his tiny movements affects my own body. "He only stepped aside to let me return because we felt...felt that you were calling for me. And he couldn't bring us to deny your call. But the wolf is right—I don't deserve you. Not when I couldn't—ow!"

Still standing on my toes, I pull my mouth away from where I just bit Shade's bottom lip hard enough draw tiny red droplets. "You are my mate," I say, low and gravelly, suddenly drunk on the coppery taste of his blood. On the roused mating bond that now twists in my chest. Inside my own veins, heat spreads through my body, quickening its circuit with every heartbeat. It's been so long since I tasted him, and I'd almost forgotten his spicy, earthy flavor, as addictive as a fine wine. "If you think I'm going to let you hide behind a wet nose and a furry tail to save yourself from feeling all the emotions the rest of us grapple with, then you've truly forgotten who in the bloody stars you got yourself entangled with."

Shade laps the cut on his lip, the tip of his tongue flicking over his canines with a predatory gleam. Balancing on the edge of his wolf shift as Shade is, I can almost see the awesome primal instinct taking hold of him, the force of it strong enough to make my own deep-lying predator break its leash.

With the next heartbeat, it's all I can do to keep from pouncing on the nearest bookshelf just to hunt down a mouse I can hear skittering beneath the stacks. Inside my chest, the mating bond drinks it all in, pulsating with blind need to secure its hold.

Shade's fingers dig into the wall behind him, his coiled muscles twitching with strain. His broad chest fills with quick breaths, his golden eyes flashing and dilating. A wolf ready to pounce, drawing on every fiber of his being just to keep himself in check. "Walk away, cub," Shade pants. "Slowly. Walk away from me slowly."

"No." I swallow, a streak of heat racing down my spine. Energy simmers inside my muscles, making heat pool low in my abdomen, rousing every scent to full wakefulness.

Shade growls, the sound more animal than fae. "Another few heartbeats, there won't be any walking at all."

My heart quickens, the echo of Shade's words rushing through my blood. *Run. Fight. Mate.* The options flash through my body without deference to higher thought, the whole world beyond us sinking into a distant fog. *Run. Fight. Mate.* A small growl rumbles through my own chest, as each heartbeat strips away another swath of civility.

My sex pulses in echo of my heart, making my hips clench with need. When I feel a trickle of moisture slither down my thigh, Shade shoves himself away from the wall.

"Go!" he hollers at me.

And so I do. Right into him.

7

Lera

We crash right back into the wall Shade just left, my nails raking the male's bare chest, leaving four parallel gashes in his perfect tan skin. Some sane part of me is appalled at the deep, bleeding marks, but another much more primal essence savagely savors the satisfaction of having marked the male. Having told his body that it's mine. I stare at my handiwork, my thighs slick beneath my dress, my sex clenching with the same savageness that spurred my hand.

Shade pounces with a snarl, his callused hands grabbing my wrists, his mouth claiming mine. The male's scent of earth fresh from rain fills my lungs as his tongue pillages my mouth, taking me in deep, possessive strokes that make it impossible to breathe.

I struggle against his unyielding grip, which only makes him shift his hold from my hands to my backside, fingers digging viciously into flesh. The small dots of pressure pierce deeply into my muscles, a predator holding prey captive. The feeling spills into my blood, rousing me to the dangers of playing with a wolf.

My hips undulate, my underthings dampening more with each moment. The bulge in Shade's trousers presses into me, his cock so hard that I can feel it throbbing. Gathering all my strength, I shove my hips against that hard cock, a jolt of pleasure streaking along my apex as I manage to connect with it.

Shade's body bucks against me in return, and he grunts as he deepens his kiss.

I reach down to tear open the flies holding him captive. The large rock-hard cock springs free with enough force to sting my thigh. The mere thought of all that power entering me is enough to make me moan impatiently, a low sound swallowed up by the pounding rain outside. I push my hips forward, and Shade grips the backs of my legs, lifting me without ever surrendering my mouth.

He takes one step forward, hoisting my slick thigh onto his taut waist before ripping away my damp underthings with the same ruthless consideration I gave his flies moments ago. The sound of the ripping fabric makes my sex clench hungrily.

Shade tears his mouth away from mine, pressing his damp forehead against mine. "Mine. You're mine."

I moan and buck, impatience almost making tears press out of my eyes.

With the next breath, Shade sheathes his cock to the hilt inside me.

I gasp, twisting along Shade's length, the great size of him impaling me somehow too much and not nearly enough at the same time. His powerful hips pump forward, sliding me along his cock as if I weigh nothing at all, the thick head of his cock striking the most sensitive spot deep inside me.

I grip his shoulders with all my strength, my teeth sinking into the side of his neck as the pressure inside me takes over my body. Shade growls and thrusts harder, faster, wildness taking any remaining finesse out of his movements.

Thump. Thump. Thump. The wet strikes of my body against Shade's rake through my core. My apex throbs, the need inside building more and more, fueled with every deep inhalation of Shade's damp-earth scent. I can't think, can barely breathe for the want of him. A deep longing so far inside my body that it drives me mad.

"Last. Chance," Shade rasps into my ear, though I've no notion how he manages the words, my own long gone. "We've things to settle. And I intend to. Thoroughly."

A shiver runs through me, the dangerous edge to his words sending just enough anxiety into my blood to make my already aroused sex clench uncontrollably.

Taking my shudder for an answer, Shade pulls out of me long enough to hook a nearby bookshelf with his ankle, his body covering me protectively as he twists us both away from the crashing furniture. Nudging a few priceless books out of the way, he grips my waist and bends me over the upturned shelf, the hard edge digging into my belly bothering me only until I feel Shade's strong arm slide beneath my hips as he settles himself behind me.

Gripping the ragged hem of my dress, the male tears the cloth just to my waist. The feeling of being half bared from the bottom somehow makes me more vulnerable than pure nakedness.

Shade growls, a sound I feel as much as hear. With one arm still firmly clasping my waist, he pushes my thighs apart and—

I gasp as callused fingers slide through my sex, top to bottom, smearing my juices so my scent fills the air. When Shade's slippery touch traces either side of my swollen bud, I discover just how unyielding the shifter's hold on my waist is, my struggles gaining not an inch of ground.

Pinned. Exposed. Excited and needy beyond logic. A strangled whimper escaping my throat turns to a yelp as a sharp crack along my backside lights every nerve ablaze. A second slap follows, this one harder. The pain turns to pulsing that scorches my skin—and is *nothing* compared to the molten heat now bathing my apex.

My breaths come in little gasps, my hands opening and closing against the edge of the bookshelf. Shade's power and arousal fill my lungs with every inhale, the intoxicating feeling driving me insane until I can't think beyond the throbbing in my sex.

I'd thought the dangerous, exciting edge of Shade's power made me the prey in this game. But as I feel everything inside me rouse and fight, I realize my error. My primal fae body is no prey, and Shade's alpha wolf instincts have known it all along. It's a predator the wolf wants to conquer, and the looming intensity of *that* clash makes my breath catch, my body bucking with renewed anxious energy.

Ignoring my struggle, Shade massages my backside. The gentleness of his touch is a new type of torture, making the clenching need gripping my apex creep away from the edge. It's not pain the bastard is after, but control. And if I ever get the upper hand in this, I'll rip him apart for it—no matter how much my traitorous body moistens for the forced surrender.

Just as my breathing begins to settle, my hands uncurling from the edge of the bookshelf, I hear the crack of another slap. The fire follows it a split second later, making me yelp.

If I thought the first two swats hard, they were nothing compared to the force descending on me now, the slaps echoing through the space, dulled by thudding rain. My yelps turn to breathless moans as the blazing heat rushes right to my sex, making me push my bottom back higher, begging for more.

"Shade." My words are strangled, my struggles useless against his steely hold. My bottom burns, my sex throbbing mercilessly, clenching around air.

Far on the other end of the library, a faint chuckle ruffles the air—and sends all the blood from my backside rushing to my face. "Oh, they can hear you just fine," Shade assures me, his velvety lips brushing over my ear just before he pushes my thighs farther apart, depriving me of what little control I still have.

Before I can rebalance myself, Shade plunges his cock deep into my channel. I scream, too far gone to care who hears me now. He starts thrusting immediately, without letting me adjust to his size, pumping hard but slow—agonizingly slow. The heavy wooden shelf creaks rhythmically under our weight. *In and out, in and out,* Shade stretches my channel, the occasional slap on my tender backside making me buck despite knowing how little good it will do—which in turn magnifies every touch.

My sex sizzles, shooting tendrils of sensation down my thighs and along the soles of my feet, which curl in desperation.

The tip of Shade's finger traces the hood around my swollen bud, making me pant with need. My slickness drips down the bookshelf, and the scent of the male's own sweat and arousal rakes through me. My breath catches as the abyss closes in on me, the tipping point of release just a stroke of Shade's finger away.

"Please!" I can't make myself care who hears us, not with my breaths coming fast, my body so tense in anticipation of the coming flood that my body trembles. The pressure building inside me grows more unbearable with every slip of a heartbeat, the wait an agony I cannot bear—and can't do one thing about.

But this time, Shade listens, thrusting faster as if his body alone is now in control. His fingers dig almost painfully into my hips, pulling me back against him so our bodies meet with a crashing force to rival the thunder outside. I groan and pant uncontrollably, animal sounds escaping me that I don't even recognize as my own.

Slap. Slap. Slap.

Shade's palm keeps time on my backside, the perfect fiery pain igniting everything with a brilliance that makes the tiny flicker of his finger over my swollen nub feel like the sun itself is raking my sex.

I scream, my voice breaking as I fall over the edge, every fiber and muscle inside me clenching in ecstasy. Wave after wave of sensation washes over my body, Shade pulling me onto his lap to hold me as I arch helplessly. As my hands and back and thighs all tighten beneath the avalanche of pleasure assaulting them, until all my strength is gone, and I pant, a little rag doll in the male's arms.

"You are beautiful, cub," Shade says, stroking my face as I recover, his touch so soothing and warm that I melt into him like a kitten, bathing in his love and scent.

At least right up until the callused hand strays across my sore backside, the sting making me jump. "You are a bastard," I mutter into his shoulder. "And I hate you."

Shade chuckles, the noise deep and velvety. "I think I can fix that," he whispers against my hair, his magic tingling like cool mint to cover my skin. Erasing the lingering ache as if it never existed.

"Stop." I push myself up, breaking the web of minty magic seeping into my skin. "I don't *actually* hate you."

Shade frowns, his thumb tracing my cheekbone. "I didn't think you did, cub—I *want* to soothe your skin. I want you to remember this moment with—"

"With something other than the full truth?" I shake my head. "I've had enough of altered memories to last a lifetime."

Strong arms wrapping around me, Shade pulls me against him in a tight embrace. "In that case, let's see if we can't give those memories a bit more to chew on," he murmurs, brushing the fallen books away to clear the carpeted floor beneath us.

Laying me back onto the soft fibers of burnt-orange rug, Shade eases off the remains of my dress and holds my gaze as he enters me gently, the glide of his still rock-hard cock along my channel pulling my mind to the here and now, very *very* effectively.

8

Lera

"Does this mean you two have made up?" Tye's voice penetrates my haze of bone-melting satisfaction, my naked body utterly content where it sprawls atop Shade's equally bare form. Shade's chest lifts me slightly into the air with each inhale, his warm sweat-soaked skin slippery and perfect against mine as I stare at the intricate woodwork along the nearest baseboard, the designs slipping and dancing.

"Mmm?" I blink away from the designs to focus on Tye. Shade's arm pulls me tighter against his chest as I examine Tye's lovely freckles and large emerald eyes, the lashes long and dark enough to make any girl jealous. Including me. Of course, if those eyes were a bit closer… "You want to join?" I ask.

Tye snorts. "I always want to join. We can't have you thinking this fleabag's feeble skills are all there is to be had in our quint. Alas, I prefer my couplings to be with sentient beings." Squatting beside my head, Tye rests muscled forearms against his knees and studies me with amusement, his beautiful wide mouth quirked at one corner.

Shade growls softly but doesn't move.

I blink at Tye again, the effort it takes to enunciate my words seeming much greater than usual. "I'm sen…sensual. Sentient. I'm whatever you said you like." My sex twinges despite my fatigue, and I run the pad of my finger along the inside of Tye's wrist.

The male tenses, looking up at the ceiling to draw several deep breaths before daring to return his attention to my face. "Right. You are bond drunk, lass. Both of ye. And we really don't have very much time for that just now, what with the Night Guard holding the kings hostage and River trying to plan an assault on the keep while Coal and I try to find a way to tell him the *other* news. And the humans, meanwhile—" Tye's words meld together, his songlike accent turning whatever he says into a lullaby.

I close my eyes, listening to the roll of Tye's Rs, the way the ends of his phrases shift beautifully to make "your" into "yer," with the occasional "aye" sprinkled in for spice. It's not until the sounds rudely stop altogether that I open my eyes again, my attention snagging at once on the sizable bulge between Tye's legs—which his crouching position gives me a perfect view of.

My mouth waters, the thought of what Tye would taste like in my mouth just now, with Shade's scent still clinging to my tongue, making my mound press hungrily against Shade's body. The shifter growls in response, slipping a hand over my bottom to help me along. My hand floats from me, reaching toward Tye's cock, my fingers already planning the quick tug that will unravel his flies. How nicely the great length of him will spring out for my pleasure.

Tye catches my wrist, his breaths quick and strained.

"What are you doing?" I demand.

"Ruining what would have been a very well-spent hour, apparently," Tye mutters, placing my hand back on Shade's shoulder before straightening to his full height and retreating from view. A part of me insists that I should care where he is going, but the rest of me can only sulk at being denied.

Turning my head the other way, I circle one of Shade's nipples with my finger, the muscles under his velvety tan skin puckering in response. "What's bond drunk?"

"It's something that sometimes happens to bonded mates when a female is with pups," River says dryly from behind me. "Given that that, at least, is one thing we do not have to worry about at the moment, you two can get your naked backsides up and rejoin reality any time now. Let me help." The last words are punctuated with a downpour of ice water.

I yelp, the shock making every nerve in my body scream with indignation, especially with a stray icy stream snaking down the crack in my bottom. I scramble off Shade—who steadies me with his strong arms before pushing himself up as well—and glare at River, who righteously sets the now-empty water pitcher on a nearby table. He's dressed now in a white shirt and blue wool jacket, his brown hair combed annoyingly neatly.

"Errr, River?" Tye drawls. "I wouldn't jump to too many assumptions there, lad." Taking off the soot-stained remains of his Prowess uniform jacket, Tye wraps the material around my bare shoulders and pulls me against him.

River turns away from Shade, who now has his hands on his thighs, shaking the water off him in a perfect imitation of a wet wolf. "What assumptions am I jumping to, Tye?"

Shade clears his throat, his gaze shifting to me, then back to River. "How is your chest?" he asks the commander, turning to fish a pair of britches from the hastily discarded pile of clothes. "I don't want you walking around if you don't have to be."

"Noted," River says dryly, one dark brow quirked. "Is something going on of which I'm not aware?"

"What's bond drunk?" I ask again, snuggling my face deeper into Tye's warm chest, his pine-and-citrus scent tingling over me deliciously.

"Pregnancy has a tendency to magnify certain emotions and senses," Tye says quietly into my ear. "Mix high emotion and mating, and the effect is well, this." He shifts to put his hard cock—which I suddenly realize I'd been reaching for—out of my grasp. "Unless you want to be doing nothing but coupling for the next few days, I suggest not going into my britches just now." He snorts. "What idiocy am I saying. If you want to—"

"Why are we still talking about—" River freezes in midsentence, blood draining from his face.

I bite my lip.

His eyes widen, the apple of his throat twitching before he steps back so quickly that Shade steadies him with a hand on his shoulder. Gripping a table's edge, River stares at my still perfectly flat midriff, his mouth moving without making a sound. Beyond the library wall, another crack of thunder cleaves the air, rain pelting the windows.

"She is..." River starts to say, then stops. His beautiful gray eyes swirl with rapid-fire thoughts, each one crowding out the next. I've never seen our powerful commander like this. It almost makes me nervous.

"The cub is carrying pups, yes." Shade tries and fails to sound clinical, his hand twitching toward me before he contains himself and sticks it into his pocket instead. "Twins."

"How?" River demands, turning on Shade with all the reasonableness of a disheveled hyena.

"Well, River," Tye says, "I'm no healer, of course, but I do believe it has to do with a cock making entry into—"

"Shut up, Tye," River snaps over his shoulder before advancing on Shade. "You said it was impossible. That being so newly fae, her body was not yet developed for…for…"

"Yes, I know what I said. As both Coal and you have now pointed out." Shade throws up his hands. "The research on the fertility cycles of a human turned fae are somewhat lacking. And before you ask, no, there is no way of knowing which of our seeds took hold. Only that it did. I suppose we might get some clue once they're born, but for all I know, Lera's weaver magic managed to blend the essences from all our seeds together."

River rubs wide palms over his face, color slowly beginning to seep back into it. The rest of us are quiet as he works through the news. "All right," he says finally, the practical command in his voice giving me hope that he'll gather his wits about him faster than Coal and Shade did. Then he speaks again. "We need clouts," he says, all business. "Where do we get clouts at the Academy? Does the infirmary stock them?"

Lera

A quarter hour later, thanks to Tye's ability to procure clothes at a moment's notice—having found inconvenient nakedness a common hazard of his former lifestyle—I stand beside River at the window in a pair of soft black fighting leathers and a warm shirt. My thick hair has been corralled into a long braid down my back, and I'm finally feeling like a version of my old self again.

In no more than ten minutes, Owalin's first deadline will pass. Not a single human has darkened our doorstep since River's offer of an alliance.

We are still two hours from sunset, but with the storm, it feels like dusk has come early. Through the gray sheets of rain, I watch the royal families huddle under a large white tent that Academy staff erected— probably repurposed from some planned Prowess festivities. They've put it as far from the Great Hall as possible to try to avoid Owalin's prying ears, which puts them close to us. Many of the women and children and even professors have taken shelter in the academic buildings ringing the courtyard, though there are still at least a hundred people gathered on the sodden cobblestones.

With nothing to do but wait, Tye and Shade have gone to the back of the library to clean up the mess, their restless energy obvious even from here in muffled curses.

I jump when the library door bangs open, the little bells cutting through the heavy tension with ridiculous cheerfulness. Coal stamps his feet and brushes water off his clothes, his pulled-back hair almost dark against his scalp. "They're giving in to Owalin's first demand. The king of Fothom is readying to enter the Great Hall."

River only nods. He's been silent ever since hearing the news of our cubs, the tension around him making the air sing.

"They're relinquishing the mortal world to a madman, River," Coal presses, glancing at me with nothing short of alarm on his face when the commander doesn't respond.

"I know," River says finally. His experienced eyes survey the situation with the calm steadiness that I have grown to take for granted, but the words lack all interest. As if the outcome of the standoff little matters to him now.

I shrug at Coal, and he lifts his hands in an "I give up" gesture, going over to the crackling fire Gavriel laid in one of the library's three massive hearths to start drying off his clothes.

"River," I say quietly. "Are you…" I search for the right word to say, my chest tightening at the one I settle on. "Upset? About the cubs." My breath halts, my eyes not daring to look at River's face. After the initial shock wore off, the male retreated behind the wall of his own thoughts with a speed that's left me reeling.

I wrap my arms around myself when the male says nothing, my jaw tightening.

"I'm upset that we are in the mortal world with no way home except through battle with the Night Guard," River says finally. With a start, I realize he's trembling. The silence on the subject, which I broke, seemed to be all that was keeping him together.

"We are *choosing* to face the Night Guard, River," I say. "We have a way home. The Mystwood key you took off me back in the beginning of the year—"

"I destroyed it." He strikes his palm against the windowsill, the glass rattling. "Katita had seen you with what was plainly a fae artifact, and I was afraid of her turning on you. With fae hunters in major towns… If she'd started something, it would be bad enough to pit her word against yours, I didn't want there to be evidence to boot. So when I took it off you, I shattered it and threw it into the fire." River swallows, turning slowly to face me. His strong, smooth face looks like marble, every hard plane sculpted to perfection. But his swirling gray eyes are a different story, the vulnerability in them striking me to my very core. "I'm sorry, Leralynn. I've been a father for less than an hour, and I've already failed."

"River." My chest tightens as I press my palm against his cheek. "River, the stupidest reasoning I've—" I cut off, the truth dawning on me just a moment too late.

"It isn't the key you're upset about," I whisper. "You aren't afraid of battling the Night Guard. You aren't afraid of battling anyone. You're… Stars. Listen to me, River. You are going to be a good father. I promise."

The male's flinch betrays just how deep a wound my words struck, his beautiful strong jaw clenching so hard that I see the muscle coil beneath his skin.

"You are going to be a good father, River," I say again. "Just as you are a good mate. And a good commander."

"You don't know that," he whispers, the fear saturating his voice now spilling into the air between us, giving a sharp tang to the dusty smell usually settling in the library. "How can you trust me when you know what kind of monster sired me?"

"Because I love you," I say simply. "Because we fell in love with each other when there was nothing to tie us together and everything to keep us apart. And because I won't let you be anything else."

River chuckles, the sounds starting off strained but easing as he gazes into my eyes. Shaking his head, he cups the back of my head with his hand, leaning down to take a slow tentative kiss. "I don't deserve you, Lera," he whispers against my mouth as my hand rests gently on his hard triceps. "But I'm grateful for you with every breath."

Before I can reply, the kiss deepens, River pouring so much of himself, his love, his strength into the connection that the magic coiled inside me rouses and *purrs* until I wonder if one of the twins isn't a shifter.

"What was that for?" I ask, when he finally pulls away, the callused tips of his fingers lingering on my cheek.

"To thank you," the male replies, a smile finally, *finally* touching his eyes. "And to make up for the bastard I'm sure I'm going to be shortly." He brushes his thumb over my lips. "If you think pregnancy is intrusive, wait until you discover what four overprotective mates are like to be around."

I snort, swatting his hand away. "Right. Well, before we discover all that—how long are you going to let the humans out there blunder about before going to talk some sense into them? I'm no expert, but handing Owalin everything he wants does not appear to be a winning strategy."

River squeezes my shoulder, shaking his head at the window. "Fair point. Let me get my coat."

10

Lera

"What do you mean they have no interest in working with us?" Tye asks River five minutes later. The rain that started with sudden violence earlier is finally pattering off to a slow drizzle, the droplets snaking down the glass like tears. "Have the human royals lost what little wits they had to begin with?"

Taking off his jacket, River hangs it on the back of the chair by the fire to dry and runs a hand through his short dark hair. From what I saw through the window, the male was barely allowed to enter the humans' command tent, much less listened to.

"They fear getting caught between two warring immortal armies." River drops into a chair, tapping his finger on the wood. "The Fothom king kept pointing out that Owalin is creating enough problems without anyone wanting to worry about our hidden intentions."

"Such as our intention to protect their arses?" Tye says. "Aye, I'm starting to find that suspicious as well."

"So what's their plan exactly?" Coal's voice is dark. "Give in to Owalin's demands like good little lapdogs and hope he gives them proper scraps going forward?"

"He has their loved ones trapped," says River, pausing to look out the window, where the Fothom king's line of attendants and clerks files slowly into the Great Hall, the latter carrying oiled satchels filled with paper and ink needed to draw up the agreements that will cede all the thrones to the Night Guard. Behind the clerks, several servants are ready with trays of food. The Fothom king himself, a blurred form through the drizzle, prepares to follow. River shakes his head. "They've bought themselves some leeway, but it's only a matter of time before the final five kings follow suit."

"Fine." Coal crosses muscular arms over his chest, his blue eyes flashing. "If the humans won't help themselves, we'll do it for them. Make entry after dark, take out the leadership cadre. With Owalin gone, the rest of the beasts will be easier to slay."

River shakes his head. "There are two dozen fae and who knows how many human supporters in the Night Guard. The five of us can't take that on without resorting to significant magic—and a battle like that is likely to bring the whole keep down. It doesn't count as a victory if we kill all the hostages."

"Isn't the Night Guard under the same constraint?" I ask. "Killing a hostage here and there is one thing, but if they explode the whole keep, they have no leverage anymore."

"Exactly right." River nods. "Magic isn't the answer since such combat would lead to mutual destruction. And when it comes to melee, the Night Guard has too many people for us to face down alone."

My hand tightens on the table's edge, the males' conversation suddenly taking on layers I hadn't noticed earlier. *Magic isn't the answer.* My heart quickens, the fledgling strands of realization injecting energy into muscle. I only realize I've spoken aloud when the males turn their gazes to me in question.

"Magic isn't the answer," I say again, already headed for the door, my skin tingling in anticipation of the chill wind and rain. Of what I'm about to do. "Being human is the answer. Which means it isn't River they need to be talking to."

"Did anyone understand what the lass said?" Tye murmurs to the others as I step out into the courtyard, lifting my face toward the command tent.

At once, I feel the wind blowing my hair free of my neck and whipping the strands while the last vestiges of rain cling to my cheeks. I walk stridently across the cobblestones, not slowing long enough to question the sanity of what I'm doing. Behind me, the soft tapping of feet betrays the males' presence behind me, as does the sudden hush of the crowd. Glares ranging from hate to fear to awe track my every movement as I survey the ground outside the tent in search of something to stand on. Finding nothing better than a charred bench that was once part of the proud arena bleachers, I set it upright before climbing on top.

"You were told to get the hell out." A man's voice hits me in the chest before I fully find my footing. Stepping out from under the command tent, the Fothom king points a sword at me. Once tall and broad-shouldered, his pale blond hair still thick under his gold-and-sapphire crown, his proud form has seemed to age twenty years from grief. "You are not welcome here. None of you."

Heart pounding, I raise a halting hand to my males, who are already reaching for weapons. The extra couple of feet of height the bench gives me are enough to make me seen, though the platform is hardly dignified. I swallow, my mouth suddenly dry, my heart quickening. Speeches are River's specialty, not mine. But this crowd doesn't need River.

"Put down your blade, Your Majesty," I tell the king, wrinkling my nose at the ornate sword in his hands. "It makes you look like a rabbit with claws, when we all know you have none."

"How dare—" The Fothom king takes a step forward before two men rush to grab his shoulders, holding him back with desperate murmurs about not provoking the immortals.

"You should listen to them," I tell the king, my words carrying over the courtyard and softly pattering rain. "After all, rabbits who get between two hungry wolves are only choosing which stomach they will end up in. Better to tuck your tail and go hide beneath the largest rock you can find while the immortals do as they please. There truly is nothing left for you anymore than to wait and mourn your dead—both present and future."

The king's face darkens, an angry murmur starting among the remaining crowd. A few steps behind me, Tye and Coal debate my sanity, neither's opinion overly flattering.

River takes a step toward me. I shake my head, and he retreats, his arms crossed over his wide chest. Grim but silent. Turning my attention back to the courtyard, I swallow, keeping my chin up as I let the crowd's newly roused fury stretch itself awake. As I drink it in.

Because anger is better than fear. Better than apathy.

"What? Don't you like what I say?" I demand, marking for the first time the one face that is listening to me with rapt attention—Princess Katita's. I let myself hold her cool turquoise gaze a moment as I continue. "I'm only giving voice to the murmurs I'm hearing," I say. "This isn't my tale. It is yours."

"Spoken like a true immortal on a pedestal," a voice yells, the crowd parting to a woman with puffy eyes, sagging red braids, and a skewed crown. The queen of Fothom, who lost her son this afternoon, whose husband is readying to surrender himself to the Night Guard for the sake of his remaining children. "It isn't your world that's shattered. Don't you dare judge what you've never experienced. You think you know what our lives are like because you feigned being a human student for a few months? You think you understand anything? Your people brought disaster on our heads, so don't you lecture us on how to take a beating with more grace."

A lump forms in my throat at the wild grief on the woman's face, my hand going to my midsection. I've only heard my pups' heartbeats, and I already cannot imagine watching someone hurt them—that this queen stands tall after the grief she faced, that she looks an immortal in the eye and holds her ground, is what makes humans as powerful as any fae.

"You are quite right, Your Majesty," I say, and mean it.

The queen, whose mouth is already open with a new insult, cocks her head.

"You deserve to make your own choices and be respected for them. You also deserve to know the truth—of who I am, of why we came here to begin with. I ask that you let me tell you, and then you make the decision that is right for your people. Better yet, don't listen to me. Listen to one of your own."

Looking over the crowd—now a thinned-out mixture of Academy cadets, Prowess athletes, staff, and those royal visitors hardy or panicked enough to remain outside—I lock eyes with the blacksmith who was ready to swing a mallet at my head earlier today. "Master Thad. There is a prisoner named Jake in the Academy's dungeons. He is the same Master Zake who has been leading the inquisition to rid the mortal world of fae. Would you bring him here and ask him about me? Ask him who I am and who I was."

Thad spits on the ground. "If you think I'll do your bidding—"

"I think you'll do *my* bidding." Katita's regal voice is smooth and polished beside mine. With her dress torn and wet, she limps as she strides from the command tent, passing by the Fothom royals as if the pair isn't even there. Coming up to my makeshift pedestal, Katita ignores my offer of a hand up as she climbs —though taking the step is plainly a painful endeavor.

"I am the crown princess of Ckridel," Katita announces to the crowd. "With my father kept captive, I am charged with the throne. And I will have no fae or blacksmith deny me the truth. Bring the prisoner and let him speak."

Turning to Katita, I search for something to say but find the young woman's gaze so filled with steel that no words come.

"My duty is to my people, not my pride," Katita says with no warmth at all, turning away.

The minutes tick by in a gut-churning wait that makes me question the wisdom of my plan more with each passing heartbeat.

By the time Thad and several guards escort Zake to the podium, I'm ready to empty my stomach into the nearest hedge and have to swallow several times just to keep my stance. When I force my spine to straighten, I find Katita watching me with a curious gaze. I almost don't recognize her without the usual scorn twisting her stunning features. Owalin's threat to her kingdom has revealed her true colors— crises have a way of doing that.

"You are afraid of him?" she asks quietly enough to keep the wind from picking up her words. "This human. Why?"

"Filthy lying wench!" Zake's words pierce the crowd from where he walks, saving me from having to answer Katita's question. "I knew the moment of truth would come. And now it has, with the whole world seeing you for the creature you are."

The princess lifts her chin, pointing to a spot on the ground right below her. "You seem to know quite a bit about this fae. If you have noble blood in you as you claim, I expect you to indulge us with an explanation that is appropriate for my ears."

Zake flinches at the command in Katita's tone, his bruised body straightening before the princess. When he speaks again, his tone is as civil as I've ever heard it.

"Of course, Your Highness. I forgot myself a moment." Zake tugs down the hem of his shirt, still the plain brown servant's uniform he was wearing when jailed. A thin layer of scruff now covers his face, matching the dark, wiry hair on his head. "Many years ago, I let an orphan girl into my home. Gave the wretched child a bed and bowl.

Taught her a trade. Taught her discipline and honesty. Or so I thought." Zake shakes his head, the disappointment hanging around him like a heavy cloak. "At the first opportunity, the wench traded her maidenhead for corruption. More than that, she took everything I'd worked for decades to create and bargained it away to the fae in exchange for being made one of them. That orphan turned backstabbing thief now stands beside you, Your Highness. And I swear on my life that, given a chance, she will take what's yours just as she took what's mine."

My hands clench at my side, even River's steady gray gaze unable to save me from the sting of each of Zake's lies.

Katita's eyes narrow at the man. "Do you mean to say that Leralynn was once human? A serving girl in your stable and under your authority?"

"That is exactly what I'm saying." Zake raises his chin in triumph as a murmur goes through the crowd. Many sets of eyes turn to me, filled with questions, before widening as they find Katita's disgusted gaze.

"Keep that filth silent," Katita orders the guards, staring down Zake as he begins sputtering. Turning to me, the princess schools her face, though the curiosity dancing in her eyes is plain to see. "Might I presume that the price of immortality was slightly higher than a maidenhead?" she asks of me.

"The price was death." I try and fail to force a smile. "I don't recommend it."

A humorless chuckle touches the princess's face. "So you were one of us. And now you are back. Why?"

The crowd's attention swings to me, the murmuring quieting. Waiting for my answer. In the corner of my vision, I catch River raising a brow at me. I've gotten the platform and audience I fought for, his gaze says. Now what? What speech have I prepared to give them?

Except, unlike River, I have no speech to give. All I have is the truth.

I draw a deep breath, letting the air fill my chest. "Because I made a mistake. We all did. Ages ago, our ancestors set up wards to ensure that no magic enters the mortal world. A few months ago, the Elders Council in Lunos received reports that those wards were cracking and dispatched my quint—under cover of a magic veil—to correct the problem. We came to secretly protect you from us, with no intention of ever telling you the truth. But that was folly."

"Because mortals don't deserve your protection?" The sarcasm in Katita's voice drips like honey.

"Because mortals can protect themselves," I say, twisting toward her, the rest of the courtyard suddenly dissolving into irrelevance. In the back of my mind, I wonder what Owalin is making of all this—if he is bothering to listen to the chattering of lower life-forms, that is. But it doesn't matter. The truth is the truth no matter how blind the bastard is to it. "We can be your allies, Katita—we can't be your puppet masters. The truth is that, for all the faes' magic and immortality, the human world is so much larger than the three kingdoms of Lunos that a battle would wipe everyone out evenly."

I look at the door to the Great Hall, looming behind the crowd and a wall of brave human guards. The place my quint cannot assault without destroying it, not by ourselves. With the rain having finally died down to a light mist, torches and lanterns have flickered on all around the courtyard, casting dramatic shadows on the towering stone. The clouds are beginning to clear, revealing a silver-blue sky, just tingeing orange on the edges.

Turning my attention back to the courtyard, I continue. "On our way here, my quint and I wore amulets to trick your mind into believing us humans. But then I accidentally tripped a bit of stray magic, which made the males believe the veil's lies for a long time. I thought it was all my fault for being careless. For tripping that magic. But that wasn't the real problem—the real problem started when we donned the amulets to begin with. When we decided to take the choice away from you."

I pause, suddenly realizing that the courtyard has gone silent, the words spilling from my soul filling the air with an intoxicating tension. For a second, all I can do is blink as I remember where I am. Who I'm talking to.

Katita nods at me, the tiny motion like a new jolt of strength circling my core.

"There are fae inside the Great Hall who hold your loved ones hostage," I tell the crowd. "We didn't bring them here. They came well before us. And we aren't going to storm your fortress, fighting a battle you do not want fought. These are your kingdoms, your lands, your choices. Just as our realms could never battle without wiping both our peoples to dust, my quint cannot battle the Night Guard without killing everyone in the Great Hall. There would be no victory for either side. This standoff will end not with magic, but with your steel. Or your surrender. The choice is yours alone."

Reaching to my back, I draw the blade I have sheathed there, the steel whispering as it's freed into the cool air. The collective breath of the crowd stills as I raise the blade above my head, letting the first rays of sunlight after the storm reflect off the shaft. "My mates and I are here to help, should you wish it. But make no mistake, the true power is with you. As is your victory." Turning the weapon, I hand it hilt first to Katita. "The fae of Lunos are in your kingdom at your sufferance, Your Highness. And we await your orders."

11

Owalin

"**W**hat in the bloody stars' name is that?" Owalin asked, staring out the bay window where a dark, swirling wall of something was forming up before his very eyes.

Behind him, the two hundred hostages has been subdued into proper order, the kings' clerks drawing up contracts along the tables set up against the back wall. His people had arranged food on the right side of the hall, where the families of the lesser nobles who'd signed an allegiance pledge to the Night Guard were allowed to go while the others watched hungrily. The five monarchs were still *thinking* things over, but it was only a matter of time. While River's wench was busy making speeches to hamsters, the Fothom king and the clerks had slunk away just as the bell tolled the deadline, the whole lot of them red-faced and shaking as they beheld the prince whose throat was a second away from being sliced open.

Owalin was a male of his word, after all—and the hamsters needed to know that with every fiber of their being. After all, Owalin required more than kings' signatures—he required their submission. The mortal world was too large for the Night Guard to hold under constant sword, and cultivating the right proxies required a proper mix of stick and carrot. It also required setting firm rules and sticking to them for as long as it took the feeble-minded creatures to learn better than to doubt Owalin's decrees. Breaking a good workhorse to bit took time.

Time that Owalin was supposed to have had plenty of. "Krum," he snapped at the silver-haired wardsmith. "I asked what that was."

"A privacy screen." Coming up behind him, Krum rolled the two spheres he always had in his hand, his face set in a contempt-filled expression. "It's supposed to keep us from seeing and hearing all the plans the king of Slait and his ilk are making out there."

"Plans? There are no plans. It's either submit the kingdoms to me or watch their offspring die one by one. Do you think I've not made that clear enough?"

"Crystal, my liege." Krum scoffed. "No matter. It's crude work. A brute-force endeavor with no craftsmanship. River was always one for brawn over finesse."

Owalin grunted. Krum's craftsmanship snobbery aside, River of Slait was known to lead one of the most powerful quints in Lunos even decades back when Owalin was still in the immortal realm. Back when Owalin had worked with River's father, Griorgi, toward a partnership with the dark realms. They'd gone their separate ways when Griorgi refused to see the reaping potential in humans, and that broken alliance had cost Owalin time and resources. Now Griorgi's bloody son was back to blunder up the Night Guard's plans.

Bloody darkened stars.

Owalin didn't think the brat and his minions were stupid enough to attack—but if they did, Owalin would have no choice but to shed human blood—possibly ruining the precious ground he'd gained with the royals, or worse—losing the highest-value leverage points for no gain. There were only so many royal children, after all.

To add insult to injury, Owalin could have neutralized River easily just that morning. How in the bloody stars' name had he not realized that it was an immortal male he'd plunged his blade into? An extra twist of the wrist, a slice across the neck, and the entire problem of River and his quint would have been resolved before it started.

Owalin's jaw tightened. Yes, the presence of the *new* king of Slait and his quint at the Academy put a new spin on the situation together. Owalin needed his humans broken, not bloody dead.

"Can you tear this *privacy screen* down?" Owalin asked Krum. "Let's see how much the humans think of their tamed fae when we tear their creation to shreds."

Krum frowned at the spheres in his hand. "Certainly. The visual effect will be closer to melting than tearing, but yes, I believe I can dissolve it."

"How long will it take?" asked Owalin.

"Thirty minutes, give or take."

Owalin grunted unhappily. "That's longer than I'd like."

"I may know something of help." Han's pain-filled voice tugged at the hem of Owalin's cloak, as if in eerie answer. "Something that might be better than tearing down the shield."

Twisting on his heels, Owalin stalked over to where Han was strung up to hang off a ceiling beam, the rope forcing him up on his toes. The dark-haired warrior, usually too slick for his own good, was pasty and limp with pain, his pale eyes glazed. Owalin might be forgiven for not noticing a detail in the heat of the moment, but identifying any fae on Academy grounds had been Han's specific assignment. One he'd failed spectacularly, as his raw back now made clear to everyone in the Great Hall.

"Speak," Owalin allowed.

"Thank you." Han swallowed, jerking his chin to the far left corner of the hall, where the last of the straggling hostages had been hauled, the irrelevant ones cowering in the back. "The last girl you brought in, the one we found hiding in the broom closet—her name is Arisha of Tallie. She roomed with Leralynn—the female who set the arena ablaze and who appears to be River's mate. She might be of use."

"Thank you, Han," Owalin said, marking how the punished male flinched even at the polite words. A few more hours hanging by his arms, and he'd let him down. Han's negligence at having failed to identify the fae on Academy grounds called for punishment, but there was a fine line between instilling fear and repentance and seeding resentment. That Han was actively trying to return to Owalin's good graces was a promising sign. As was the information. This Arisha might know more than she realized.

"Bring her to me," Owalin ordered two of his males, pointing them toward a slightly chubby girl in the most hideous dress he'd ever laid eyes on. The ugly little sunflower made a feeble attempt to fight off the immortals, but settled down easily beneath a casual slap. By the time the males deposited the trembling creature at Owalin's feet, she was as docile as a trembling mouse.

Squatting down to bring himself level with his prey, Owalin made his voice gentle. "It seems your day has become fortunate, Arisha of Tallie. Do you know why?"

The sunflower shook her frizzy brown head so violently, her glasses nearly fell to the floor.

Owalin smiled. "Because you get to tell me all about Leralynn—and in doing so, ensure that we can all finish this business in a way that no one else gets hurt."

The sunflower glared at him through her skewed glasses.

"Leralynn is the one who set an arena full of people ablaze," he continued. "Don't you think it wise to halt her antics before more innocents get hurt? I, for one, think the humans' safety needs to take priority over all else."

"Crows take your eyes." The words rang clearly enough through her shaking voice, though their power deflated quickly as one of the guards raised a hand to administer correction.

Owalin halted the guard, regarding the girl from above. "You seem like a loyal friend to Leralynn. Is that right? A *very* loyal friend."

The girl frowned, plainly trying to work through the trap in the question—never realizing that her hesitation had already given Owalin all the information he needed.

12

Lera

"Deep, easy breaths, cub," Shade says, guiding my magic alongside his across the shimmering screen of darkness.

He and River rigged it to keep the Night Guard from observing the mobilization of the newly formed human army, nearly a hundred strong. They cross the courtyard in neat rows behind us, royal athletes and trained cadets shoulder to shoulder with footmen, strong male and female guards, and even the gray-haired mathematics professor, all armed with whatever weapons they could lay their hands on. Many of them watch the towering wall of earth with wide eyes, mouths open in astonishment, reminding me of the first time I saw River wield his earth magic. Breathless tension fills the silent air, so thick you could cut it with a knife.

The screen is a risk—possibly a flat-out provocation—but River is gambling that Owalin won't be quick to take new lives with the kings' allegiance still hanging in the balance, and the element of surprise the shield grants is apparently vital for a successful assault. As for the plan itself, it is as simple to understand as it's difficult to execute.

A surprise entry made from the balcony, with the males' shields taking the first volley of arrows from the Night Guard archers and drawing Owalin's forces toward the mezzanine. A minute after that, a second, larger force will enter through the side doors of the Great Hall, half of them keeping the Guard at bay while the other half focuses on getting the hostages out. River, meanwhile, will seek and take down Owalin. The importance of that last part all the rulers agreed on—a male like Owalin likely holds all the reins himself. Take out the driver, and the team of horses will scatter. Or, at least, stop.

Inhaling as Shade instructed, I savor the calming lungful of his earthy scent. The screen the males concocted is actually made up of bits of sand and dirt, held together by Shade's silver magic that slides about like honey to keep everything in place. The healer makes the shifting magic look easy, but I know it will take all I have in me to replicate the smoothness.

"Pull the magic, don't push it," says Shade. "And don't focus on the whole thing at once, just concentrate on any holes that start to show."

"I know. You've said it five times." I try and fail to sound annoyed —though Coal, stepping up beside us, has no such difficulties.

"She'll be fine," the warrior snaps, forbidding as usual in his head-to-toe black, his hand wrapped tightly around a sword hilt as he surveys the columns of brave mortals. "And unless you get your ass into position, Shade, the rest of us are going without you."

When River first outlined the assault plan, my hackles had risen at the notion of staying behind to keep the screen powered while the males entered with the mortals, but the indignation settled quickly. One look at the males' faces made it clear that they'd fight any suggestion of me joining the battle and—more importantly—would be incapable of keeping their wits about them on the mission if their pregnant mate was alongside. And even if there was a chance in hell we could have gotten past that, the fact remained that *someone* had to stay behind to keep the screen up, and the males were still the better swordsmen.

And less likely to lose control of their magic and accidentally bring the keep down on everyone's head.

"The threat would carry more weight if the *rest of you* weren't all here as well," I say, pointing behind Coal to where River and Tye are feigning invisibility, their faces tight. For all the battles we've gone into together—for all the battles the four of them have had over the centuries—this one feels different. As if the stakes are so much higher.

I swallow, forcing a smile for the males. My chest is tight, my heart a thin beat against my ribs. Clearing my throat, I stick my hands into my pockets, lest the males catch the slight tremble at the tips of my fingers. Shade takes complete control of the thick, wavering wall before us without a blink.

Stepping forward, River takes my face in his warm callused palms. "We've done this before, Leralynn. But we will be careful, I promise you that."

"I know you have." I nod quickly at him. "I'm just worried you'll enjoy yourselves so much, you'll forget I'm out here."

"Verra good point." Taking my hips in his wide hands, Tye spins me away from River. "I'm easily distracted. Better give me something to remember you by." Before I can say a word, he lifts me easily to cover my mouth with a thoroughly pillaging kiss that sends a jolt of melting arousal through my core, making me want to purr against his mouth.

I'm still savoring the male's dizzying pine-and-citrus taste when a knife whizzes by Tye's ear to impale the ground behind us. I jerk in Tye's arms, but he holds me closer still as if to make a point before pulling away leisurely and raising a brow at Coal.

Walking past Tye and me, Coal retrieves his knife from the ground and sheathes it inside his boot. "Let's go. I want to kill something."

"Evidently." Tye touches a small cut on his ear, and my eyes widen at the realization that Coal marred more than just the damp ground. Setting me down, Tye traces my chin with his finger, his red hair glowing like fire under the lowering sun. "You did it, Leralynn. The mortals are ready to make entry with us. Together."

"They're ready to make bloody entry *without* us," Coal growls.

Tye rolls his eyes, and—stealing one more quick kiss—follows River toward where the teams of human warriors are shifting on their feet.

"Keep the shield up, mortal," Coal says, our eyes locking. The brilliant blue hue in the male's gaze flickers for a moment, the purple specks there promising he will fight to keep our quint safe. As much of a leave-taking as Coal can manage.

"Don't show off too much," I tell him roughly. The male snorts before turning to stride to position.

Turning to Shade, whose attention has been on keeping the screen powered through my good-byes, I put my hand on the healer's forearm. "I'm ready."

"I know you are, cub," he says, the magic he's been holding sliding over to settle around me like a cloak.

I gasp in surprise, and Shade brushes a light touch over my back, a soft, soothing motion that I dare not let distract me from the task. "Count to one hundred," he says as my power fills the dark shield. "That is all the time we need to get into position. Then save your magic."

"Easy." I force a smile. "I've counted to a hundred dozens of times."

"I love you, cub." His voice is husky behind me, his damp earthy scent comforting the jagged edges of my mind. "And I will see you soon. I promise."

I nod, not daring to turn to watch Shade lope off to join the others as I focus all my attention on feeding my magic into the shifting screen, the inferno of the burning arena all too vivid in my mind.

Despite how easy Shade made it look, the screen grows heavier with each heartbeat, as if I'm holding up a bucket of water. No, not just a bucket—a bucket full of living liquid that constantly shifts left and right in an attempt to slosh right out of my grasp. It rises into the sky so high, it almost seems to bear down on me, a thick, shifting curtain of debris. Rocks and dirt collide with small clacks inside it. My body is so tight, the muscles of my core shake with effort, my immortal senses barely aware of the receding footsteps announcing the others' departure. How can something that looks so effortless be so bloody difficult?

I draw a deep breath, imagining myself in a sparring match with Coal, reminding my body to pace itself while my arms cramp with effort. I don't bother to count since I've no intention of taking down the screen while there is any strength left in me. Shade may have said they'd only need a hundred to get into position, but I've listened to enough of River's battle plans to know that is the best-case scenario. If I can't be with the males in battle, I will sure as hell give them every possible advantage to come out safely. And victorious.

My thoughts are still on the ache in my arms and core, the strain of keeping my power even and steady making it impossible to know whether I've been at it a minute or an hour, when I feel something ripple through the magic screen.

I blink, the sweat dripping into my eyes, making them sting.

The tug comes again, this time so harsh and deliberate that I'm certain it's coming from the shield itself rather than some phantom pulse of my own fatigue. I frown, my offended magic lashing back at the intrusion—

And feel it ricochet right back at me. My breath stops, my body tensing as tiny little claws grip the magic cords I've been twining through the screen.

"It's called a mirror weave, Leralynn," a deep voice says. A male voice that seems to travel through the cords of magic itself echoes inside my core. Inside my magic. Not Owalin—someone else.

Tearing my eyes from the dark screen, I turn to check whether anyone else hears the words, but the two guards standing closest to me seem oblivious. My gut tightens, but I at least mark that the males and the assault units they were leading are well clear of the courtyard the shield conceals.

And whatever this is—whoever this is—I want no part of it.

Stepping away from the screen, I let my hold on it drop altogether, pulling my magic back inside me.

The little claws hold fast, keeping the screen and my magic in place. "Relax, little one. I only want to speak with you," the voice inside me says.

"Who are you?" I ask, feeling absurd as I speak to the air, one of the guards turning to give me a quizzical look.

"I can see your lips moving, but I fear I cannot hear a word you say, my dear," the voice tells me. "Fortunately, that is of little consequence. You need not talk to me. You simply need to listen. Nod your head if you understand."

I keep still.

The claws holding my magic dig in and yank, the pain spreading through my insides like a thousand exploding needles.

Stars. The pups. I nod quickly, breathing a sigh of relief when no repeat demonstration comes.

"Very good. Now then, it seems that I have something you might want. And I am more than happy to give it to you—all you need to do is come and get it." The magic gripping my core starts burning again, the strands taking shape into an image I see not with my eyes but with my body itself. A figure, kneeling on the floor. A knife above her. A horrid ugly dress spilling around her knees.

Arisha. The bastards have Arisha. The magic image releases and I stumble back, able to stay on my feet only because of the stranger's grip. "I am more than happy to trade you for her. Please make your way to the back of the keep and I will ensure you enter unharassed."

The magic's grip disappears, leaving me on my knees, the dark shield I'd been holding now staying up by the power of the Night Guard male. Keeping anyone inside the Great Hall from seeing my movements as I start toward the keep.

13

River

On the roof of the keep, River stopped at the edge of the rough stone parapet, the Academy and Great Falls spreading away before him, brushed in dusty pink under the lowering sun. Turning, he surveyed the warriors a final time. A hundred faces looked back at him, scents ranging from excitement to desperation, from steel to sweat. He didn't envy the mortals who had loved ones inside, who'd be fighting two battles at once—one with their swords and the other with their hearts. It was only the stars' fortune that Leralynn was not beside him now. That she was safe.

Putting his hands behind his back, River made his movements slow as he turned back toward the wall—and the Great Hall below. Slow was smooth, and smooth was fast. Battle was about being slow quickly, and the few extra moments it took to instill that in the ragtag mortal army before him were worth the time.

The Great Hall's layout was as much a boon to Owalin's position as a liability. On one hand, five doors leading inside—including the main entrance and the various servants' passages—provided five points of entry for the hostage takers to guard. On the other hand, each of those entry points was a killing funnel, allowing one or two of Owalin's warriors to stanch a whole flow of River's fighters streaming through.

Which was why the initial force would make entry through the wide balcony, rappelling down from the roof on ropes Coal and Tye had snuck in and set up earlier. It made River slightly unsettled to be taking untested humans through a difficult entry. He needed them here—especially since he intended to extricate himself from the fighting on the mezzanine in favor of hunting down Owalin.

Hoping the rappel would leave no broken necks, River started to raise his hand to give the entry signal when his gaze landed on a pretty girl who was supposed to be elsewhere.

Swallowing a curse, he beckoned to Katita, the girl still limping as she came over. She wore her gray cadet uniform now, her blonde hair pulled back into a high bun for battle. "Your Highness—"

"If the next words out of your mouth have anything to do with sending me back to herd the onlookers, you might as well save your breath for the fighting, sir. I'm a trained warrior, more experienced than many of the men here." Katita crossed her arms over her chest and studied the structure.

Brilliant. Getting the one person who was able to make humans see reason killed off was going to be a great start to the venture. "There is no need to address me as sir, Your Highness," River said politely. "And there is likewise little need for your aid here. Keeping the masses contained may not sound glorious, but I assure you that it is paramount. It's where we need you most, and not because I don't trust you with a blade."

Katita turned toward him, lifting her face, the emotions there hidden well enough for a human to miss—but plain enough for River, who'd spent centuries in court, hiding his own. Desperation. Fear. Bravery. A need to protect what was hers. "I chose my form of address for a reason. As you made clear with your mate, there can be only one commander on a battlefield, and I yield that flag to you. If you are ordering me to go to the courtyard, I will obey. But is that truly the message you want to send to my people after all the trouble Leralynn went through to grant them ownership of the problem?"

River's brow tightened, and he let himself rub his hands over his face. "Fine. But stay with Coal," he said finally, turning back to give the go signal before any more news came his way.

THE ROPES SLID EASILY beneath River's gloves as he rappelled down at

Tye's side, Coal, Shade, and a dozen of the humans sliding in just behind them.

"Now," River said softly. He and Tye released the rope despite being several feet from the ground. Tye's hands rose with shimmering magic before they landed, heating the air, still damp with recent rain. By the time River's boots landed on the balcony, a thick cloud of fog concealing him and the others, his heart was beating with steady hard beats that sharpened all his senses.

The light *tap tap tap* of others landing safely behind him made River nod in approval, though no one could see him—which didn't mean the Night Guard archers would not loose their arrows, just that they'd not be able to aim. Would not know just how many of them were here to cause trouble.

As if in answer to his thoughts, the tip of a nocked arrow shimmered with reflected light.

"Shields!" River snapped, his own magic reacting on instinct. A moment later, the *clank clank clank* of shafts falling harmlessly to the stone mirrored the soft taps of warriors' feet landing behind River's wide back. The second dozen fighters had made it down the ropes, then. Good.

"Bows!" River ordered, the bowmen stepping forward out of the fog to take aim at the Night Guard below. Unlike Owalin's archers, who were firing horizontally over the mezzanine, River's people had the advantage of shooting downward. "Aim." He held his breath, giving the humans an extra second to acquire their targets before dropping the shield. "Loose."

The bowstrings loosened, the arrows whistling as they cut the air.

In the Great Hall below, Owalin shouted orders dispatching forces to the mezzanine, the magic shield around him keeping him safe from the fired arrows.

"Remind me to compliment Owalin for that bellowing voice of his," River murmured to Coal, the dark warrior unsheathing one of the swords strapped across his back. If the humans counted correctly, they'd be making entry thirty heartbeats from now, while most of the Guard were distracted with the mezzanine assault.

Heart beating a steady rhythm, River pulled out his own sword in time to meet an overhead strike from a newly arrived dark-haired male whose eyes burned with murder.

Steel met steel in a resounding ring that sent welcome vibrations through River's bones. *Stars,* he'd missed this. The feel of the blade in his hand, the way battle made every one of his senses alive and hungry.

Twenty seconds, then he'd have to go.

The lingering ache inside his chest faded to a distant, irrelevant throb as the scent of *now* filled his lungs. Kicking the male away, River grabbed the next assailant, using him as a shield against a straw-thin fae warrior whose eyes widened as he realized he'd sunk his blade into his own comrade.

Ten seconds.

Sensing the fight, magic inside River roared for the freedom it had been denied so very long, kicking him like a crazed stallion determined to escape the stall. Tightening his jaw, River gave the magic no leave as he peered over the rail to survey the Great Hall below.

The place swarmed with predictable chaos, cowering hostages and scrambling Guardsmen. Owalin was in the corner now, an oblique magical shield around him preventing archers from landing a shot.

"River," Coal called behind him. "Three, two, go."

River vaulted over the mezzanine rail just as the second contingent of his mortal forces rammed down a side door and streamed inside. Absorbing the landing, River rose into a defensive crouch, the sounds of the melee rising around him in a familiar cadence. Clash of swords. Grunts of fighters. Screams of the wounded. The latter were intense but surprisingly few for the numbers involved.

Out of the corner of his eye, River marked Coal engaging several of Owalin's minions together, the blond warrior's sword moving with a lazy precision as it sliced the air, reminding the world of why their quint was feared throughout Lunos.

On River's other side, Katita was leading another assault—the warriors with her doing their best to put themselves between the princess and her attackers.

It was going well.

It was going too well. River blinked as one of the Night Guard warriors twisted in the air to avoid harming a hostage instead of running the young princess through, while another of Owalin's warriors actually pushed a confused noble out of the way with an admonishment to stay the hell down. River's heart started to speed. If Owalin gave orders to protect the hostages, it meant he was certain he'd still need them after this assault.

Owalin was certain he'd win.

Cursing under his breath, River forged his way toward where he'd last seen Owalin, the bloodred cloak of the Night Guard leader like a beacon amidst the fog. He had to take out Owalin. Whatever was truly happening—and something was—it would not stop until River had the Night Guard leader's surrender—or his head.

River carved his way forward, clashing blades only enough to throw the others from his path. Closer. Closer. River's heart pounded against his ribs, the sounds around him dulling as he approached his prey. Now he could see the tall body rising above the rest, his back turned to River. Another two steps and Owalin would be within sword's reach. River could already see the face beneath the deep cowl, sharp and— pleased? One step.

"River." His name, said with a sharp desperate inhale, came from a voice so familiar that it stopped his heart. Froze him so completely that someone's sword managed to leave a long gash along his shoulder before he was even aware of the attack. Because suddenly, the attack, the hostages, the battle, all stopped mattering.

Because there, in the middle of the ring River had just penetrated to get to Owalin, stood not only the leader of the Night Guard, but also Leralynn herself.

14

River

River's world stopped. Leralynn stood weaponless, her beautiful face fallen, her shoulders hunched in apology.

"I'm sorry," she said, her voice shaking. "They had Arisha. I couldn't leave her. Not her."

Cold fear wrapped itself around River's soul, the noose tightening with each heartbeat. His sword arm fell to his side, his fingers still gripping the steel but no longer willing to move. Afraid to make any motion that might threaten the female standing so, so close to the self-satisfied Owalin. The latter's hood was off now, his long white hair and blue eyes gleaming under the light of the remaining chandeliers.

"And did I do as Krum promised you?" Owalin asked Lera. "Did I let the little sunflower go when you came in?"

Leralynn nodded, looking up at River with large pleading eyes, beautiful chocolate eyes he was planning to drown in for the rest of his life. Though dressed in her soft fighting leathers, the girl looked anything but ready for battle, her arms hugging her chest, her thick auburn braid mussed as if she'd been in a struggle. "River, I had to," she whispered. "Please understand. Please forgive me."

"There is nothing to forgive," said River, though his voice clearly named the words a lie. "We'll work something out."

"Of course we will," said Owalin, a genuine smile spreading across his artfully sculpted face. "It is all about finding a solution that fulfills everyone's true desires, isn't it? You, for example—as much as you want to lead these humans into needless slaughter, you want to keep this little female out of said slaughter just a bit more. Isn't that right? Because we can work with that. We can make it happen just as you wish."

Bile rose up River's throat. Around him, the sounds of battle continued in a distant, dull sort of way, the fighters closest to him and Owalin slowly catching on to the change in atmosphere. "What would you have me do?" River asked.

"Start by telling everyone to stand down." Owalin gestured to the ongoing battle. "Provided you have some measure of control to make that happen."

River's jaw clenched.

"No, don't do anything he says," Leralynn said, taking a step toward him—only to have Owalin's arm block her path easily. Weaponless. Leralynn was utterly weaponless, even her boot knife having been confiscated. *Bloody stars.*

River's eyes locked on where the bastard was touching his mate, the magic inside him roaring hard enough to take down the entire keep. Tamping the power down with all his might, he sent a thin pulse of magic whispering through the stone, down into the earth beneath the keep itself. The ground shook, the fine tremor enough to get everyone's attention without collapsing the structure.

Beside Owalin and Lera, a silver-haired fae toying with a pair of spheres raised an appreciative brow as the keep quieted in confusion, the occasional groans of wounded warriors and the clash of rogue swords the only sounds to be heard.

"There has been a change of plans." River raised his voice to fill the Great Hall, though his eyes could not bear to leave Lera, who now had Owalin's arm around her. The girl's own arms had moved down to cross her midsection, her hands buried in the fabric of her coat as if she might use the cloth to hide herself from the dark reality. River forced himself to straighten. "Owalin and I have decided to come to a more peaceful resolution to the conflict. Put down your weapons."

"Excellent," said Owalin.

"Coward!" Katita's voice rang out over the room as she limped forward. "I took you for many things, River, but a coward was not one of them. To think you would fold beneath—"

"He has my mate!" River roared, spinning to the princess. "My mate who is carrying pups. I will protect them over your kingdom. Over the world. Over anything."

Blood drained from Katita's face, Owalin's laugh in the background salting the wound. "I'm glad you and I are of the same mind," he told River. "Now then, let us have you set the right example for the mortals here. Clerk! Draw up a contract granting me the right to the throne of Slait."

"No," River breathed, twisting back toward Owalin.

"Don't worry," the male said, striding toward where a trembling clerk was already pulling a sheet of parchment from a pile. "You will still rule Slait in my absence. I am not about to take you—or anyone else—from the throne. You will simply answer to me on matters of coordination. Most importantly, you will have your mate back. Unless —" Owalin spun around so quickly to put a knife against Leralynn's belly that River's vision blurred. "Unless you don't care for her as much as I thought?"

"Draft the documents, Owalin." The words on River's tongue were the hardest he'd ever uttered. "But I want my mate back before the ink touches the parchment."

"No!" The yell came from Katita, echoed by voice after voice. By everyone except the males of River's quint, whom he could feel around him, just as frantic as he was. River ignored them all.

"We'll do it at the same time," Owalin offered, smiling when River stepped back with a bow, allowing Owalin to turn his attention to the writing desk along the nearest wall.

And turn his back to Leralynn.

Hands flashing, the girl drew something from her pocket with speed to rival a striking adder. Too fast for a single Night Guard to even shout in warning. River's throat closed, his heart racing. One minute, her hands were crossed protectively over her midsection, and the next—the next, they were clasping something around Owalin's long neck.

The broken pieces of Leralynn's old amulet, longing to be whole again, clanked together in a blinding flash of flickering light.

The air around Owalin shimmered, the male screaming as his hands went to his throat. A sizzling sound of burning skin mixed with the sudden scent of sulfur filling the air.

River blinked, his vision taking a moment to recover. By the time he could see again, Owalin was twisting around in a confused circle, like a dog who didn't know which way to run.

"Where—" Owalin's words broke as he clawed at his neck where the broken bits of Lera's amulet were still melding into his skin, the pattern as deranged as the look in his eyes. Owalin whimpered, the pitiful sound turning to the crazed shouting of a broken-minded man a moment later. "Who are you? What's going on?" he demanded of everyone and no one, sinking to his knees when no answer came, his red cloak pooling about him like blood. "Where's my horse? Who took my horse?"

15

Lera

Pop. Pop. Pop.

In mere moments, almost all the Night Guard have shifted into their winged forms, taking screeching flight through the open mezzanine doors. They may be evil, but they're far from stupid. Without Owalin, they're mere foot soldiers in a hall of kings.

Some circle overhead as if indecisive, almost majestic in the warm light, their burnished-gold, black, and tan feathers catching the brilliance of the setting sun.

But a volley of arrows from some of the human warriors below has them swiftly rethinking.

"Didn't Gavriel warn you off playing with broken magical artifacts, lass?" Tye says, swaggering up to me through the bewildered crowd, while River braces his hands on his thighs, his breath heavy. My own breathing is little better, the wave of relief washing over me intense enough to make me sway on my feet. Tye's pine-and-citrus scent wraps around me a moment before his arms do, the male pulling me against his chest with a desperation that betrays his lingering tension. "By the looks of it, Owalin's memories of his own self have been destroyed entirely—he may never recover now."

A few paces away from us, Coal already has the babbling Owalin in his steel grip, bare muscled arms bulging as he lifts him to his feet. Over the male's silver-blond head, Coal gives me a look of such desperate fury—mixed with heart-stopping tenderness—that I know I'm in for some sort of reckoning with him later. Shade bends over several of the injured, his silver magic flashing while Katita quietly orders her forces to secure the premises in case any Night Guard decide to circle back.

It's over. Almost over. I turn my face to River, meeting his haunted gray gaze. "Are you all right?" I ask.

"I don't know whether I want to kiss or kill you right now," River whispers, running both hands through his hair so it stands up in dark spikes. "Do you have any notion how terrifying that was?"

"A fair good one," I say blearily, Tye's hands wide and comforting around my middle. With the adrenaline faded, all I can feel is the exhaustion left behind, pulling at my body and words. "When did you figure out what I was doing?"

"I didn't." River rubs his face. "I didn't know what the hell you were doing until you did it—but I trusted you had something in mind. I trusted you." He straightens, the force of his attention on me blocking out the slowly growing buzz of the Great Hall letting out its breath. In the corner of my vision, I see the doors flinging open, loved ones streaming into each other's arms—Katita apparently having decided that the Night Guard threat is really, truly finished. Weeping and shouts of joy collide against the Great Hall's high-raftered ceiling, making my tired heart lift.

I know that River and Tye and I should go help, talk to the most traumatized hostages, organize food and beds and medical supplies, but I can't bring myself to move. No matter what River says about having trusted that I had a plan early on, the terror I saw in his eyes when I stood beside Owalin was real enough to hurt us both. To hurt still.

River holds out his arms toward me, the motion as vulnerable and desperate as the gulps of air I still pull too quickly into my lungs. Tye releases me with a gentle push, spotting me as I fling myself into River, my body savoring his woodsy scent on the heels of the bloody charade.

When I lift my face to him, River presses his mouth over mine, his tongue sweeping in with a single conjuring stroke that shatters all inhibitions. Twisting my hands through his hair, I push the male back until I have the king of Slait pinned against a marble pillar, his body willingly surrendering everything to the bond between us.

Somewhere beyond the moment, someone whistles, applause filling the scorching air. I don't blush. I don't care. Not about the blubbering Owalin, or the escaped Night Guard, or the entirety of the immortal realms.

"Not that I'm not enjoying the show," Tye drawls, interrupting the kiss just as River's fingers start slipping into my waistband, "but is the rat with the spinning balls anyone of importance?"

"That's Krum." I pull my head back only enough to mutter the words. "Owalin's wardsmith. Why?"

"Because he is currently making his way out the back door," Tye supplies.

"So go fetch him," River says, his lips already returning to mine. "I'm busy."

~

"You've been busy." Taking the chair opposite Krum, River lays his forearms on the table and cocks his head as if he had all the time in the world for this conversation. And to be fair, he is immortal, so there is that.

Around the elegantly appointed suite, which was Sage's receiving room only a day earlier, the other males of my quint as well as Arisha, Gavriel, Katita, and the mortal kings all listen in attentive silence. The humans' faces run the full range of emotions, from Arisha and Gavriel's morbid curiosity, to Katita's fury, to utter fear and confusion—the latter especially prevalent on guests from kingdoms on the other side of the continent, who've never been close enough to Mystwood and Lunos to give the immortal realm much thought.

"I've never been one to idle, true." Krum tries to open his palms in an irreverent gesture, but the chains Thad forged to shackle the fae wardsmith will not allow the motion. With his silver-gray hair swept back and easy, smiling eyes, he still makes more than enough impact. "There is little more enticing to a magic scholar than working with ancient wards."

"Then we have fortunate news," I say, crossing my thighs and smiling at him. With River, Krum, and I the only ones sitting at the interrogation table, I feel like a fish fluttering about a glass bowl for others' entertainment, but River insisted I sit beside him. "You now get the pleasure of closing the wards back up."

Krum gives me a condescending look, an impressive feat for a shackled male with a split lip. "That can't be done."

My stomach tightens, an uncomfortable shiver running across my skin. Somehow, I believe him. This, the wards, was the entire reason for our coming here. For all that we went through in the mortal world. To hear that it can't be done...

River's hand flattens on the table's wooden surface. "I little like what I'm hearing, Krum." His words, while quiet, ring with enough menace to flay open a soul. "You are the one who wedged the wards open."

"I meant what I said, Your Majesty." Krum shrugs, nary a flicker in his pale eyes. "Your displeasure can certainly rearrange my face and bones—but it will do nothing for the wards." He purses his lips, regarding River and me as if we're a pair of slow-witted students he has no time to school. "Oh, stars take me. The only reason I was able to drive a wedge into the wards is because they were cracking already."

"We are aware of the crack," River says. "Fixing it is the reason we came to the mortal realm to begin with."

Krum laughs. "*Fixing* it? You swaggered from Lunos to the mortal realms thinking that you would, what, patch up ancient magic created in a time when any dozen fae warriors were more powerful than today's entire world of Lunos combined? How exactly were you planning on accomplishing this feat? A bit of putty, perhaps? A needle and thread?"

My jaw tightens. We needed to find the leak before we could assess how to close it, but saying as much out loud just now sounds more defensive than anything.

"I discovered the leak in the wards dozens of years ago," Krum continues. "It was how I convinced Owalin to bring the Night Guard here, to live in the mountain in wait for when the gap opens wide enough to be useful. Maybe back then, if you'd been smarter, if you'd studied and paid attention as I did, you might have been able to slow the ward's breaking. But now? Now there is nothing to be done."

"But *you* put in a wedge," I say, my mind jumping to the time when magic flickered in my blood for a moment before disappearing again. "You can take it out. You've done it before."

"I am happy to encourage it." Coal takes a step forward, the carved angles of his face so deadly, even I want to shrink away.

"Wallop away," Krum tells the warrior impassively before turning back to me. "A test, yes. I've run several of them during the decades. But did you wonder why it was so very short? Did you ask yourself why, if I was going to test something as important as the return of magic, I didn't let it stay open for several hours? Enough to perhaps give Owalin and his warriors a chance to exercise the power held in shackles for so long?"

"He didn't dare hold it open longer lest the flow of magic shattered the gateway completely," Arisha says quietly, her face coloring when the entire attention of the room shifts to her. Eyes widening, she tries to step back—only to hit Tye's large body instead. The male puts both hands on her shoulders, squeezing lightly.

"Go on and tell them, braids," he mutters into her ear.

The girl swallows. "He knew that once the magic started flowing fully, he could no longer stanch the flow. And he didn't want to release the dam until Owalin's warriors were ready—especially since they knew there were other fae somewhere in the vicinity."

"Ah, so you do have a thinking being among you," says Krum, nodding to Arisha respectfully—before swinging a gaze that is anything but to River. "But no need to take our word for it. Wait until Lunos sends *experts*. It little matters. The truth is the truth: there will soon be no mortal realm, and the humans can return to their rightful place as servants to the higher beings."

Silence grips the room in an icy wave that seems to freeze everyone in place. My own blood chills with Krum's words and with Arisha's fallen face that tells me she believes the male. That everything we sacrificed to come here was for nothing. Even River's face is a frozen mask, the sparks of failure dancing in his gray eyes twisting my gut.

"We need to raise an army," King Zenith of Ckridel says finally, his words hitching as he shatters the silence. A murmur of slow concern echoes from the other monarchs in the back of the room. "There might be no stopping magic from coming into our world, but we can stop the magic wielders who bring it."

"No," I whisper, softly at first, then with force. "No. Whatever the answer is to this, it isn't war."

"She's right." Stepping forward, Katita stands beside the table with River and me, regal and polished once more in a simple forest-green gown, her golden hair gathered in a nest on top of her head. "We don't need to build an army. We need to build an alliance. This Academy was built to bind together the children of the powerful continental families, and it has worked. And this year…this year, we've been fortunate. Because we had yet another family join us. A deputy headmaster. An instructor. A healer. A student. And even that rogue over there, who should by all rights have been banned from the Prowess trials." She jerks her head toward Tye, the small quirk at the corner of her mouth taking the sting out of her words.

"When we were going to lie down and surrender, it was Leralynn who reminded us that the power lies in our own hands. Our unions. Our alliances." She turns to Arisha. "Now that the wards are open, how quickly will the magic spread throughout the continent?"

Arisha bites the end of her braid, her blue eyes glazing in calculation. "It's hard to say," she mutters, "but given that it took decades to spread from the rip on the mountain to the Academy, I would imagine it will be years until it creeps through the Ckridel kingdom. Decades before it covers the continent. But it will."

Katita nods, turning back to her father. "Then I propose we open the Academy immediately to our friends in Lunos. If King River would agree, let us invite faculty and students from Slait to join us here, to learn and grow together." The princess turns slowly, until it is me she speaks to alone, our whole complex history laid out clearly on her face —competition, rancor, partnership, and finally, respect. "Maybe, if we do this right, if the Academy becomes a place of learning known throughout both our realms… Then when your children come of age, you will want them to come study here. To spar and learn and fight and discover truths with the royals of our world. With the children I will one day bear."

I only realize I'm on my feet when my arms are wrapping around Katita. After a moment, she pulls me against her. "Thank you for coming here, Lera," she whispers softly for my ears alone. "Thank you for protecting my world."

16

Lera

"*D*o you need help, lass?" Tye asks, climbing through the window of my bedchamber to land with a flourish on a small open spot in the middle of the floor—a feat made more impressive by the clothes and bags spread on every other surface. Minion, testing each item of clothing for rip-worthiness against his claws, arches his tiny back and hisses at the guest.

Arisha rolls her eyes. "You've been able to use the door for months now. Do you just enjoy making this seem…illegitimate?"

"Yes, of course." Tye blinks in surprise at the question, his messy red hair and sparkling grin making the image irresistible—and he knows it. "Why wouldn't I enjoy it?" After picking his way across the room, he grasps my hips and lifts me up for a thorough kiss that sends tendrils of warmth all over my skin, the little prickles of fire heading right down to—

I smack him, wriggling down to the floor as I close my thighs quickly.

That wasn't my own heat tickling my sex—that was the bastard sending tiny sparks of literal fire sneaking toward my apex. Right in the middle of my packing. With Arisha watching. Thanking the stars that Arisha's mortal nose lacks the ability to scent just how quickly my body

273

roused to Tye's intentions, I give the male the best glower I can summon while pressing my legs together.

Arisha snorts. Clearly, what my friend lacks in smell, she makes up for in eyesight—my heating face clueing her in to exactly what instincts are pulsing about. Gathering the remaining shreds of my dignity, I brush down my light blue gown, which arrived in a chest of at least a dozen others in River's sister Autumn's luggage three weeks ago.

Once Katita's plan was affirmed by the other rulers, the choice for the initial cadre to the Academy turned out to be the simplest one to be made yet. Retrieving the Mystwood key the Night Guard once used from their mountain lair, Shade shifted to wolf form to deliver the news to Lunos. A week later, he returned with Autumn and her mate, Kora, along with Kora's quint, to take on the Academy billets for the coming semester.

With her brilliant mind, Autumn will make an incredible deputy headmistress to the Academy, taking the place River was now vacating. As for physical training, anyone who thought trading Coal for Kora would bring about a more pleasant experience in the sparring ring was going to enjoy a shock. Although River decided against sending fae students to the Academy this year, we both hope to identify a handful of candidates to start the following semester.

"Any word on the new headmaster?" I ask Tye. "I imagine Sage will no longer be gracing these halls with his brave leadership."

Tye picks the hissing Minion up by the scruff of his neck, the kitten clawing the air in indignation. One set of green eyes locks on another, and Tye lets loose a low feline growl of his own.

Minion goes limp and cute at once, licking his little nose piously with a pink tongue.

"River is proposing Princess Katita for the post," Tye says, dropping the cat onto a pile of my lacy underwear. Of course. "Given that it's her vision, after all—which goes to show the importance of keeping your mouth shut, lest you get tagged with extra work."

"Katita?" I frown. "Isn't she a bit—well, young?"

"She'll have plenty of old arses around her to make things appropriately stuffy. With the Academy on Ckridel lands, the humans see it as fair, and she does have more experience driving immortals out of their minds than anyone else. She'll have things sorted out here quickly enough. Or not. It will be amusing either way."

Arisha makes a small choking sound, turning away quickly when Tye and I twist toward her.

"What are you hiding, braids?" Tye asks. "I don't think it's hair ribbons."

"Autumn asked Uncle Gavriel and me to stay in the Academy," Arisha mumbles.

"My condolences." Tye leans back on his heels, his hands going to his pockets. "Though I am not clear as to why you find that uncomfortable, given your odd sense of humor. Plus, weren't you always going to stay?"

"Not just as a student." Arisha cringes. "River's sister wants me to liaise between the fae faculty and human students. She thinks surviving sharing quarters with Lera counts as qualification. She'd not mentioned the Katita factor before I agreed."

Tye throws back his head to laugh. "Don't worry. I'll get you something to help."

"What's that?" I ask, frowning at the male.

"Wine, of course," Tye says seriously. "A great deal of wine."

"What are we doing here?" I ask, following River through the once-more regal Great Hall up to the mezzanine balcony where we danced on Ostera. As if in reminder of those times, the Academy bell strikes midnight, the sleeping grounds drawing a collective breath of cool night wind. Under the full moon, the balcony looks like something new altogether, vases of flowers and silk ribbons in the blue and gold of the Slait kingdom now filling the space.

Stepping up to the rail, I see the beautiful mortal world sprawled lazily for miles in every direction, the sheep fields once more free of soldiers' tents, the rolling hills disappearing into the darkness. Somewhere far away, the Great Falls waterfall cascades down through the silent night, an echo to the phantom violins that once played an intoxicating waltz.

"Saying goodbye to the place where we fell in love with you all over again," River says. The other males step out of the shadows to stand with us, their stunning moonlit faces stealing my breath.

"Isn't that what the farewell feast tomorrow is for?" I ask, curling my hands around the smooth banister, my voice light despite a lump forming in my throat. Deep inside my abdomen, a tiny body shifts and yawns. The twins are no more than three months along, but I feel them already.

"I wanted a night with just us here." River's hands brush my shoulders, sending ripples of warmth over my bare arms. "Us and our memories. Before our lives change forever." His palm slides gently over my midsection, my fingers closing over his.

"If you've not noticed, River, our lives have been changing forever every few months since the lass walked into them," Tye says, snatching me from River's arms.

Now that I look closer, I see the males are all dressed differently. Tye wears the red-and-gold colors of the Prowess team uniform, Shade the soft gray cashmere he wore as the Academy healer. River's tailored coat is as regal as all his clothing, but the garment he chose for tonight is the deep red one he wore the most during our time here. And Coal... Well...

He is in black fighting leathers, though his blond hair is loose to his shoulders. I grin. "I see that nothing so small as lost memories and freed magic can get you out of these."

"Oh, I imagine something that can," Tye murmurs loudly enough to make Coal glower. Tye flashes him an impertinent grin before tracing a thumb along my cheek. "Or someone. Unless you are shy now that you are with cubs?" The last is said with enough of a challenge to have me striding up to Coal to unbutton his leather jerkin one brass clasp at a time.

Click. Click. Click.

The male stands rock still as I slide the leather vest off him, the hardness building inside his breeches the only sign of my effect on him. The only outward sign, that is. Inside me, my magic wakes to Coal's rousing purple power, the two forces pulsating with the need to connect with their mate.

Swallowing, I brush my hand down Coal's muscled chest, resting my palm on the hard squares of his chiseled abdomen.

Coal shudders. "I don't want to hurt you," he whispers, his hands opening and closing at his sides without ever touching me. "When we... Things tend to break when we couple, mortal. A lot. I don't want to add you and the cubs to the list."

"Good thing we've three other males to keep us in line," I say. The male inhales sharply when my hand drops to his waistband. Lower. My heart quickens, my body already warming with a need that makes every details of the male's face stand out in sex-clenching clarity. The powerful square jaw. The sculpted muscles that shift like liquid silver in the moonlight. The musky metallic scent that makes my toes curl.

"One problem of toying with your food, lass," Tye says as his sensual drawl caresses my back, "is that you miss the predator behind you." The male's hands deftly undo the little hooks along my dress, the *click click click* an invitation for Shade and River to help ease the fabric off my shoulder until it spreads on the balcony floor like a pool of midnight. Until it is me who stands naked before the four males, the barely noticeable bump on my taut belly drawing the starlight to itself.

Dropping to his knees, River runs his lips across my abdomen, my sensitive skin caught between his heat and the chill of the night. When I opened my mouth to draw breath, Shade is there with a low growl, pressing his full lips over mine, his tongue stroking the inside of my mouth in deep possessive strokes that have heat spreading through my entire core.

Down lower, River pushes my thighs apart, the chill air brushing my open sex for a moment before his hot tongue slides between my folds. I gasp against Shade's lips.

And moan when Coal's warm mouth closes over my neck from behind, nipping lightly with his teeth. His callused hands knead my bare bottom, his fingers traveling dangerously close to my back opening. He thrusts his hips against me right as he bites my neck harder, the hard bulge against my flesh making me desperate beyond reason to be filled by it.

My eyes widen, my heart already gasping with the sensation coming at it. Twining my fingers in River's hair, I whimper against Shade's deepening kiss, which grows more primal and possessive with every stroke of the shifter's tongue—River's echoing licks down below trapping the storm growing inside me, making me buck. The male grips my hips and pulls me against him hungrily.

"Seems you need to learn to be cautious about the scraps you start," Coal says gravely into my ear, the amusement peeking from beneath the stern tone doing nothing to soothe my racing pulse, my body lifting desperately on its toes as River flicks his tongue right over my aching bud.

17

Lera

I scream into the night, moisture slithering down my naked thighs as the tip of River's tongue traces the hood around my swollen bud with quick *lap lap laps* that send jolts of sensation zinging through all my nerves. That would have me falling flat on my face if Coal and Tye weren't now bracing my shoulders, Shade nipping my lips gently before pressing a string of kisses along my jaw.

Down my exposed throat. Along my swollen, aching breasts.

Shade's tongue circles my nipple, the sensitive tissue already peaked and hard. When the male suckles on it, the slight ache of the pull shoots right to my apex. To where River teases me so so close to the looming release that my whole body shakes with the need of it, my sex, the backs of my thighs, my breaths, all trembling beneath the males' unyielding hold.

"I do like those sounds almost as much as I like the lilac taste of you, lass," Tye says with approval, now circling my other nipple with his tongue. "And I *truly* like where we have you just now."

"Bastard." The words come in pants, my body so aroused, I can barely breathe for the need.

"Oh, you've no idea," Tye says, rising to whisper into my ear. "I'm just gettin' started."

Pulling me away from the others, Tye frees himself in one practiced tug, the tip of moisture on his pulsing cock catching in the starlight. The thick shaft is so long and thick, it curves slightly, the velvety skin stretched with taut, mouthwatering deliciousness.

Hooking his hands under my slick thighs, Tye lifts me easily into the air—and lowers me right atop himself. The large head of his cock penetrates my channel with slick precision, Tye sheathing himself fully a moment later before pausing to let me adjust to the great size of him. Before… Before nodding over his shoulder.

The emerald gleam in the male's eyes is enough to send my heart racing, my channel gripping his cock as if that can help anything. I know it can't, not beneath the males' unyielding hands. And that somehow only feeds my need, whipping my throbbing sex to a new frenzy.

River's woodsy scent touches me before the male does, coming up from behind to lather his fingers in my moisture while Tye holds me impaled on his cock.

"I will be inside you soon, Leralynn," River promises, his hands now sliding to massage my backside, spreading it apart to the chill air and his slickened fingers. When he traces my rim, I clench it closed on instinct, despite longing for the feel of him there. For the feel of them all.

"That won't work, and you know it," River murmurs into my ear, his commanding voice as intoxicating as the feel of Tye's cock filling my channel.

I wriggle anyway, though there is nothing to be done.

Slowly, keeping me wrapped tightly around him, Tye lowers to his knees and then his back with me astride him, his eyes glinting mischievously in the moonlight. Before I can so much as adjust my knees on the cool balcony floor, I feel a firm hand on my back, pushing me forward until my nipples brush tantalizingly against Tye's hard chest.

With both hands now firmly on my bottom, River positions himself at my back hole. My heart races with anticipation, each beat echoing through my core. Through the magic that makes every touch a thousand times more exquisite. Intense. Unbearable.

Tye seizes my mouth, distracting me with his wicked tongue. I whimper against him. Draw a breath.

And that's when River pumps into me from behind.

I feel a burn as his cock stretches me wickedly, the pain morphing at once to hot liquid pleasure. To a glorious fullness that fills my backside and my magic and my soul. River's breath is warm and unsteady against my neck, his grunts of pleasure tickling my skin. Driving me mad.

For a moment, he stays there, letting me adjust. Then, as one, River and Tye start pumping in tandem. Slowly, sensually, filling my channels again and again with powerful thrusts that reverberate through my whole body. The heels of my hands dig into Tye's rock-hard shoulders, the double fullness of his cock filling my sex while River's claims my back hole stealing both my breath and my sense. Pleasure ripples through me in growing waves, the world swimming more and more with the powerful twin thrusts echoing through my core.

The heat of the males' bodies wraps like a cocoon around me, their two cocks pumping in intoxicating harmony.

Thrust, thrust. Thrust.

They move faster as my body adjusts. Harder. The wet sounds of slick skin striking full force echo through the night, the males' groans joining my breathless sounds in the night.

Thrust, thrust. Thrust.

The stars dancing in the sky meld with the ones waltzing before my eyes, my body a bouquet of sensation I can't keep up with. Heat. Fullness. Desire. A slow, unrelenting climb up to the parapet of the highest cliff I've seen yet.

Without warning, River pulls me off Tye and up to my knees, still buried deep inside me. I growl at the loss of Tye's pounding length, but River slides onto his back, leaving my pale breasts and belly—and sex—splayed wide open to the moonlight. Without hesitating, Coal kneels between my legs, his blond hair loose around his fiercely beautiful face, every ridge of his formidable body tightened with want. Purple specks already dance in his eyes.

My mouth waters at his long, thickly veined cock, twitching with his heartbeat.

He pauses at my opening, longing and uncertainty warring on his face.

"Trust me," I whisper. *You won't hurt them.*

With a groan, he plunges into me, his hard cock striking deep with a wet slap.

I scream and buck my hips, silently begging both males to move faster. Coal starts pumping hard, this new angle sending him deeper than ever before, filling me again and again. He tweaks my nipples with rough, callused fingers, shooting fire straight to my bud. River's powerful arms lift me along his hot length, my tight hole clutching and pulsing around him.

When I blink to find Shade and Tye standing naked, their hardness bathed in the moon's pale light, my mouth waters with a want so great that my plea comes out strangled and high.

The males answer my call at once, kneeling by my side, their dripping cocks moving toward me like two grand desserts, tempting me with a thousand promises.

My heart pauses as I grip the shafts, one in each hand, savoring their hard feel. Savoring their glorious taste as I lick one head, then the other, until I'm sucking each cock in turn with a greediness to match the demanding pulsing filling my sex. My bottom. My soul.

Shade's and Tye's thick thighs shake violently, their hands gripping my shoulders. Supporting their bodies as much as mine. Our quint holding one another up as magic and arousal batter us with a tsunami's force.

Somewhere in the forest's darkness, a pair of owls exchange hooted greeting, the trees rustling their branches in the chilly night breeze. Somewhere, this is just another night. But not here. Not on this balcony, where the mating bond pulls me toward my males as fiercely as my need does.

River's thrusting deepens, his hips bucking up with a rhythm that Coal matches with unrelenting force, his eyes glowing purple now, making my own magic rise to its call. In and out, in and out, hitting every nerve. Sending me closer to soaring with each wet strike of thighs and sacs.

The next time I breathe in, I am no longer sure whose cock it is that is so wonderfully salty and thick and sweet as it tightens inside my mouth, and whose bunches just as fiercely inside my palm. Callused hands grip my sensitive breasts, a pair of cocks filling me in a final, grand pump that comes just as Coal's deft finger brushes my engorged bud.

Molten heat rushes through me. My magic, my muscles, my channel all spasm as I tip over the edge of the grand abyss. Agony grips every fiber in my body—agony that melts to equally unbearable ecstasy a moment later, with release echoing through my core.

I'm in free fall, my back arching over and over. Sounds that have no meaning escape my throat, while four males shout my name in unison, their seed exploding inside my channel and backside, coating my mouth and breasts. Filling me with warmth and love and promises of forever.

1 8

Lera

"You know, the one thing I still don't understand is how our original Mystwood key ended up in my change of clothes back in the beginning of the year—after Coal had taken me for a punishment run. There was a note, but I didn't recognize the writing." I try to make my voice light despite knowing this is the last conversation I'll have with Arisha and Gavriel for a long time. "River said he'd given it to you to examine, Gavriel—but what happened after that?"

Behind us, the males are triple-checking the horses, Coal having decided at the last moment that he wants to lunge my mare, Sprite, before we ride out, while Shade and a female healer debate the safety of my sitting in the saddle at all. At the top of the keep, the last bell I'll hear at the Academy tolls its own farewell.

"Seeing how the key disappeared right after I saw Arisha eye it, I'd assumed she'd taken the artifact to study in private," said Gavriel. "Is that not what happened?"

Arisha shakes her head, Gavriel frowning down at his niece in surprise.

"I had considered it," Arisha admits, chewing on the end of her braid, "but changed my mind. Other things seemed more pressing at the time. I certainly did not put it into the clothes River asked me to send over to the infirmary for you."

"Well, it was in there by the time Rabbit brought—" I stop, my eyes widening. Rabbit. The little boy who knew the truth all along. "Where is Rabbit?"

Arisha looks over my shoulder, wincing. "I'm no powerful immortal, but I don't imagine your bags usually move of their own accord."

Turning, I mark a large bundle shifting around beside our other gear just as Coal walks Sprite back and clips the mare into crossties. Before I can step forward, Coal yanks the living luggage open. Rabbit's thin, shaking body pops free of the cloth. Even standing twenty paces away, I can see the tears running down the child's face, his cheeks white with fear beneath Coal's ice-blue gaze.

My chest tightens as Rabbit tries to take a step back and Coal's hand clamps down hard on the boy's shoulder.

And then Coal is down on one knee, saying something too quiet for me to make out, his face never giving sign of seeing either Rabbit's tears or the boy's valiant attempts to dry his cheeks with his sleeve. When Rabbit nods, Coal holds out his hand, the two shaking in an unholy alliance that sends a warning shiver down my spine.

"River," Coal calls over to the stable as he unfurls back to his full height, his hand still gripping Rabbit's shoulder. "We need another horse saddled. I'm bringing a training aide back to Lunos with us."

"What? Never mind," River's exasperated voice comes from the stable's darkness. "You can take a training aide, Tye can take a brothel, Shade can take every bloody potion in the Academy for all I care by now. If we can just please go."

"What exactly do you think he wants to train in?" I demand of Arisha, my hand tightening on my friend's wrist as Coal pulls a boot knife from his leathers and hands it to Rabbit.

"Parenting, I think," Arisha mutters, just as Rabbit tosses his new blade into the air. My eyes widen as the sharp knife twists blade down before falling right back in the boy's hands. Blood spills from cut palms, an ear-piercing shriek bringing all the males out with weapons drawn to correct the problem. Arisha clears her throat. "Well, they do say practice makes perfect."

I laugh, the first true joyous laugh I've had in a long time. Looking around at my males, my friends, my future, I decide that I like the world into which our twins will be born.

~

READY FOR A NEW reverse harem romance by Alex Lidell? Check out LAST CHANCE ACADEMY, The Immortals of Talonswood Book 1. If you are reading an ebook version of this book, please continue for a FREE preview.

THE CADET OF TILDOR

SIGN UP FOR NEW RELEASE NOTIFICATIONS at https://links.
alexlidell.com/News

ABOUT THE AUTHOR

Alex Lidell is an Amazon KU All Star Top 50 Author Awards winner (July, 2018). Her debut novel, THE CADET OF TILDOR (Penguin, 2013) was an Amazon Breakout Novel Awards finalist. Her Reverse Harem romances, POWER OF FIVE and MISTAKE OF MAGIC, both received Amazon KU Top 100 awards for individual titles.

Alex is an avid horseback rider, a (bad) hockey player, and an ice-cream addict. Born in Russia, Alex learned English in elementary school, where a thoughtful librarian placed a copy of Tamora Pierce's ALANNA in Alex's hands. In addition to becoming the first English book Alex read for fun, ALANNA started Alex's life long love for fantasy books. Alex lives in Washington, DC.

Join Alex's newsletter for news, special offers and sneak peeks: https:// links.alexlidell.com/News

Find out more on Alex's website: www.alexlidell.com

SIGN UP FOR NEWS AND RELEASE NOTIFICATIONS

Connect with Alex!
www.alexlidell.com
alex@alexlidell.com